Wylde at Heart

by

Rosemary Foy

Fernsby Ladies Literati Series

Wylde at Heart

Cover Art by *Debbie Taylor*

The Wild Rose Press, Inc.
PO Box 708
Adams Basin, NY 14410-0708
Visit us at www.thewildrosepress.com

Publishing History
First Tea Rose Edition, 2016
Print ISBN 978-1-5092-0884-5
Digital ISBN 978-1-5092-0885-2

Fernsby Ladies Literati Series
Published in the United States of America

Dedication

For Andrew, Emily, and Margot
~*~
Thank you also to the friends from my critique group,
Winsome, Kerry, Sue, and Joanne,
who have made writing a pleasure
and gave me encouragement and support.

Author's Note

Writing historical romance creates a wonderful opportunity to weave fiction with fact.

One of Joseph MW Turner's (1775-1851) last paintings, mentioned in chapter twenty, was entitled *The Angel Standing in the Sun* (1846). Indeed, Joseph Turner said of Margate, "Dawn clouds to the east and glorious sunsets to the west...the loveliest skies in Europe."

I have also been fortunate to research newspaper articles circa 1789 when writing *Wylde at Heart*. The items mentioned in this story have been adapted from actual published accounts. I hope you enjoy the rich authenticity of the language in these snippets, which is not generally available in today's popular literature.

Chapter One

Sunday, April 19, 1789

Public Debate: "Is it justifiable for a man to fight a duel to vindicate the honor of the lady he loves, or under any provocation whatsoever?"

While facts are known to only a few, a recent circumstance reported in various public publications of the near fatal rashness and subsequent injury to one of society's brightest ornaments, the Earl of Rochester, this question was commended for free debate to the respectable citizens attending this hall, to investigate the passions of noble combatants.

Numerous members of the fair sex attended, forsaking their dallying and trivial amusement to attend this grave question, the audience deciding dueling a mistaken principle of honor, an evil arising from a refinement of manners.

Next week's debate: "Is it probable that a reformed rake will make as good a husband, as the man whose life has been uniformly consistent with prudence and morality?"

"Ohhh, what I wouldn't give, my lord, to be called society's brightest ornament." The naked woman sighed as she stretched on a bearskin rug, idly threading her fingers around the butt of a gentleman's walnut-handled pistol. "Ain't it the truth, though, wot they've written then? England is terminally dull when you're on one of your voyages."

Slouched in a wingback, dressed in a black silk gown knotted at the waist, the Earl of Rochester, John Wylde, let the scandal sheet drop beside his chair to watch afternoon sunlight flash red and green in the prisms of his half empty snifter. He wanted to tell her he was too drunk and heavy headed to care, that England was always terminally bloody dull, and editors and scandal sheets were liars, but before he could speak, the bed linen rustled, exposing the white globed buttocks of another female, who agreed with her playmate in deeper, throatier tones.

"They don't need a fancy debate when I could tell 'em sweet that any man worth his salt is always plain immoral." She winked. "So come 'ere and do justice to your bedroom reputation, you big ornament you." Her hands patted an invitation on the plump emerald silk duvet as she barnacled deeper into the four-poster.

John cursed the scourge. "It's no use."

But the wench on the bearskin rose onto her knees and, with a sultry toss of her auburn mane, cupped the pistol in her palms, opening her thighs with clear intent. "We ain't the sort of ladies for refined manners, my lord. We'll do whatever it takes to cheer our favorite customer."

John doubted his personal presence at the birth of Venus could cheer him, and yet his member stirred. The black metal gleam of the pistol beckoned. Dearest, reliable friend who kept him safe and ensured his heart remained beating behind his bony ribs. He was almost certain it wasn't loaded, but what if a shot was fired? What if the wench brought down the chandelier in a glittering rain of chaos, drama, and screaming mayhem?

His sluggish blood quickened. God, what a delicious diversion from this dead calm. He'd known one lady with the bright-eyed teeth-clenching daring to wield such a weapon and cause blistering sweet havoc. An elegant noblewoman whose aim with a pistol was lethal to its target, who relished hazard more than life itself. A dark-haired siren, an avenging angel, whose skin enriched the soft sunlit luminescence of pearls from a fathomless sea. His shaft tingled and pulsed.

He scrubbed his hand across his eyes. Why did the memory of Anne always grab him at his lowest, a reminder he would never be honorable or manly enough for a lady such as her?

"My lord, I hold the weapon, so you must do as I command," the wench purred, taking skillful advantage of his arousal by pushing her thighs further apart. "And I think you're ready to fire. Come here, my sweet, and feel my weapon."

He wanted to take the vixen, plunge into her moist warmth, and rock in the cradle of her white hips, lay his head on the swell of her breasts, close his eyes, and float. Could he? The fantasy enticed for one second of perfect bliss, too vivid to ignore. He wiped the back of his hand across his brandy lips and dropped the snifter onto the Persian rug better to brace his arms and lift himself from the chair.

But one shuffled step, and fire shot up through the floor, the devil's hot hold pincering into his right foot and calf, squeezing the fleshy tissue, raising the tendons in a vicious cramp. He collapsed back into the seat where he pitched and rolled, gripping the wasted muscles as if holding together the shards of bone.

After five damnable months, he should be used to this. His shaft withered and died as he fought back the bile. Five months cursing the pirate captain with his rum-skewed aim who felled him once, yet felled him a thousand times. Alive, yet dead to the advance of one naked woman who might fulfil a fancy—and all society debated his reputation as a rake! His life was a bloody joke.

A miserable bloody joke.

A sharp rap on the door ricocheted through the room like a shot.

"Enter, Donovan," he rasped. "Well timed as usual. The girls are bored. They itch for a new playmate."

His manservant filled the oak-framed doorway, the man's gaze avoiding the women as he brought the scent of pine and cool air into the stuffy bedchamber.

"My lord. You asked to be reminded about the visitor from the Fernsby Ladies Literati. I believe someone will be arriving within the hour."

John shuddered. The humiliation of a painful dressing session to meet a cold old biddy, or stay ambushed in his suite with two hot wenches when he couldn't perform?

"My Lord, this engagement has been scheduled some days now and a selection of small cakes have been prepared by—"

"All right, Donovan! Don't go on so. I'm coming." And so the manservant dictated his master's duties for the day. "Society's brightest ornament" would take tea with an interfering old matron in some fucking rural England backwater because making love with two whores cost too much exertion. A bloody joke.

4

He struggled to stand, slower this time, frowning away Donovan's movement to aid. "See the girls are well compensated. Oh, and, I'll need the pistol." He held out his palm, trusting everybody would ignore the tremble in his fingers.

The amateur actress yielded with a dramatic pout, some of her heat transferred in the barrel. Snatching the silver-topped blackthorn cane where it rested against a nearby table, he limped from the room.

"God's humor is wondrous, is it not, Donovan?" he snarled, as he inched to his dressing room.

The Scot walked in front, his back as solid as a brick wall.

John thumped his walking stick into the wainscoting. "Do you hear me? A narrow house is preferable to this hell—you can give your God that message in your next prayer. Tell him I prefer a speedy exit."

The big shoulders heaved, no doubt muttering prayers for his bloody salvation, or sending him to the devil.

In his dressing room, John's shirt and cuffs were straightened, his wardrobe attended to with grinding efficiency.

"I hate England and this cold weather," John said through clenched teeth. They both knew conversation was a poor diversion from the terror raking his body, at those long hessians pulled over his foot and up his leg. On bad days like these, he was convinced Donovan prolonged the agony in hopes of mitigating his time in Purgatory. Bastard.

"My lord, if I may. You love England. It is these women with their antics. They wear you dreadful."

"Everything wears me. Even you. Especially you." John panted to stop himself from crying out as the brown leather hessian clamped around his leg, bracing his shattered bones like a vise. He fell back into his chair and gulped for air, wiping sweat from his brow, while Donovan tied a white silk cravat around his throat with dexterous ease for a man so damned ham-fisted. "I should be in Otaheite beneath a palm tree with a dozen native women ministering to my wishes instead of dressing to meet a village prude. You have the fire burning in the reception room?"

"Aye, my lord."

"Remind me what fit of generosity prompted the donation of two books to this literati group in the first place."

Donovan lowered his head with due deference. "If I remember correctly, my lord, you said nothing could be learned in letters, that couldn't be learned from the pulpit."

John snorted. "Obviously I was well advanced in my cups at the time, and you made good advantage of my condition! You know I'm a useless faithless heretic doomed to the fires of hell who does not attend church—despite your best attempts to get me there. Pistol." He held out his open palm.

"No soul is lost, my lord." Donovan handed him the weapon.

"Get fucked." John nestled his friend under his belt at his back. Beneath the white silk waistcoat, the hard metal pressed into his kidney as he stood. He didn't need God to damn a man's soul. Only a bullet.

One final glance in the mirror. An invalid with gypsy looks, whose dark circled eyes saw too much of the world to settle. Even the hair at his temples grayed as if tired of growing, a public proclamation that the sands of time were emptying in his hourglass of a useless existence. He turned away.

The stairs were an obstacle, needed to be navigated crabwise, using his stick and gripping the massive Elizabethan balustrade while Donovan drifted behind like a tender on a rope. At the landing, John rested. As his body gathered air and blood, his fingers traced the wooden ebb and flow of the grain on the oak rail.

"I fear I am scuttled," he whispered into the echoing hall where gold-framed paintings of his ancestors stood stoic and stared at him with oceans of disdain. "The leech dictates I must avoid the salty air and all exercise," he told them, "and I have complied these past five months, yet my blood should be encouraged to surge." Before I end up an oil on canvas, he might have added.

His eyelids grew heavy. He needed a tropical sun to warm his marrow, waves lapping against a rolling creaking hull, a sharp breeze in his ears, tingling his cheeks. Gulls crying. Forever horizons… He took a deep lungful of briny sea air. Then choked and spluttered on beeswax and dust.

"Donovan, I can't take this confinement a moment longer. It would be no greater loss if I attempt recuperation myself or died in the attempt. How long would it take to organize to depart to sea? Four weeks?"

Donovan's bushy red eyebrows lowered. "My lord, with all due respect, the leech would object—you being in such a fragile state an' all."

"The leech has had me these months without success. I say we organize a ship."

"A journey to the Isle of Man, my lord?"

John didn't bother gracing the suggestion with a nay. "Port Jackson."

"New Holland!" Donovan's right eyebrow lowered till hair covered his eye. "With all due respect, my lord, it would take nigh on a year sailing an' conditions are primitive at best. It might be more prudent to wait till you be healed. It is madness to think you can take such a journey where…"

But John was already shuffling away. "If I can muster a pinch of energy in such a feeble condition, the least you can do is rouse yourself to enthusiasm. The decision is made. *Lady Juliana* leaves within a few months and a second fleet is set to follow, but I'm not waiting. I'll go ahead on my own with supplies."

Limping into the reception room, he stood before his collection of primitive ash-blackened weaponry adorning the walls, his heart beating a tribal rhythm in his hollow drum chest. What arms might the Aborigines of New Holland brandish? What curios might be discovered and traded? Better to have his old bones parched under some foreign sun or sunk in Davy Jones locker than resting in this tomb.

Ah, but damnation! He had the visit from the old woman to get through first.

"Blood and wounds, Donovan, where's this visitor?"

"Not arrived yet, my lord," Donovan said from behind. "Perhaps you would like to wait, or if you would prefer me to assist you back up—"

"No. No. I'm not going back upstairs. Show the old trout in when she arrives, and Donovan"—he tapped his finger to his lips—"serve cakes to keep her mouth busy

but"—he pointed at Donovan, narrowing his stare—
"don't make them too flavorsome. I don't want her
sitting here all afternoon guzzling when we have plans
to make. In the meantime, ensure my study is ready for
work, get rid of those women upstairs—stop—no. On
second thought, I need to celebrate my decision. Let the
women stay. Methinks they will be my last hurrah to
old England before I am gone forever."

Donovan's eyes rolled, but he bowed out.

Mumbling about upstart bloody servants, John
eased himself into his chair and, walking stick safe
beside him, hoisted his leg onto a tapestry footstool. He
patted Hermes, the faithful old carriage hound who
stayed by his master's chair without need for God-
fearing lectures and moral condemnation. He crossed
his arms, leaned his head back, and gave a deep sigh. A
change of strategy, back to the usual rhythms, made his
bones hum better than any bloodletting. He would order
Siren's Song out of dry dock and speak to the
Maritime—

"My lord. The lady from Fernsby Ladies Literati
has arrived." Donovan bowed.

"Right. Show her in." John sat up and poured a
drink, downing it in a gulp. Might as well be
lightheaded to see the meeting through, before the real
work began.

"Lady Anne Dankworth," Donovan announced
with a bow, moving aside as the door opened.

His stomach hit the floor. His heart stopped. Dead.

He couldn't stand like any normal man. Could only
gape and blink, a gasping fish with a bloody big slack-
jawed mouth, struggling on the end of a line, gills
flapping, as Lady Anne Dankworth, nee Anne Gastrell-

Smythe, if you please, entered his life, hooked him bad, and reeled him in.

Not today.

He thrashed in his chair as she glided into the room, glided on essence of sweet violets.

Her dark liquid eyes quelled him. It was too much. Her step faltered, suggesting a grave air he had never seen in her before, like a hurricane looming and twisting on a morning horizon, deciding which path to destroy, majestic in its power. Dear God, how she drew him into her violent avenging squall.

But he could not even begin to guess her motives for this irregular appearance when her flashing dark eyes ravaged him, her braided chocolate brown hair swept up from her long white neck like a cresting wave, where his tongue had once flickered and tasted the salty soft downy curls at her nape. The dipping plumpness of her pink lips parted, inviting him to breathe into her. Translucent skin clearer than coral shallows set him a-shiver. His hands clenched into fists.

Oh yes, he remembered all the little things…yet he couldn't take a breath.

Twenty years he'd wandered the globe for all the reasons that embodied this cold bitch, and still she brought him to his knees.

This female whose deadly aim murdered his younger self, killing his soul.

The devil's pincers shot up from hell, straight into his ribs, cramping the air from his lungs with the hot power of hell's bellows.

She would never be his, yet he might have once laid the treasures of the world at her feet. "Anne." He panted—a lifetime in a name.

And already he had said too much.

All he heard in reply was the pounding ocean of his rushing beating heart.

Chapter Two

John Wylde.

After twenty long years.

She should have had the presence of mind to note the collection of primitive weaponry menacing her from overcrowded walls. Ash-blackened masks and spears. If she had, it might have given her due import of the dangers to come.

But today she had other worries on her mind. Anyway, the man sitting in the chair before her deleted all peripheries.

Strange how he sharpened her senses, buckled her knees, bringing her to the ground at his feet. Exactly where the rake wanted her, no doubt! She ordered her heart to slow. No need to be a bitch when he'd said one word. In truth, he had not changed. Apart from the obvious differences, his leg raised on a stool, a darkness to his pallor, strain about his broad shoulders, hair flecked with white at his temples as if he had risen from sea foam.

Those sea-blue eyes were the same, running over her, alight with speculation, surprised at her sudden appearance in his home. Although the tight drawing of his lips suggested a cynical determination he had never possessed. Her focus scrolled down where the skin at the base of his throat beat with pulse. Who ran her fingers over his rough and smooth skin, through his sun-bleached hair? Who calmed his tempers? Who gave the energy to his life blood? And who else but her could ever notice all the nuances of this man?

Did he remember all those years ago, at their last private meeting, on the drystone wall at midnight? What a wild and headstrong fool she had been. Her breath hitched as she clutched her reticule. She girded her hands under her bosom and sat in the chair opposite. He may still retain his good looks, but this meeting had nothing to do with the mistakes of their youth. It had everything to do with her future. Her family's future.

"Anne," he said, and her body betrayed her. All thirty-eight years curled as her name reverberated and rolled over his rough sandy wind-swept lips, dissolving her purpose before she had even begun.

"What are you doing at Elfleet Hall?" His eyes numbed like an arctic wind, yet her pulse ran swift like a warm ocean current beneath his ice. She swallowed and tried to look away, to break the intensity of his gaze, but instead caught the scent of him—a hint of sandalwood mixed with clove and rich cracked leather. Damn him. Why did he have to be so vivid? She shouldn't be so vulnerable. Yet the sensations were intoxicating, thrilling. She shook her head and forced herself to concentrate. Dragging up some pretense of a self-possessed military wife, she lifted her chin. "I have a request to make of you. It's important and…and a secret."

One eyebrow arched. "The good wife seeking assistance from a rake?" A corner of his mouth squeezed with contempt. "Please, indulge my limited sense of propriety for a minute, and tell me how your little life goes. We last saw each other at a distance at the opera, in London. Some six years past, isn't it? Too busy for conversation, as I recall."

Her face heated. The bastard had been surrounded by a bevy of women, as he well knew. His lips twisted with smug enjoyment at her discomfort. "Ah, but that is right, Anne, you laced your décolletage with a diamond necklace, yet when we were younger you always favored pearls."

Her hands were sweating now, clenched so tight they slipped on the bone. Of course a rake would remember her attire, and she should berate him for it, but instead her mind slipped back to summer afternoons in fields when she'd whispered all her hopes and dreams to him, his strong bare hand rolling the favored pearls at her throat, grazing her skin, his thighs hard pressed against hers. Damp earth, fresh breezes, long days—and bitter broken promises.

"My husband prefers diamonds."

"Ah. Yes. Your husband."

Enough said, it seemed, for he let his arm drop to the canine beside the chair, to fondle a silky black ear. The kind ministrations of his fingers on soft flesh stabbed her. What would it mean to feel a touch so gentle?

Thank heavens the servant entered at that moment with a tray. She must endeavor to exert some small portion of control, to halt her imagination from running away with such immature fancies. She drew a deep steadying breath, then stared at his raised brown booted leg till her eyes ached, until a crippled forty-one-year-old man sat before her, a rogue who owed her one discreet, not-so-honorable task before sliding into his next bed.

"You walked from Graystone Manor?" He broke into the strained silence, as he indicated the pot of tea and iced cakes. "You must be thirsty. You will have to pour. I can't pass. It's my leg, you see. Useless thing."

"Yes." She set her reticule aside to organize the tray, anything to keep her hands busy and delay the inevitable.

She excelled at pouring tea, so everybody told her, although her stupid hands wavered as she lifted the silver pot. When she offered him a steaming cup, he took it with a nod.

"Thank you. My, how we have grown and the years have passed. Adults sipping tea." He paused, then frowned. "Do you know, I don't drink tea. This pot was for you." He placed the bluebell-patterned saucer on a table by his elbow, where also sat a decanter. "It must be the unexpected nature of your visit, Anne. It hasn't been a good day. I have been exceedingly busy." He grabbed the decanter by its neck and sloshed two fingers into a glass, then downed the liquid in one gulp.

She sipped at her insipid tea, sneaking an assessment over the rim of her cup. Too many years had passed to make him predictable. Alcoholic? She'd heard no rumors of such vices, but rogues and seafarers did have a reputation for drunkenness.

"So, what secret business premeditates this auspicious little visit? People will talk, you know. They will have seen you skipping across the field." He straightened his double-breasted waistcoat, then giving a small wince, leaned forward to massage his knee, long fingers stroking and pulling the cream leather breeches as he looked back up at her. "I hope you haven't come to discuss our past. Too distant and disappointing, wouldn't you say?" He smiled, though no humor reached his eyes.

"Yes." She cleared her throat. "I have two reasons for this visit. The first is a trifle, a pretense for any gossipers. The second is rather more serious, requiring some of your skill, time, and discretion. I require the support of an old friend, and you…you are a man, the only man, I trust."

He inclined his head. His eyes glittered. His lips twisted with distaste. "Old friends? Such a description would imply we kept in regular correspondence. Wouldn't it?"

She ignored the poke. She did not need an argument when she merely attempted to be polite. Hopefully, he didn't see her hands shake as she retrieved a piece of green cross-stitched linen from the depths of her reticule. "The ladies of the Fernsby Literati have embroidered you a bookmark, in appreciation of your recent donation. They have taken considerable effort over the gift."

He gazed at her, a long stare of disdain. Eventually, he reached across to take the material. In the quick exchange, the rough tips of his fingers grazed hers, causing her heart to trip as her fingertips burned, lingering hot, as if she'd held her hand above a white flame, as if the adventure in his blood, despite his injury, smoldered beneath the surface and blistered her soul. Damn him. Damn him. He would unnerve her at every turn.

Her hand dropped, singed, scalded, into her lap.

"Thank you so very much," he cooed. "This is just what I need. A pretty little stitched bookmark when I read."

"Yes. One can always use a bookmark." She held her hand tight. "I volunteered to bring the gift since I was visiting Father here in Fernsby, and my friend, Lady Claire St. John—do you remember Claire from church? Claire invited me to the Readers Circle whilst I was visiting, and when I heard they were thanking you for your donation, I took the opportunity to represent them. Claire had meant to accompany me, but one of her children took ill so she couldn't visit." Babbling. She forced herself to slow. "Which leads me to the second reason for this visit."

One eyebrow arched with devastating effect.

Bastard. No doubt he practiced the move in his looking glass.

"I require your delicate assistance with an urgent, confidential situation I find myself in." She stopped and swallowed. She sat on the precipice, teetering on the edge of social and personal annihilation before a man who could read the soul of every woman he met. Dangerous ground for a good little wife.

Dear God—all her fears about to be given voice.

All her trust placed in a man whose accidental touch burned into her soul many years ago and burned there still.

"My daughter, Charlotte, is to marry the Honorable Joseph Chichester in two weeks' time. It's a love match," she said nervously. "You must know the Chichesters. Joseph's father, George, holds a baronetcy. They live a few miles away. Of course you know—you live here. It is a worthy match, and Howard and I, mainly myself, have been in Fernsby four weeks already, helping her prepare for the wedding, though I haven't been kept too busy. Enough time to join the Ladies Literati. I'm babbling again, aren't I?" She paused and looked up at him, his clear blue eyes boring into hers. "I-I…I apologize. This is difficult for me."

A muscle in his jaw tightened, pulling his lips into a thin line. "Arduous for me too."

His small admission might have made her smile once. Today she could not find amusement. "You know Father and I have never been close. However, he has agreed to have Charlotte's wedding at Graystone Manor."

He took a mouthful of whiskey, then grimaced. "I heard talk of your daughter, Charlotte's, match. I suppose congratulations are in order."

She cursed her stupidity at blathering on about Charlotte. Of course weddings would not be a comfortable topic for a rake. After all, how many marriages had he ruined with his lovemaking? A vision of his muscular naked body curled around linen sheets brought a burning to her cheek. "I'd be ever so grateful for your expertise and guidance."

He splayed his hands inviting her to proceed, strong hands which molded and positioned other women's bodies to his purpose.

She shifted her skirts. The material rustled. "Remember when we last met, I was with my husband?"

"As I said, the opera." His hand rested on his knee, working across the breeches in a slow caressing rhythm.

She readjusted her shoulders. "I suppose you would have met Howard at some function or another?"

He scratched his left eyebrow. Then he crossed his

arms high across his chest, the material of his shirt and waistcoat pulling taut across well-defined muscles as one elegant hand fingered the forgotten bookmark against the broad landscape of his biceps.

The bastard touched himself in too many places to give her comfort. No wonder the women loved him. His slow deliberate mannerisms, the long skilled fingers gliding, probing, caressing, all might have touched her skin, set her nerves to spark like flames in a whoosh of hot combustion.

"What is it in particular you fish for, Anne?"

"Well, I-I-I must first discern how well you know my husband, Howard. Whether you might be friends or engage in business over the years. It has an important bearing on the purpose of my visit."

He shrugged, then looked to the fire unimpressed, though he seemed to answer honestly enough. "Your husband is in the military, and I am a merchant with my own fleet of ships. Our paths do not often cross. Like the rest of England, I know he has the approval of the king and is an awarded hero of the first order. That is the extent of my knowledge." He stopped, stared back at her then added, "My voyages take me away for too long to keep up with all the latest developments, and his campaigns lead him in different directions." His voice lowered. "But you know all this."

"I need to make sure."

One eyebrow arched in disbelief or disdain. "You may rest assured, Major General Dankworth and I are barely acquainted. Are you seeking me out now—after all these years—for a dalliance?"

"No!" She shook her head, even while the muscles in her neck and back loosened a fraction. "No. I require the assistance of a civilian, someone who would be in a unique position to make delicate enquiries, a person who can keep confidentialities and who is not connected with the military or Howard. Discretion is vital. Someone like yourself."

"I usually create the marital problems, not solve them."

She held up her hand. "My concern comes from another quarter. I need the aid of someone who is not swayed by public opinion or my husband's regimental accolades."

"Ah. Yes. Well." His lips twisted. "The public hold a definite opinion about me. I trust you have seen the latest public debate?"

"Naturally. It was the impetus for my visit. You are an adventurer, a rogue, so you will not mind if the task I set is ominous, or not *de rigueur* and as a rake I can trust you to be discreet. In fact, I believe you would be tempted by the adventure."

He flashed a wide white smile, joyful, sincere for the first time since she had stepped into his reception room. In an instant, he took her to the day behind the gravestone of Stephen Jones Dearly Departed, when he'd asked to see the top of her knee. He smiled the same way when she had complied. One dimple crevassing his left cheek. He became the small reckless boy whose eyes glittered with energetic mischief. Who wanted her to come and play.

"It is like our childhood, isn't it, Anne? You and me, sharing secrets and adventures? Sneaking away from our fathers."

And in an instant he had pulled through her uncertainties. Those dimples of humor curled a historic intimacy around them like warm honey. His arms gathering her in, molding her to him, a place she craved, safe and protected yet wild and unknown. She closed her eyes, hearing his laughter ripple the air and a time when honeysuckle bloomed at night and summer days were long escapades. If only they existed in a bubble of time, never growing up, growing old, making mistakes, or knowing regret.

But her problems had nought to do with sweet memories. Those were better remaining in the past where they belonged. She could not be deterred from her purpose any longer.

"I fear Howard may be duplicitous in his dealings with the army," she said in a hurry, paused, then concentrated on keeping her pace measured, the way men talked politics—precise, unemotional. "I need a man who is familiar with shipping and Margate. A man who appreciates the constraints of my family, in particular, Father. Foremost, I need discretion with Charlotte's wedding just two weeks away."

He said nothing, perhaps still smarting at the squashing of memories. Yet his silence invited some sort of disgruntled confidence, the worry of months coming loose in large peeling flakes of explanation, shed from her body like a toughened winter bark. "The delicate matter of which I speak relates to the military. I believe Howard may be involved in some sort of subterfuge."

He held her gaze. Did he believe her? Did he think her a fool? She broke his stare, looked down, at her hands, where the nail on her forefinger had broken— she could not remember how or when—but it made her imperfect, imperfect the way she must now admit her family and her husband, the national hero, might be something less, the poor reflection on all wives who pretended one ideal of a perfect married life and secreted something else.

"Whilst I have been in Fernsby preparing for Charlotte's wedding"—she pressed on—"Howard has been making frequent trips to Margate. He has been saying it is for the baths or to see his military acquaintances. Three days ago, he received a note." She opened her reticule and removing a dirty sheet of paper, held it out to him.

He met her stare, then spat, "You think I am some prying maid who sinks to reading a man's private correspondence?"

The terror of her husband kept her in her seat, while the indecency of John's anger, instead of repelling her, made her long to move closer to him and absorb the heat of his fury into her flesh. She needed this energy to feed her courage.

"Please. I do not risk this visit lightly. He must never discover I have taken this note. Howard's temper is cruel."

He glanced away, dismissive, yet there sparked something else—she hoped it might be a grain of respect. After all, what she suggested wasn't uncommon, the physical world where men beat their wives. Did he understand?

He rubbed his chin, then reached out, snapping his fingers.

Anne passed him the note, careful to avoid touching him, watching his face as he read, the way his dark eyelashes fanned his pale cheeks, the faintest flicker of a muscle revealing his thoughts as he scanned the few lines.

"What of it?" The paper floated onto the table.

"I stole this note and must return it to his pocket. It was delivered late at night by some wretch and asks my husband to start preparing his eulogy." She took up the paper and folded it. "The note says a boat will collect my husband from Margate one week after Charlotte's wedding."

"I know what the letter says. I want to know why it matters to you." He barked, something in his manner changing. The atmosphere warming a fraction, as if despite his misgivings, his interest was piqued.

"Because Howard isn't going to die, is he? So why would the message refer to his funeral preparations? It makes no sense. Also, none of us are staying the week after Charlotte's wedding. Father wants us gone from Graystone. Aunt Bess and I are organized to leave the day after the wedding and Howard was to accompany us. Yet this note implies he will be staying on an extra week." Her hands collapsed in her lap.

"Ask your husband for an answer, not me."

"I have asked. That is why I am here. Howard's reaction was extreme. He bawled that if I continued prying, he would trump up a charge and with his judicial connections, have me imprisoned, then deported to Botany Bay. A lifetime in penal servitude. He would have me shackled in the bowels of one of your ships in an instant. I am at his mercy. However, you can make enquiries in Margate, talk to people, and find out what he plans, and with the knowledge you deliver, I can protect myself—know when to stay out of his way, and if there is any underhanded goings-on, I should also be able to protect Charlotte from gossip."

He shrugged. "I feel for your situation. I also hate gossips. However, all you have brought me, in essence, is a note about a eulogy." He shifted in his chair. "Speaking as a man, Anne, it is clear he is making over-emotional threats toward you because he is experiencing a patch of melancholy. You must remember, he participates in gruesome battles, has seen bloodshed. Dankworth's burden of guilt may not rest easy on his mind. It never does. It is not to be expected that a wife, sitting at home by the hearth, would appreciate the moral dilemma of taking a human life, even in war."

What? She shook her head to clear the ridiculous notion. "John, you underestimate Howard's determination if you consider his mental state enfeebled. Bloodshed is his business, and to even suggest he might labor under a burden of guilt is preposterous."

His eyes flashed. "Anne, you've been married twenty years. He's hardly likely to deport you after all this time. What would be the point? There is none! So I will repeat, you can't be sure of any man's state of mind. Even a hero can succumb."

"I may not know much about my husband, but I know he's of sound mind, and if he makes a threat, he carries it out," she snapped, then paused, drawing a deep breath. "I apologize. I am not explaining myself as succinctly as I should. There are other incidents…incidents that make me suspicious Howard is either involved with miscreants or is planning to involve the family in some sinister deal." Anne moved to the edge of her chair and lowered her voice. "He travels constantly. I am not privy to his whereabouts.

He comes and goes seemingly on a whim, yet not three months ago he thrived on strict routine. Also, I have seen someone sketching me." She whispered, "Hiding, following me. Drawing pictures of me. Why the subterfuge? Why me? I feel I am in danger in some way, that Howard means me harm. Please. Help me."

She waited, desperate for him to read in her face and manner, all the things this good wife could never admit to another living soul.

He rubbed his face.

"Please, John. It will not amount to much commitment of your time, yet would make a world of difference to me."

"You are another man's wife, Anne."

"I am a woman pleading for your assistance! Does your reputation extend to refusing aid to a woman in distress?"

"Not if your distress were real," he retaliated. "However, you come here with neurotic fancies. Your daughter is about to get married, and you are back at Graystone Manor living with your father who has never been easy, indeed, appears to despise you, and a husband who needs assistance from his comrades about issues beyond your ken. You are anxious and fragile. Who can blame you?"

"You maintain this is in my mind? That I am shallow, some poor mother of the bride, insipid in thought, delusional like my poor mother? Is this what you believe?"

He labored up from his chair. "It was never my intention to offend you. I apologize if you have misconstrued my comments as a reflection on your mother's health and death. However, as an advisor, a man who has experience of this world, I tell you your family, the military, or perhaps the advice of a leech, are better placed to answer these concerns. Not me. Anyway, I am in the midst of preparations for my next voyage." He turned away and began walking to the door.

His indifference sent her reeling. The scandal sheet had the facts of the matter—he was an ornament, but hardly brilliant. About as useless as the weaponry adorning his walls.

"You've changed." She remained in her chair. "Where is the man London talks of, who loves adventure and danger? Are you so exhausted by your thrilling living? Is this what life has done to you? One sore leg after an altercation with a jealous husband and you're a cripple? My request would require two hours of your time in Margate."

He turned to face her, his gaze like stone, his hand curling and uncurling on the stupid walking stick. The John she knew would never have admitted to such infirmity. She needed his influence and damn him, but she would demand it.

"John, there are rumors in Fernsby that you do not leave the house. Making these enquiries would give you something to do. You can hardly walk, let alone balance on a ship's deck in rough seas."

In an instant, his expression went blank.

Empty as a pocket.

She closed her eyes. She'd pushed too far.

He leaned on his stick, turned, and went through to the hall, the stick tapping an echo on the cold marble tiles, his voice colder. "Unfortunately, the cripple can't help," he called over his shoulder. "I have heard nothing of artists in the neighborhood, and I repeat…your husband, as head of his household, is better placed to make inquiries."

She retrieved the gloves from her purse, taking her time to stand and exit his horrible reception room. He put her in her place—at the feet of her husband.

"Either way, it seems someone is admiring your beauty from afar," he continued, his clipped voice echoing from the main hall where the marble tiles bounced and slapped his cruel sardonic quips in her face. "A romantic notion that should keep your marriage alive, as I am sure your visit to my house will inspire your husband's affection once he learns of it. It does for most women, even with the reputation of a cripple."

She fitted her gloves, pushing each finger into its stall, fiddling with the shiny yellow buttons which were too gay and dainty. "You must not ever mention this visit to my husband," she called back. If he could not bother, neither would she.

"Oh, believe me, this visit is forgettable." He laughed humorlessly.

Her hands shook as she placed her reticule into the crook of her arm so as to readjust her hat as she followed him out to the hall. "You haven't changed, John. Always running away when situations became tough. Even now. I did wrong to believe more of you."

"That was always your problem, wasn't it, Anne? You never believed in me at all."

"You never gave me reason to." At his growl, she let her mouth break into a gaping hole making hollow sounds. "So, thank you, on behalf of the Fernsby Ladies Literati, for your kind and generous donation." She paused, letting her eyes rake over him one final time. She wanted to unglove her hand and hold it out to him, to have his angry hot lips graze her bare knuckles. One last touch to brand his name into her bones.

But she also longed to slap him. Hard. To hear her hand crack sharp against his arrogant stubbled cheek. To have it hurt him red stinging sore, to leaving him feeling, but for a moment, some of her pain.

Instead she nodded, turned, and crossed the hall to the door his manservant held open.

"See you in another twenty years," John said, his tone full of boredom.

His stick tapped on the tiled hall, and she turned at the doorway determined to have the last word.

But all utterance died.

Two young women waited halfway on the stairs, holding their arms out to him, crimson and indigo dresses falling off their shoulders, disheveled hair, smiles wide, inviting him up in lewd whispers. He stretched out his arms to them, then leaned forward to get his foot balanced on the stair, his vest rising against his white shirt, as if already undressing. A gray pistol nestled near his spine, close to the hand of the coaxing woman. Not so crippled.

Stinging needled the back of her eyes, her ears hummed, her throat gripped tight, and her chest hurt to breathe. She turned and stepped into the afternoon sunshine, while a pickaxe mined rock-hard ruby chambers in her heart.

Dear God, the agony of scars ripped bare. Neither good enough, nor bad enough.

Forgotten.

Chapter Three

From the upstairs landing window, he watched her slippers pattering across his pebbled drive as she took the old secret path to Graystone Manor.

The only woman to lead him down secret paths and then walk away as if the drama of her visit were nothing.

He leaned his forehead against the cold pane, ribs aching with a desolate chill as if in ague. True, the angles of her body had softened. Age and motherhood curved her into sweet indulgence. Even the white lace on the edge of her skirt danced around her ankles. Oh, but her personality sharpened waspish, her manner fit for boots, spurs, and savage kicks. A moment of his pain and she would know the truth about being a cripple! He had done well. This rogue did not play at rescuing damsels in distress.

He paused and frowned. Once she would have rebelled against a tyrant of a husband, as she rebelled against her father. Her husband must have had some success in taming her for she showed but a small glimmer of the feisty nature he'd once adored.

He pushed himself away from the window. Let the hero husband and her controlling bastard of a general father sort it out. Fuck, the husband had ruined her…

Better he remember violets, pearls, and a fine décolletage, than the hard cold diamond she had become.

"My lord, are you coming?" The auburn wench pulled at his hand.

"I want both of you. Get into bed."

Good little wives were none of his issue.

Chapter Four

Tuesday, April 21

Anne stood beside Aunt Bess and the vicar in the chancel, the reluctant audience to an ensuing row.

"Mrs. Snell. You will arrange the flowers for my wedding day as I instruct, or I will find somebody else!" Charlotte's clipped voice rang from the nave.

Anne shifted from one foot onto another, noting both Bess's obvious eye-roll, and the vicar's acute interest in the flagstone flooring.

"Lady Charlotte." Mrs. Snell's voice boomed from her ample bosom. "I do my wedding posies with rosemary and roses. It is tradition, and everyone else in the county will tell you the same. I'll suffer no argument or interference."

"I am the bride, Mrs. Snell, if you care to remember, and so you will suffer me!"

Nobody dared interrupt. However, a convenient intervention was provided by a dull thud and the obvious sound of someone knocking into a pew in the dark recess of the church.

Charlotte, possessive of lightning faculties, called into the shadows, "Is someone there?" Receiving no response other than the sound of quick, soft steps, she turned to her audience. "Well, Mother? Why are you all just standing there? See who it is, as I must reason with

Mrs. Snell's petal-filled brain"—she turned to the florist—"that my wedding dress is an angelic vision and the flowers must be…"

Anne required no further encouragement and touched Aunt Bess's elbow to join her. The vicar also followed as they hurried past the choir stalls and screen to the back of the church.

It occurred to Anne as she scurried away, that at the best of times Charlotte's temper could be overbearing, but with the wedding looming in twelve days, the bride had become sensitive to provocation. A small part of Anne sympathized with poor Mrs. Snell, but then again, too many on the distaff side had been simpering fools, including her mother and herself.

The poor vicar, however, unused to anyone except God questioning the skill of the parish florist, looked pained and shaken.

"Hello? Is anybody there?" he called into the wax-scented shadows as they moved between the pews. "I can't see anyone," he added under his breath.

They turned their attention to the front of the church where Charlotte and Mrs. Snell, framed by the morning sunlit gold and blue of a mighty stained glass quatrefoil of the Blessed Virgin, battled.

"Matthew 6, verse 28, says 'Consider the lilies…' " Mrs. Snell lectured.

"I'm not marrying Matthew," Charlotte interrupted, "and I don't want lilies! I want jonquils. Can you acquire them or not?"

"In the cemetery they abound, Lady Charlotte."

Anne turned to Aunt Bess and the vicar. "Perhaps we should take a look outside?"

The vicar had already begun making his escape as

Bess said in a loud whisper, "You look outside, but I think I'll stay, dear. Just in case the ladies need monitoring."

Anne nodded, knowing Aunt Bess would be hard pressed to leave an entertaining argument. Anne, however, followed the vicar out into a peaceful spring day, where the residents of lichen-covered gravestones were silent and the perfume of freshly turned soil from one of the village gardens carried on the lightest of breezes.

Despite the muffled dispute raging inside St. Ursula's, Anne and the vicar ambled down the main church path, making no pretense of conducting a search. Instead, they enjoyed a quiet discussion about guests when their attention was diverted by a large black steed drawing to a frisky halt outside the lych-gate, the stamp of the hooves conveying urgency. The identity of the rider, blocked by budding yew trees, meant the reverend needed to hurry down the path if he wanted to divert unsuspecting parishioners from the turbulence inside the church, and Anne followed ready to assist.

"Ah, my lord, what a pleasure seeing you this morning!" The vicar stopped short at the gate and clapped his hands.

Anne felt no such desire to applaud.

John Wylde remained on his horse, man and beast looking as if they had erupted from the bowels of hell. John's gaze bore down on the vicar with warmth, which changed to cold stony arrogant disregard as he took in Anne.

"Good morning, Vicar." Then, after a slight pause, "Lady Anne." He tipped his hat. "It is fortunate I have met you, Vicar. Apologies for not dismounting. It's my leg, you see."

Anne crossed her arms. As far as she could tell he mounted a few different beasts. Cripple? Hah! It didn't take more than a glance to see John looked stronger than he had two days ago when she'd visited him. Maybe it was the thick gray jacket that accentuated his shoulders. His hair was ruffled, and his color too seemed brighter. Bastard. She knew why his skin glowed, and the idea of it curled her toes. God, how she itched to let the good reverend know what his favorite parishioner was up to.

Under her disparaging scrutiny, his smile tightened, and his hand snaked down to his knee. Oh, yes. She prayed the vile man was in tremendous, gut-wrenching pain. To be out here in front of the lych-gate as pious as a bloody saint, when just two days ago he had his arms strung around two doxy whores. She had thought him a man worthy of assisting her! What a fool she'd been. The devil take him and burn him and eat him alive! Why had God ever breathed life into the wretch?

"What may we do for you, my good friend?" the vicar asked.

Before he answered, John frowned, his eyes travelling to the church where faint raised voices penetrated the air. "Have I caught you at an inopportune time? There is no urgency in my request. I am preparing a voyage, and as is our tradition, I came to ask if you might spare some holy water to bless our ship at the Chatham launch. I've arranged for Vicar Sommers to do the honors."

"No, my lord. Of course you're not interrupting us.

It's a romantic tradition using St. Ursula's holy water." The vicar clapped his hands. "I heard rumors you were leaving soon. Botany Bay, I believe? I'll get a vial and be back in a twinkling."

The vicar hurried off, leaving Anne alone with the hell-hound on a clear spring day, in the grounds where their childhood memories of play and tomfoolery, were most poignant. The yew tree to John's right where they climbed and scraped as high as the clouds while she would pretend to fall so as to have his strong arms tighten around her. Dear God, she wanted to throw up at her innocence. It was disgusting how the man could set her shivering with loathing. Too bloody vigorous for her liking. Sandalwood tinged the air like sulfur. Even the black steed looked too spirited for its own good. Indeed, everything about the man suggested the spilling of seed!

"Good heavens, Anne." He smiled too damned wide, his teeth too damned straight and white. "How charming you look this morning."

Anne gave him her shoulder.

"Remember"—he leaned forward in the saddle, his voice lowering—"when I taught you every black word I knew? Right in this churchyard. I can tell you wish to aim a few at me this minute."

Anne acknowledged him with a penetrating glare. "How perceptive of you, my lord. My compliments on your well-chosen memories at the lych-gate. Once again, you prove yourself a bastard of impeccable bloody style."

He threw back his head, his laugh ringing over the green. "I wonder what has you running hot today. During our last discussion, you ran ice cold."

She cut him a withering look. "Perhaps it is because when I last saw you, I sought the assistance of the young honorable man I once knew. Clearly that person no longer exists." She looked away. The saddle creaked beneath his shifting weight. The horse's tail swished the air.

"Ah, and all the while, I despaired your husband, daughter, and household chores had robbed you of your spirit."

She pressed her lips together, still keeping her gaze averted. "I've kept my spirit, although I believe your antics eclipse the devil's own."

"My antics? Now how would a good wife like yourself know about my antics?"

He laughed again, and despite not wanting to look at him, she cut him a scowling glance, noting the way his countenance broke into the familiar easy smile while the mighty black beast between his legs stamped and snorted with his rider's sudden shift in balance.

John patted the horse's neck, gloved hands making wide sweeping arcs, the same tender way he'd patted his canine. "Hush, Sparks," he ordered, but before he could say more, Lady Charlotte erupted from the church, bearing down the path toward them, burgundy and white skirts tangling and flapping in her wide stride, Aunt Bess following like a wizened bridesmaid.

"Charlotte, Aunt Bess." Anne welcomed the diversion. "Allow me to introduce you to Grandfather's neighbor, the Earl of Rochester. My lord, may I present my daughter, Miss Charlotte Dankworth, and my mother's sister, Miss Belet."

"Good morning, ladies." He dipped his hat, his cold gaze following Charlotte. At least Anne did not have to fear interest from such quarter. Her daughter would be more woman than any rake could handle!

"Good morning, my lord," Charlotte snapped. "Would you kindly mind moving your horse, my lord, as it is blocking access to our carriage and we are in rather a hurry."

"My apologies, Miss Charlotte." So saying, John pulled on the reins, bringing his horse back a few steps to allow the ladies to pass.

Charlotte swept aside her skirt to march to the carriage, but Bess made an independent assessment of John verging on indecent as she stopped before his beast. "How lovely to meet you, my lord," Bess drawled, her eyes raking over the man as she patted the umber ostrich feathers in her wrap. "Of course you know our Anne. I have not visited Fernsby often over the years. However, I have a vague recollection of supervising you at play in this churchyard when you were young. Anne, your father would have a conniption if he knew you associated with his hated neighbor." She smiled.

"Then best not to tell." John winked.

Bess tittered. Anne groaned. The man and his secrets were vile. "We best be going," Anne snapped.

"Anne, dear…" Bess laid her gloved hand on Anne's crossed arms. "Give me a few moments in the carriage with Charlotte alone, would you? She's most upset." She laughed merrily at John. "A pleasure to meet you, my lord."

"The pleasure is all mine, Miss Belet."

As Bess climbed into the carriage, Anne had no intention of lingering. She didn't care a fig about Bess and Charlotte's privacy; she wanted to be gone. So with a perfunctory curtsey and injecting a carefree note into her voice, she said, "Every success on your voyage into your boiling oceans."

She stepped aside to follow Bess, when some pressure touched her upper arm. She turned. John's plaited stock connected them and for some nonsensical exasperating reason, her heart soared. Perhaps he had reconsidered her appeal. Please, God let him offer to help.

He drew the chestnut brown leather away with a seducing slowness, bunching the fine blue cambric in her sleeve. Dear heaven, he was practiced with how to thrill a woman—the vibrations sank beneath her skirts, deep down. Was this an example of the artifice of a rake? She lifted her gaze to meet his.

Leaning in his creaking saddle, he said with quiet reason, "Lady Anne, it strikes me we have much—" His head angled away from her, he frowned, his body tensed as if his interest had been arrested by some situation over her shoulder. "Strange," he whispered.

"I beg your pardon?" She followed the direction of his gaze. Headstones.

He turned to her, the frown deepening. "I remembered I'm supposed to call on someone. Tell the vicar I'll collect the water later." Delivering a hearty kick to the horse's gut, he pulled the reins hard, turning the animal's head about. A whip on the flank and the horse leaped away. Sitting firm in the saddle, John Wylde galloped off leaving a trail of dust hanging through the village.

Anne stood gaping.

The vagabond! Remembered one of his Jezebels half undressed lolling all over his bed, or did the headstones remind him of hades? Rude arrogant swine of a man, ignoring her yet again—and he had the last word!

Clenching her teeth, she gathered her skirts in her fist and stomped to the carriage digging her heels into the soil. Her ridiculous plea for his assistance had brought her closer to the man, and she did not seek proximity! God knew he was incapable of a civil farewell! She was bloody well rid of him.

"Wasn't he the neighbor Grandfather complains of? Believes in the freedom of slaves, or some such nonsense?" Charlotte said as soon as Anne flounced into the carriage. "I hadn't asked him to the wedding ceremony because of his reputation. However, now I fear I should have." She screwed up her nose. "I've heard he has much influence with the king, although I didn't want a guest who would be an irritation with walking sticks and the like, guests tripping over them and so on. Always burdensome."

"There's nothing crippled about Lord Rochester," Bess observed.

Anne brushed at the material of her skirt. "He is a rude bore. I cannot believe how bloody rude he is."

"Don't swear, Mother. You know I detest it. However, I agree. He is a complete bore."

Bess rolled her eyes.

"Perhaps not a bore." Anne pursed her lips. "But he is rude. Undoubtedly rude. Horribly rude. Cruel."

Bess's eyes lit up. "Anne, you used to be very good friends with him when you were children. In fact, I thought you would have made a fine couple when you were older, but your father would have none of it, of course." Bess smiled conspiratorially. "It gave me untold pleasure to allow you to spend time together. I never told your father. He would have blown the roof off if he knew I'd allowed you to play with the Rochester boy. That's why I did it, of course."

"Great-Aunt Bess." Charlotte's voice dripped with disapproval. "I'd appreciate it if you would keep you memories to yourself. The last thing I need is anyone in Fernsby learning my mother cavorted with a rake."

"Charlotte, they were children at the time. All this happened some thirty years ago!"

"I don't care. Keep your memories to yourself."

Bess tittered, then fussed with her reticule, pleased at creating a stir, which sank the other occupants into frustrated silence.

Anne moved her shoulders, straightened them, and made them loosen. Why were people always taking liberties with their tempers and tongues? At least she maintained a sense of quiet dignity in her dealings. People today were too free with their emotions, and men like John Wylde accentuated the fault. Men like him undermined the whole of society with their devil-may-care attitude, no plan or consideration for anybody but themselves. Never a care for the poor village women whose washing was now dusty from his galloping escapade! Or the vicar left waiting at the lych-gate. No compassion. Selfish. Two women when for any normal man one would be enough! They were all selfish. Including her daughter and Bess. Why did they need all this fuss about flowers? If it hadn't been for the bloody flowers, she wouldn't have had to tolerate the awful man's smirk. If Charlotte had just agreed with Mrs. Snell, they would be home by now. Instead… Instead…

"Charlotte," Anne bit out as the carriage jolted over a deep rut, "I let you have your head organizing the wedding because I wanted you to have the opportunities I wasn't afforded. I had no say in my nuptials and at the time it upset me dreadfully. However, I fear—"

"Mother, I have heard all this before." Charlotte held up her hand. "I understand your wedding was a dismal failure performed in the dead of night, meeting none of your expectations, but all this has nothing to do with the earl and his walking sticks at *my* wedding."

"No, of course not, Charlotte. Dear. I am simply requesting you temper your interactions with people. The flowers—"

"Please, Anne." Bess interrupted with a shudder. "We have discussed flowers enough for one day. However, the earl is a different matter. I believe he has been outspoken about the freedom of slaves."

Anne had her interest piqued, despite the fact he was a philandering bloody bastard. "Does he indeed? Well, as much as it pains me to say it, I would agree with him."

"You must tell him then, Anne." Bess's eyes glittered. "When you next meet, explain we are of the same opinion and would be most supportive of any action he would deem necessary. I think the ladies of Fernsby would agree—"

"Mother! Aunt Bess!" Charlotte screamed. "Are you saying these outrageous things to spite me? I would be furious if I discovered either of you had been talking politics with a rake! What would people say? You never think of me, do you? You only ever consider yourselves."

"We can and will talk politics with whomever we

choose," Bess retaliated. She opened her mouth to say more, but Anne gave an imperceptible shake of her head. Bess grudgingly pursed her lips and gave a *you must take your child in hand* stare.

Anne ignored her aunt's unspoken advice, straightened, and took a moment, her hands squeezing together.

"Charlotte. Dear. Granted the earl is the most stupendous rake I have ever had the misfortune to meet, but even rakes and women are entitled to express an opinion. I have raised you to hold sentiments, and Aunt Bess here is a shining example of how women can be informed, independent, and—"

"Mother! I am about to be married." Charlotte's blue eyes popped. "I know my place, and what's more, I am grateful for it, having been instructed in its appreciation by *you*. Do not think it has gone past my notice how changed you are since we've been back in Fernsby. I am sorry I agreed to Grandfather's plan to have the wedding here at your childhood home. As it is, I am prepared to give you some movement because I can see you had no parental role, your mother having died of a nervous disorder when you were twelve and Grandfather being so involved with his own military authority. Obviously, my wedding and leaving the nest has upset you. However, it is wearing looking after you and Aunt Bess like recalcitrant children at a time when I need you to be observant of protocol." Her voice rose with a hard edge. "In truth, Mother, I have enough to do without also watching over you. This is my wedding. This district will soon be my home, and you'll do well to remember it."

Bess's left eyebrow rose as she pierced Anne with

a *your child is out of control* glower.

Anne sighed and turned away, looking out the window at the fields and distant hedgerows, which were now apparently her daughter's fiefdom.

But there lay the bitter truth.

Bess wanted Anne to control the headstrong daughter, however Bess didn't realize the awful secrets Anne guarded. Secrets that would see her family's destruction and her daughter's dreams crashing if any of it came to light.

Secrets of a younger, impetuous Anne—desperate for affection—who loved John Wylde, offering him her virginity, yet he would not return her love. The secret of a resentful Anne, a brat who had been so distressed at John's cold dismissal she'd sought petty revenge in the arms of the stable boy.

The secret of the foolish naive Anne who fumbled sex with the stable boy in a hayloft, a humiliating pregnancy, then the stable boy's death—Charlotte's natural father, murdered by thieves.

The horror of a dead man's seed growing in her belly, an unwed pregnant woman in her father's precise house. Anne wrapped her arms across her stomach; the pain and loneliness of childbirth might have been only yesterday.

"Mother, did I tell you about the monogram Joseph and I had designed? The Chichester name has been entwined with strawberry leaves and…"

Charlotte chatted on, but Anne couldn't concentrate on the prattle about monograms. Names. Howard Dankworth. What a dreadful name, yet it reflected the man's unnatural persistence—crusading savior of family honor with his offer of marriage during

Anne's pregnancy. Always the hero. The fact that twenty years of national fame and wedded bliss, in secret, was twenty years of isolated hell and shame, was her penance as his wife.

"Joseph's father said he was impressed with the new design because it echoed…" Charlotte continued.

Anne looked to her daughter, studying the straight blonde hair and proud tilt of her chin. The carriage rocked, but Charlotte sat tall, unaffected by the shuddered ride. Hadn't it always been so?

Poor Charlotte, daughter of a stable boy and a noblewoman, oblivious that her natural father was a commoner. If the truth were made public, Charlotte would be shunned from society, her upcoming marriage ridiculed, the girl's dreams for a bright future, a love match, shattered, why? The mistakes of the mother made years ago. Anne's heart trembled, an all-too-familiar sensation, for hadn't the women in this family paid price enough? Her own mother chained to a tyrant till he broke her sanity and drove her to the grave. Aunt Bess never married, refusing to relinquish her independence while also giving up all the happiness of bearing children. Her own marriage a social charade. No. Arranged marriages never succeeded, but kept men like John Wylde in active employment. Charlotte loved Joseph, and they wanted to wed. This was what mattered. She would not let anything or anyone undermine her daughter's union.

And she would not judge her daughter's argument about flowers. In fact had no right to judge anyone at all.

"I told Mrs. Snell the flowers on my gloves had to match my bouquet, but the silly woman…"

Anne let her daughter's voice flow over her, concentrating instead on putting the events of the day into clarity and order with simple logic. What did flowers matter when the poor girl's adopted father might be conspiring some further madness? Howard was up to wickedness, of what, how, where, or why, she wasn't yet sure. However, if danger threatened from some future event, then today Charlotte should be able to demand whatever flowers she wanted in whatever manner suited, without suffering Anne's lectures. She would do well to remember her daughter's needs at this delicate time, instead of acting so selfish.

"Twelve days and counting till Father walks me down the aisle."

The simple words were spiked, breathed into the air, dangling like sharpened icicle blades over her head. What did Howard have planned?

She had needed John.

Anne's heart went silent. She closed her eyes.

Forgotten.

Alone.

Chapter Five

Friday, April 24

Try as he might, he couldn't forget Anne.

John pulled down the carriage blind, retreating into the dark cocoon, giving his body over to the vehicle rocking like a cabin in a ship. It was a short-lived romantic notion, for the noisy rabble of London town was unlike any ocean ever heard, and the carriage soon stopped, brought to a halt by a muddy sea of people draining across streets and lanes.

He gave a heavy sigh, running his thumb over the silverwork on his walking stick, the familiar grooves and scrolls from some undecipherable pattern secure, while foul-smelling rotting vegetable matter assailed him from beyond.

For God's sake! She was married to a national hero, had a daughter, a family, possessed her own unfathomable problems which concerned him naught, and yet, like a knight compelled by some higher purpose, he'd been drawn into her affairs.

He still wasn't sure how it had happened, except he was so bored he'd been diverted by the first sign of adventure no matter how paltry, for it was paltry.

Three days ago he'd been talking to Anne at the lych-gate, had seen someone following her. She hadn't noticed the person, had her back to the cemetery, but from his height on Sparks, he spied a boy watching her from behind a gravestone. When the child ran, John followed—too easy a task on horseback, he collared the boy in a nearby lane—a child holding a bevy of sketches of Anne. At first he thought the pictures part of some present for the upcoming wedding and might have left things, letting the boy go, except the child seemed too terrified for so innocent a commission, and when questioned, it became apparent someone was paying for the sketches.

What man, other than himself, might be interested in Anne? It somehow seemed, after all these years, inappropriate. Distasteful. Had he brushed away Anne's portent of evil too hastily? She certainly lacked the joyous energy and quick humor he'd once loved. Perhaps she did have a real concern—

A snaking pain slithered across his belly, gone before he could catch hold of it. Anne made his feet stumble on land in ways the pirate captain with his rum-skewed aim had not. Far more dangerous than any weapon, she glided into his life like a serpent constrictor, wrapped herself around his soul, and squeezed. The infamous Earl of Rochester, rake, rogue, adventurer—she snapped all his lies like the spine on a rat's back, left him withered and without form.

But now came the depraved part. Like an obsessed fool, he had rushed to Margate and spoken to the boy's uncle, offered money for the name of the person who commissioned the sketches. The uncle had been pleased to be rid of it, didn't want to involve his nephew, a creative, brilliant child, in anything untoward. He handed over a leather pouch, and so taking the child's pictures, John now went to meet the owner and commissioner of these portraits.

Three o'clock at White's was the appointed meeting time. Ten minutes to wait.

John leaned his head against the deep leather rest. He'd given her a gift once. A whittled boat he'd made after her mother died. A naïve present filled with splinters and nautical inaccuracies, it had been the first and last gift he ever gave to anyone. Of course the boat would be long perished, yet his mind played with it. Why couldn't he let go of childhood reminiscences? She had moved on with a husband and family without care for him.

He gave a long sigh and shook his head.

He should have made love to her back when they were young, when she begged for it and wore pearls, and no impediment but pure violent lust prevented him. Instead he pleaded his honor, valued her virginity. His one regret.

Even now, he should be on a ship. Pack up and leave England. Forget her. Exercise his passions with other women and remember her as a piece of unsympathetic baggage, leave her to her national hero "till death did they part."

But the question burned. Who wanted these pictures of Anne? Of course, he wasn't doing this for her—he was doing this for himself, an entertainment to shift the devil of her pleading dark eyes. He did, after all, want to rid the chit from his mind, and this little jaunt provided a diversion of an hour at the most before he met his man of business about *Siren Song*. Yes. He would lay her little mystery to rest and leave England for good. When he died on some foreign soil or in the watery deep, his conscience would be clear of Anne.

Barking an order for the driver to wait, he disembarked with difficulty, giving a curt nod to the doorman. The arrangement had been to wait in the foyer with the sketches, so John duly waited, standing uncomfortably, leather pouch in hand. It wasn't long before another man, not so tall as wide, aged in his mid-fifties with gray wig askew and red wine cheeks entered, seating himself at a secluded table placed for gentlemen to meet non-members.

John, certain this was his quarry but not recognizing the stranger, thumped around the side of the Palladian window, brushing peacock feathers out of his face, pouch tucked under his arm, which he threw onto the small table, introducing himself without formality.

The gentleman registered John's identity, brown eyes dancing with keen pudgy interest.

"Lord Rochester, how delightful! Captain Oscar Barton." The man held out a chubby hand. "A pleasure to meet you. We can go into the club if you like. Not enough time today? Well, here is as comfortable as anywhere. I was waiting for someone else. However, since the pouch comes in your possession and is mine, it seems you are the delivery boy. You will have a drink, yes, while you explain how this came to be in your custody. I'm sure there's an interesting story involved." Before John could respond, Barton called a waiter and prattled on. "I have heard of your extensive merchant ships, and of course, I've just come back from India where your ships pass all the time. Agricultural equipment. Read about the duel. Over some married wench. Of course, bullets are nothing to me. I was with the military, you know. Served under Dankworth. Your best brandy for Lord Rochester, thank you." This to the waiter, though John hadn't been consulted. "Yes, ten years abroad. I'm a regular Odysseus." He laughed. "Mind you, it was as dull as ditchwater. Hated it. Needed a rum to get out of bed. Not that I'm going anywhere now. Those days are behind me. It's old London town for me. I'm forty-eight years, you know. I know, I know. I don't look it. Not a day past thirty, but there you go. My mother was the same. Now, enough about me. What about these pictures, ah?" He opened the pouch and flicked through the charcoal sketches. "She's a beauty, isn't she? And the young boy Turner? He isn't so bad as an artist. Mind you, if I had skill, I think it would be the life drawings which would interest me the most, a lot more interesting than the landscapes, what!" Barton laughed.

John itched to whip out his pistol and terminate the man's damned voice box. Instead, he said with due brevity, "At White's, one doesn't discuss business."

Barton gave a small shrug. "I am not sure how a man of your considerable stature has become involved in my worthless affairs. However, I'm not doing business. These sketches are settling some gambling debts. I'm rather good at gambling, even if I do say so myself. Do you know my secret?" Barton leaned forward, tapping the side of his nose.

Despite his better instincts screaming for him to jab the man square on the snout, John moved closer.

"Routine," Barton whispered. "I will sit here in the foyer, watching all the comings and goings for ten minutes, then I will order a whiskey sour, then I will walk upstairs to the tables starting my ascent left foot first."

John sat back.

Barton frowned; he wasn't so stupid as not to notice John's displeasure. "It was your father who had the reputation for enjoying a wager, if memory serves. A man after my own heart." Barton's voice became sterner. "So how did you say you came by this pouch?"

"I didn't. However, the contents must be important for a personal delivery to such an establishment."

Barton's frown deepened, yet his voice was silky smooth as he said, "You can have no idea why I want these sketches. However, I am a man who likes to play at games of chance, and your reputation as a rogue precedes you, your lordship. I believe we might understand each other's interest."

John stilled. "Are you suggesting a financial interest, Captain?"

Barton waved his hands. "Nothing so obscene. Let us call it a business interest—far more polite, wouldn't you agree?"

John neither agreed nor disagreed, but if a man like Barton were paying this much attention to the phrasing of the word interest, then there was something illegal about it.

"How shall I explain it?" Barton's voice silked on. "I have spent every minute of my life in service to the ton, to the king, to my country, to generals, and even my horse, which I had to shoot in India. So now I am home, but I am lonely. So lonely my heart is breaking. With Mother gone, who will look after me in my old age? Oh, I know what you're thinking. I have a small stipend, and I do well at the gambling. Increased my fortune, even if I say so myself, but I need more. I need a son, which requires a woman, which requires money, which requires a scheming mind to make the right match. As I am getting older, it is the essential business arrangement of marriage to which my mind turns. Ha. I don't expect one such as you to understand the yearnings of a man to settle."

A large knot of contempt twisted in John's gut. He pushed it aside. Barton alluded to something. Blackmail?

John's knee tremored, a cramp seizing him as if the devil wanted to haul him back into hell. He shifted, massaged his knee, breathing through his nose. Beads of sweat formed on his brow with the concentration of not wincing.

"I believe your last utterance sums this conversation." John spoke under his breath, dragging out a kerchief and wiping his brow. Weak when he needed to show strength. The dead pirate's skeletal fingers reached beyond the grave into White's, into his private affairs. Curse Anne and his own stupid inquisitiveness.

The captain's eyes glittered, his voice dripping with insincere concern. "You are in too much pain, my lord. We might continue our discussion at some other time perhaps? When we might reach a full and meaningful understanding?" Barton smiled. Then he reached into his pocket and brought out a gold watch. "Oh dear. It'll be a bad night if I don't get a move on. Boy!" he called to the attendant, "a whiskey sour. A pleasure to meet you, my lord, and I hope we can catch up again soon. Where did you say you resided now?"

"Fernsby," John bit out.

"Fernsby, you say? Well, I never! I'm planning a journey down there in a few days' time. Perhaps I can visit? What a coincidence, eh? We can catch up then. I'd love to. Ah, here's the boy with my drink. Best be off then."

Holding out a puffy hand for his drink, the captain was already waddling toward the stairs.

"Barton!" John called.

The captain turned.

"You forgot your pouch."

Barton beamed. "So I did. Good show." And taking the package, he went up the stairs, careful to put left foot first.

John watched him, in no doubt they would meet soon.

He thumped his hand on the chair, the physical pain hampering a statuesque departure. Instead, he limped his way out of the club, clambering into his waiting carriage. He wanted to go to the park, sit in open air, to ruminate on what he had learned, but the afternoon was too risky a time to meet some female he'd rather forget, or already had, and should have remembered. Anyway, he was too tired to walk, too confused. Instead, he ordered his driver into a backstreet, where a small inn known to locals had a worn and grubby exterior advertising its existence for the grog, not companionship.

The benches were hard, but the low blackened beams and quiet talk of men cozied him like a ship's cabin. He found a secluded spot to raise his aching leg. Having fasted for some hours, he ordered rum and whatever food was available. Porridge? Well, he'd fared on less. He ordered a bowl of the stodge, and when his stomach was a little fuller and the owner had exhausted his interest in the limping gentleman, he shut his eyes and considered all he now knew.

What could Anne have done in her life to warrant such dubious attention from a blackmailer?

It didn't seem connected with any scandal sheet, but it must be sordid to attract a scoundrel. So what then? Gambling? No. Gambling scandals were as common as a fouled ship's bottom, not fodder for a blackmailer. No. It must be related to something more personal. Extramarital affairs? Her husband Dankworth? Possible, but it didn't explain the pictures of Anne.

Perhaps it was Anne who had the affair? Also possible—but with a man like Barton, the idea was laughable. No rumors circulated about her enjoying flirtations, but it didn't mean she hadn't enjoyed numerous romances. Men stacked in her bedroom the way he stacked women in his, and she had thrown herself at him all those years ago. His juices boiled, although he wasn't sure how he could count such a reaction as holding any integrity when she wasn't throwing herself at him now.

Perhaps she had some other lover? No. He shook his head. She didn't have the sexual poise or confidence of a woman balancing both a husband and a lover. Yet, Barton wanted her picture. Why?

He called the attendant to bring another rum.

What of Anne's life could concern a scoundrel?

As a child, she'd been spoiled. Her mother always fussed around her after church on Sundays, straightening bonnet or curls. He had been an only child too, but his mother died in childbirth and his father never recovered from his wife's death. Didn't want the son around to remind him. Perhaps their upbringings weren't so different—a situation made ironic when their families had ignored each other for a century. When he and Anne played, it involved lies and subterfuge. Probably why she trusted him now.

Which was misplaced.

Their lives could not be more different.

She kept house. A few bricks and mortar up north where there wasn't a seaport.

Meanwhile, he conquered women, himself, and the whole wide world. Ports drifting by in an explosion of color, smells, and lust where he proved he was a lover every day of every year. Where the women needed him, and he strode away when he tired or the fancy took him.

Until the damned shot bought him down.

Until Anne glided back into his life.

Damn, but if she didn't make him feel as nervous as a virgin.

He took a swig of rum, but the alcohol that had at first numbed his mind, now left a bitter aftertaste.

While Anne might be the mistake he tried to forget, he'd watched the illustrious career of Howard Dankworth with more than a passing interest, although he hardly cared to admit it to Anne when she asked.

Major General Howard Dankworth. National hero of the first degree, tireless in campaigns, a savvy negotiator, and an exacting commander who demanded the best from his troops and was loved or loathed because of it. The man marched from one part of the globe to the other, following skirmishes and political unrest. As far as John knew, he'd never even been wounded. Dankworth's luck even had a name: Dankworth's Duck. Never failed to raise a smile—with the right crowd. Fucking bastard. How do you go through battles and come out unscathed? Belly to the ground—that's how.

He'd heard it whispered aplenty, when the drink ran free, that Dankworth might be victorious in campaigns, but the disarray he left behind always negated the value of the triumph. Not a criticism to be made in elite circles when England and king hailed the hero. John dragged his hand across his lips. Well, the marriage wasn't based on triumph or trust. Perhaps Dankworth's taste ran to men? He scowled. He could not dwell on the thought, and still did not explain the pictures of Anne.

He knocked back the remainder of his rum in one quick hit, slamming the cup on the table.

So what to do about this Captain Barton?

He should forget the whole stupid mess. Escape. Yet his life meant nothing if he didn't lay her memory to rest once and for all. Dear God, of course. There was the rub. He had always dismissed her as a young lad's passion. Yet today, in this fetid land-lubbing bar, the hidden dangerous treasure shone as soft and luminescent as it ever had.

His blood stirred at the notion, igniting him where two women in his bedroom days before had not. Anne's softness in his arms, her voice moaning against him, her breath across his cheek, violets, the way she had looked at him at the lych-gate, her eyes full of soft yearning. Pearls...

Here were the perilous uncharted waters of his soul.

His body radiated a heat that had been dormant for five long months. His shaft swelled. He didn't dare move, his groin aching for the woman after years submerged.

As always, in his lap, he found straightforward purpose.

He would assist her on this quest, and his payment would be an unholy satisfaction of urges. Their memories were unfulfilled, unfinished, and incomplete. A knot needed to be added, a conclusion, a clasp, to keep those pearls from disappearing into the ether. Then he could live, and die, a satisfied man.

Years of pent-up frustration demanded respect.

His plan was clear. He would stay in England a few weeks longer, enough time to assist her by telling what he had discovered. Then, he would seduce the hero's wife—take the investment he had buried long ago—show her the man he had become, what she had forfeited when she ran to another's arms, and bury the image of her which haunted his lovemaking.

Leave her regretting him.

The answer to a rake's prayer.

It was all so simple.

His lips twisted into a half smile.

And an old tremoring hag with black broken teeth, who'd been appreciating him with a rheumy gaze from a far corner of the bar, smiled back.

Oh, blood and wounds! Anne had him so tightly wound he'd forgotten his appointment with his man of business about *Siren Song*! He still had time, if he hurried.

Chapter Six

Monday, April 27

Three days later, a chill harkening back to winter rode the air, transported by a brisk breeze chopping and changing its mind about which direction to travel, tugging the spring blossoms off their buds and swirling them into faux snowflakes. The sort of wind to make ears ache after church, flap washing on the line, and send obstreperous children into frenzied squeals. It was a good day to tuck a blanket around one's knees and listen to the windows rattle.

Too busy to notice the weather, Charlotte organized the presentation of jellies for her wedding breakfast—not a job for her mother. So Anne availed herself of the rattling peace, ensconcing herself in the library window seat to ponder the question that mattered most. Her husband. She wished she were ornamenting jellies. Howard was never so transparent. These days he had taken to closing his eyes during conversations, as if blotting out the identity of the participants, snapping at her without provocation, going off for days on end without notice, ignoring even the young lieutenants when they spoke to him. The inconsistencies mounted. Yet she could not enquire about the change without incurring his wrath.

And what of the letter that stated, "The scheme for

Howard Dankworth's funeral must be begun." It made no sense for her husband, the great and famous Howard Dankworth, to receive a letter with such oblique commands. Military orders were delivered with a grandiose flourish of pomp and ceremony, a snappy click of polished heels and shiny buttons, not squirreled in a torn jacket, delivered after dark by a wretch with grubby hands. She would have explained all to John if he had have given her a chance. His rejection cut deeper than any of Howard's fists ever bruised.

A budding rosebush outside the window pushed against the wind, its prickles scratching impotently across the glass. Planted as a deterrent for thieves, it seemed to want in, yet her father's house contained no nurturing atmosphere for precious blooms.

Just then the library door flew open, letting in a cold wave of air along with everyday sounds: broom bristles scratching their rhythm against the floor, a maid's shoes tapping smart on the tiles. The door closed behind her father. Heavy silence.

"I'm in here to escape my awful sister-in-law. She keeps badgering me about cakes," the general barked, his gaze assessing a Wedgewood vase with its mate further down the reading table.

Even at this angle, Anne could see the vases' alignment was off.

"As though I don't have enough to worry about with Cook still unwell! I told the interfering biddy, if it weren't for my generosity giving everybody beds and feeding your gullets, this wedding would not eventuate!" He closed one eye, then the other, checking the orientation, moving the vase closest to him a nudge to the right. "Other than when Howard deigns to appear, it's my burden to be surrounded by hens!" He stood up and, tugging down his sleeves, added, "Even your mother's exit was an agonizingly slow piece of dramatic ham-fisted theater."

"Death will do that," Anne observed.

He humphed. "You always were a disappointment, Anne, and don't think your presence here for this wedding doesn't remind me every second your mother and you both had the temerity to give birth to girls instead of the boy I deserved." He shook his head. "For God's sake! This is a military household. Have you even considered how it looks when there is no male heir? My family home going to some distant nephew?" He tugged harder at the sleeves of his jacket, then went to his desk where he removed a pistol box. "Even the old nitwit Wylde, with his big fancy title of Earl of Rochester, managed to produce a son. What a jest! I may be a viscount, but by God I've done more for this country than that sod." From the box, he raised a mother-of-pearl-handled dueling pistol. His fingers were soon wrapped in clean white cloth, scrubbing the metal and shell to a gleam. "The compensation is at least your hen-brained daughter is making a worthwhile match instead of getting pregnant like her time-wasting mother. Let's hope she can produce a son."

Scratch. The wind blew the rose across the glass. Anne tucked the blanket tighter around her knees. The library door opened again. This time Haversham entered, placing himself before her. "You have a caller, madam."

"Who?" the general snapped.

"Your neighbor. The Earl of Rochester, my lord." Haversham turned to his master.

"I had no notice of his call, did I?"

"No, my lord."

"After one hundred years, what reason did he give as the purpose of his visit? What?"

"He didn't say, my lord. Only he wished to see Lady Anne."

The general threw down his cloth and stood, straightening his jacket sleeves. "Show him to the front reception room."

While Haversham bowed out, Anne fixed the white frill on her chemise, harnessing the flushes riding through her veins at the mention of John's name and a history of family rivalry about to climax. What would John want, to visit Graystone?

The general marched out of the library, across the hall to the reception room. Anne followed at a pace, her slippered foot stopping her father's intended exclusion before he could close the door on her. She slid sideways through the small opening behind him. He cut her a withering look, but she didn't care, for she had caught the scent of sandalwood and her heart sung that John, the rude rake who slept with two women and championed the freedom of slaves, should be so daring as to enter their reception room and ask to speak with her. Her father would burst a blood vessel if he guessed the scandalous deeds occurring next door when he still raged about the Dissolution that had separated the two manor houses in 1538.

The general gave a sharp nod as John, who had been ensconced in a fauteuil, struggled to stand.

"Good day, General." John greeted him.

The general frowned. "In this household, Rochester, the Gastrell-Smythe household here at

Graystone, I expect social protocol to be observed, even if it is from one of the merchant class. I have received no notice of your intended visit, otherwise I would have declined the offer. I am assuming this appearance relates to some of your errant sheep?"

John's right eyebrow arched, a quick glance at Anne to confirm her father behaved as remembered, then he bowed his head. "I didn't realize you were so observant of the rivalry between our houses, General. Even I can barely remember the stories regarding the circumstance of the original dispute. In any case, I came to visit Lady Anne Dankworth."

The general's bushy gray brows drew down over eyes narrowed to fort-like slits. "I am respectful of the politics of our ancestors stemming from the Dissolution. State your current business."

"Please, feel free to resume your former occupation, General, for I didn't intend you to be disturbed. As I said, I'm here to visit Lady Anne Dankworth. Lady Anne is not a member of your house since her marriage, so we can allow our feud to continue for the future." With this, John sat back down, stretching his injured leg into the middle of the floor.

Anne closed her eyes, her heart bursting into a battle refrain. John Wylde, Earl of Rochester, may have the disadvantages of being lame, a merchant, seated, higher titled, and the first of his forebears to visit them in a hundred years. However, his presence was more commanding and vibrant than any man she had ever met—a sense of capacity and intense power emanated from every pore—as if during the few days apart he had found some inner strength. While she might writhe with jealousy as to what had increased his joie de vivre, she had no doubt such arrogance would drive her father to distraction and possibly even herself in the end, but for the moment, she welcomed his company.

The general, blotched cheeks glowing, took a step forward looking down on John and spat. "You, and your father before, might hold the titles, but you are nothing except middle-class traders. So the question begs"—the general turned toward his daughter as if comprehending the visit involved a female—"why would a Wylde visit you, Anne, when you know I never engage socially with my neighbors, especially this vile rogue and rake?"

Anne dropped her gaze to her hands, heat erupting in her cheeks. "Father, is this necessary?"

"If I might interrupt, General…" John spoke with authority. "My business with Lady Anne involves my generous donation to the Fernsby Reading Circle of some books. I have come here on their instigation."

"Generous?" Her father repeated, his face taking on a purple hue, spittle flecking his lips as he took a step toward his daughter. "Pray, what generosity could this foreign-loving cripple offer the ladies of our district? Or should I guess."

"Father, I am a married woman."

A loud cannon boom erupted in the room. Anne started and the general jumped, but it was John's walking stick fallen to the floor. Retrieving it, Anne caught a conspiratorial glint of devilry in his eye. The small moment of sanity somehow reached deep into her soul, giving solace, confirming why she had sought John's assistance in the first instance. For all his vices, he never required explanation of her family. It was as if he just understood and came to her aid.

"General, the reason for my visit is but a trifling matter of a poem," John said. "And you may rest assured, I would never have afforded myself the opportunity to visit Graystone if it could be avoided. However"—he paused—"Fernsby Ladies Literati have requested a copy of a poem, *The Fable of the Bees*, which I had offered to acquire for them, to be delivered to your daughter."

"You have come here to deliver a *poem*!" The general stiffened as if he had caught a whiff of some unpleasant odor.

John didn't hold a book or paper in his hand. Would her father believe it?

But John patted his leg, saying with absolute authority, "Being incapacitated, I am too poorly to travel further than your property—a position to which I am averse, as much as yourself."

Anne gulped. The ruse might yet succeed. For the military-obsessed general, verse ended with Homer, so by extension, anything published after 800 BC was drivel, the whole charade made more plausible by the admission John visited Graystone under duress.

Already the general turned and marched to the door, forgetting one hundred years of household rivalry in his hurry to escape the company of a man who was malleable to poetry and the hen-brained ladies from Fernsby Reading Circle. At reaching for the door handle, however, the general stopped and turned to his daughter. He was, after all, a military man. One last parting volley.

"The good Lord knows you seldom do the right thing, Anne. In future, I suggest the reading should be selected by myself or, better still, your good husband, for then it will be without vice and keep your mind pure. I don't trust anything a Wylde might choose. Then again, I'm sure none of you women can read." He shot a superior look at John adding, "You think you're aristocracy, but you can show yourself out when finished, and don't expect any food or drink. Our cook is off-color. Once your transaction is complete, I forbid you entering this house again."

When the door closed, Anne stared at the floor, listening to her father's clipped retreat.

Then she raised her head and smiled. "Thank you for your intervention. You have always been a reliable ally against Father, but whatever possessed you to mention that book in particular?"

"I must admit, the years haven't mellowed him," John observed dryly with raised eyebrows. "You know the poem?" He indicated her to sit.

Anne made herself comfortable, her heart beating from the eccentric camaraderie that settled between them. "I have indeed read it. In truth, any book, as soon as it is banned, hits my reading list."

"A politically subversive poem on economics?"

She conceded his point. "If we were to ever discuss politics, I might mention I have a soft inclination for the socially disenfranchised."

His gaze swept her fresh and cold like a wave. "Strange. I would not have believed a woman who wears diamonds because her husband prefers them, would either know or care about social disenfranchisement."

"You do not know me very well then, but in any case, you would not care for my thoughts on the matter—being just a woman."

"But, Anne, you judge me wrong." He gave her a devilish smile. "Indeed you will find I exhibit exceptional appreciation of the qualities belonging to the fairer sex." Once she would have whimpered to see such a smile. Not now.

"Would those be for the ones you paid?"

His eyes sparkled. "I didn't realize my liaisons interested you. We can discuss this later, I promise, but for this minute, I have other matters on my mind. Don't you want to know why I broke a hundred years of tradition?"

"To garner my best wishes for your voyage?" She straightened her shoulders, clasping her hands in her lap. "You waited for little else when you dashed off at the churchyard." Discuss his bloody liaisons! The man had lost control of his senses! Definitely too much rake in him today! It must be the wind addling his brains.

John leaned forward. "I had good reason for galloping off as I did. The person following you is a mere boy." Anne gasped as John went on. "I saw him in the churchyard hiding behind a headstone and collared him. No more than thirteen years. Shy. He lives with his uncle but has taken up art. His name is Joseph Turner. You will have been away from Fernsby and the district too long to know of the family. The boy's father is a wig maker in London, but his mother is poorly, so the boy schools in Margate this past year. The boy's genius for art is astounding."

Anne blinked. "A mere boy was following me?"

"Yes." He gave a self-satisfied grin.

"You might have told me sooner. It has been some days since we met outside St. Ursula's."

"Oh no." He chuckled. "I don't expect you to

understand. In these situations, a man must act. There is no time for discussion. Discovery of information is vital, and in any case, I have been busy. Believe me, I had no intention of assisting you at all, and it would have remained so, but when I saw the child behind the gravestone and you looking so forlorn at the lych-gate, I seized the opportunity. Events have a habit of unraveling quickly when a matter becomes of concern."

"So, you developed an interest in my affairs? After having me plead, no, beg you, and you took great delight in refusing, you suddenly change your bloody mind?"

He stared at her, smile fading. His jaw ticced. "Anne, your freedom of language was always inspiring. I notice you use it in my company. Perhaps it should have alerted you all those years ago that I am a rogue of the first order—instructing a young innocent girl to swear was my fault for which I take blame. Ah... No. I am not being swept up in detouring arguments." He leaned forward. "Blood and wounds, woman, I followed the Turner lad. You should be grateful."

"Naturally, I am grateful for your assistance. However, I didn't expect your help, ever, and now you show up at Graystone saying you have discovered a child drew my picture? It makes no sense." Her heart pounded in her chest, her nerves tweaking to some message he had yet to convey. "What did this boy say?"

"Well, before I continue, perhaps I should also come clean. It was hasty of me to dismiss you so callously when you first asked my assistance." He inclined his head. "I apologize." His jaw ticced. "The boy himself said nothing of value. However, the uncle has a small house in Margate, so a few days ago, when the Turner family were away, I availed myself of a quick sneak around and—"

"On your lame leg." Anne's eyes darted from his knee to his healthy countenance. "You had a quick sneak around? In Margate? Already?"

He lounged back in his chair, the ticcing jaw muscle replaced with a superior smile. "You will be pleased to hear my crippled leg is healing, and anyway, I wanted to act. The boy's room was filled with pictures, but on his cot were sketches of you. About six. Some were drawn when you were in St. Ursula's church; others when you were about Fernsby."

"No. Please say you didn't trespass or steal those pictures."

John inclined his head. "I'm not a common thief, Annie, but I know how to enter an abode quietly. The boy is talented. I know a little about art, enough to recognize talent." He paused as if remembering a sketch he liked. "Portraiture is second to his interest in architecture and light, I think. Turner is gifted, and the pictures do hold an exacting resemblance. This is not all. I orchestrated a meeting with the uncle who told me he was taking the boy to Sunningwell, Oxford, to another uncle, but they would be travelling through London to finish some business with the pictures first."

"John"—she leaned forward to whisper—"No. You should not have done this. Not in Margate. Howard visits the town regularly. I wanted your enquiries to be discreet." She shook her head. "This does not bode well."

He sat forward, whispering, "Don't fret. I had plenty of time to break in." He smiled, full of bonhomie, spreading his hands wide. "The portraits of you were the only existing portraits and held in an expensive leather pouch of an Indian design which the uncle gave me eventually. I knew it meant something, Annie. Ah, but I see the direction of your concern. Yes. You were always portrayed clothed. There were no fig leaves. Do not concern yourself on that count."

"Fig leaves!"

"Well, one thing led to another, and before I knew it"—he clicked his fingers—"I was offering to deliver the sketches to London myself. I had an appointment with my man of business later in the afternoon on Friday the 24th, about the upcoming voyage, which was fortuitous, and of course I was also able to give the Turner boy and his uncle a ride into the city. They were most appreciative—a lovely family. It all fitted in nicely. Oh, I also paid the Turners what they were owed for the pictures, and then just ambled over to White's in their place."

"What!" She stood. "What!" She could not even countenance the discussion. "John, I asked your help in making discreet enquiries in Margate, not to go gallivanting around the clubs of London." She turned away from him, turned back to face him, not knowing where to damned well turn!

John smiled and made himself comfortable, like a brilliant raconteur with a captive audience. She wanted to kill him. Strangle him. Put a bullet through those shiny white flashing teeth! She'd repeatedly told him she required discretion. Had he not been listening to a word? Bedding two wenches was preferable to this! Dear God, what had she unleashed?

"My initial thought was some London rag requiring sketches of you for a society gossip column, and I was thinking I would take the matter up with them, at how they have disturbed you and my good self, with their scandalmongering—"

She battled for breath.

"Annie, one wonders, is the written word not enough anymore? Do people need sordid drawings to illustrate what they read?"

Her scalp constricted. She had wanted him to make a few quiet enquiries in Margate about Howard's activities, military or otherwise, that might be happening around the time of Charlotte's wedding. Not this. Damn him. Damn him. Damn him. Dear God. This was her own fault. She should never have asked.

She turned and walked to the window, gathering sensations, forming them into some sort of idiotic jumble. Charlotte would disown her at the hint of a scandal. Why hadn't she planned this better? Why hadn't she anticipated the reasons she approached John in the first place, his knowledge and fearlessness, would be the same qualities he would use to his advantage if the quest inspired him! Suddenly, it seemed far better he was on one of his ships in the vast ocean, than causing trouble in England, trespassing roughshod through her life and talking about her wearing fig leaves and illustrated scandals in London clubs! Calling her Annie as if he cared.

When she turned around ready to ignite a fury such as the world had never witnessed, John disarmed her by asking, "Are there many men who would value your portrait, Annie? A lover? Or perhaps your husband wishes a portrait for himself?"

She blinked. Howard, who couldn't look at her without his face becoming a blank mask of hatred? She wanted to vomit. She wanted to breathe. She wanted to curse John to the devil. She wanted to faint dead away on the floor. "No." She half gulped, half groaned.

"It's not inconceivable your husband might?"

She said nothing. He could draw his own damned conclusions. He hadn't wanted to help her when she'd first asked. She wasn't about to refer to the man now, for if these pictures were connected with Howard, and if Howard had twigged or learned of John's artless escapade through Margate and the Turner's property, then God knew what cold fate awaited her. Transportation to New Holland in shackles would be the best she could expect. He'd hit her and hit her and never stop. The pain and bruises would be unimaginable—Oh, but if her punishment was to be delivered with cruel authority, what then might happen to John?

She cringed, her eyes red hot and sore as she gazed at the man sitting at ease in the reception room. By involving John, she'd excited a harmless gadabout bedroom rogue, expert at trespassing through boudoir windows. John could never match the vile desolation of a military man like Howard.

Her heart boomed, the blade of destruction swinging too close, leaving a sinister breeze spiking the hairs on the back of her neck. She had done wrong and now must prepare to take whatever steps necessary to make John stop. Her only option was to drive him away. She had done it before and would do it again.

Oh, but her soul ached.

Their reunion had been too painful. Too short.

****

John's heart lifted. Confirmation. She had no lover

and didn't believe her husband commissioned the pictures of her. So far, so good.

"Forget your husband then," he said, trying to lift her from a fog which she had descended, "because there is more I have discovered."

"More?" she echoed, her face pale.

"Do you know of a Captain Oscar Barton?"

"No."

"Pity. I hoped something he said would give us a clue. You'll have to think hard to draw conclusions that may not be clear, but the man was an inveterate gambler. It was he who commissioned your picture."

"I don't know him."

She was telling the truth. Indeed, she looked relieved not to know him.

"Barton had many scheming bones in his body. He was in your husband's regiment. I wondered—" He stopped, studied her. She had gone deathly still. "I wondered if the solution was in blackmail."

"Blackmail?" Her voice held a screechy edge. Disruptive to his ears.

"Has it struck a chord?" he ventured politely.

"No." She answered too quickly.

"Well, in that case," he said, "I suppose my next step will be to invite this fellow Barton down here to talk. Maybe I could even bring him face to face with you or your husband."

She pitched forward, clutching at her skirts, holding the material in fists so the material bunched and shimmered, revealing shapely ankles and calves. Alas, her eyes were urgent. "Neither Howard nor I are meeting anyone."

"No?"

"No."

"Mmm"—he lowered his voice, taking the liberty of a peek at her ankles—"will you tell me why you're so afraid?"

She swallowed, let the material fall, smoothed her skirt down, then went and stood by the window, looking out with concentration, as if searching for a cairn on some far hill.

He missed the sight of her ankles already. "Annie, the plan from these conspirators isn't obvious, but I know when treachery is afoot."

She was quiet.

If he could stand, he would have walked to her and grabbed her. As it was, he stamped his cane on the floor making her jump and turn.

"Annie, you are connected with a blackmailer. You can't ignore the truth."

She nodded and crossed her arms, as if holding her emotions whilst deciding what to say. Eventually she licked her lips. "John, you've been sailing oceans whereas I am a married woman who runs a household." Her tone was reasonable. "In asking your assistance, I now realize I have made a terrible mistake. It was ill-mannered, inappropriate, and unconsidered to seek your succor with a military matter which might concern my husband. Thank you. You have helped me greatly with your enquiries, but you can do no more. I must finish this on my own."

He stood. Took a faltering step toward her. "Is it me? I know you believe me a cripple. However, I am recovering, and I admit, I allowed you to believe reports that it was a jealous husband who caused my wound, but in actuality, it was pirate who boarded our ship. I shot him, then dropped him into Davy's hand. I am no slouch, if that is your concern."

She blinked, took a step backwards, shaking her head. "I didn't know you were so intrepid."

"I will face my enemy and protect what is mine." He held out his hand, though he was too far away to take her in his grasp. "I don't understand your concern, Anne, but perhaps I can guess." He inched closer. She turned to him, watching him as if committing every detail of his features to her memory. He lowered his voice to barely a whisper, all caution thrown to the winds in his zealous desiring. "Your husband doesn't know of your previous feelings for me, does he? Have you ever told him how close we came to being lovers? That you were the one who almost took my virginity?" He stopped mere inches from her face, breathing in the sweet violets, his body aching in all the right places, straining to get at her. "I owned you before you ever knew him. We could put our demons to rest once and for all. Here. Now. One quick dalliance before I sail."

He reached for her, but in an instant, his face stung like a Portuguese man-o'-war's barb. Damn her eyes, the woman had strength! He had never in his life been slapped—and who was she to dare! She was fantastic!

Even still, the vixen held her hand in place, her palm giving them a connection, however tenuous. The ache snaked up to the pit of his belly and tore at his innards. Fuck! She played him!

He placed his hand firm over hers, keeping those long overconfident fingers pressed to his cheek. "You still know how to incite a man." He dragged her hand across his face toward his mouth, flicking his tongue against her pulsing wrist, kissing where the skin was white and the veins threaded blue, so the fire would erupt in her belly and make her ache hot and moist, in the place she would open for him. Her eyes faded from oak brown to black.

"Go to the devil, John Wylde." Her voice shook, her hand ripped from his grasp, her steps taking her away, shaking.

He stared at her. For fuck's sake, he was hard in the daylight of her reception room and she played the paragon? No woman possessed such strength of virtue against his seduction. She wanted him—every tremor in her body screamed she wanted him, and she pulled away like a fucking maid with her virginity to protect.

"Doxy whores will relieve your boredom," she snapped. "I've real problems to contend with."

He blinked. What on earth was she doing? She was as changeable as the monsoon tropics. One minute she needed him, the next tossed him away with insults.

Her breasts heaved, her knuckles white, clasped the back of a chair. "You are too crippled to continue with a pursuit that involves not children with charcoal, but able-bodied men, England's finest. You have never been fit enough to pursue my husband. I should never have asked you to help. I expected a few enquiries in Margate around the regiment. Not this."

Suddenly, the truth became apparent.

He stopped.

An ice descended. No communication, no noise. The eye of the storm.

He stared at her, the poise of her body, the arch of her neck, her large seeking eyes and soft black hair. Any normal woman would be swooning in his arms, thanking him for his protection—any other woman and he might have taken his time seducing her, but there was nothing normal in this room between them. She kept still and silent, as if to disappear.

Her husband.

He stepped back. What had the bastard Dankworth done?

"You feel better because the bloodletting has stopped," she said with quiet bitterness. "But my husband is the hero, held radiant aloft before all of England and the world. You can never compete. Enjoy your freedom and your women, John. Bon voyage."

She turned and left the room.

Left him.

He stared at the closed door. The poor woman wasn't nervous. She was terrified!

He walked to the door, grabbed the handle, and then paused. Did she think him scared of a few shiny military brooches?

He threw open the door and marched out of Graystone into a boisterous windy day and his waiting carriage. He would call his man of business immediately. *Siren Song* was going back into dry dock, in favor of another voyage through the filth of England's society.

Dankworth had ruined the woman of his dreams. He wanted to know how, and why.

Chapter Seven

Friday, May 1

She stood at the Fernsby Ladies Literati May Day stall answering enquiries about Charlotte's upcoming wedding and listening to the clucking about the famous Dankworth being on business for the king.

"Good afternoon." John came upon them, a self-deprecating smile playing across his lips.

She started at his sudden appearance, then took a step away, better to observe him while her heartbeat slowed, or quickened, she was not sure. For it seemed strange in polite company to think their conversation had ever become so heated she had used her hand, or he had ever been so kind and patient at her cruel words. She cringed, wishing their relationship might have been otherwise. If the situation had been different, who knows but she might have enjoyed John's flirtations, taken up his offer of coquetry in a heartbeat. She looked away, rubbing her hand. Her wrist still ached deep where his lips had trailed and his tongue flickered.

Yet she could not feign disinterest for long. Today he contained a vitality, as if on some mission, and it drew her to him, her feet daring to inch closer to the carefree abandonment and dominance he exerted. A casual impertinence and arrogance, the way he used his cane, not as an aid, but a prop to his presence, the way he studied the women and spoke with them, while appearing not to notice them at all, his laughter and easy banter. Oh, but he had grown overconfident. She smiled, and of course he noticed. He nodded to her, touching his fingertips to the narrow rim of his black hat, his eyes alert like a fox. Impertinent rogue. Dressed in a superior lavender tailcoat, he cut a fashionable figure amongst the country folk, all the women fluttering under his charm. Had any of them noticed the slight bulge in his back? All eyes seemed to be focused on another part of his person. He was dangerous no matter his direction.

"Good afternoon, my lord." Everyone bobbed, nodded, sighed, and smiled. Anne kept her hands clasped, silent, and waited for him to leave.

"Lady Anne"—he drew her out for attention after other avenues of small talk had been exhausted—"how lovely to see you once again in Fernsby. Your daughter's wedding is on the fourth of May, so I've been informed."

Anne lifted her chin. "Correct, my lord, and we anticipate my husband, Major General Dankworth, will be arriving within a day or two." At her husband's name, John's jaw ticced.

"About the wedding"—he indicated the other side of the common with a generous sweep of his arm—"I was wondering if I might show you some blooms in the flower stall, which I believe your daughter would find both perfumed and ornamental. I did overhear her mentioning to the good Mrs. Snell she was after something special."

Anne held herself still, noticing everyone else also paused, waiting her reply. No doubt gossip of Charlotte and Mrs. Snell's argument had already circulated. Whatever he planned by referring to the affair, she had no idea except he looked like an absolute nincompoop, and she was obligated to point it out. "I didn't know you were interested in flowers, my lord?"

He blinked. His lips pursed. He did a small bow. "I have been on ships far too long not to appreciate the beauty of the forest."

Now he was talking absolute nonsense, but some of the women were tittering at his brilliance. "Yes. What flowers you must have picked, my lord. Rather a reputation for it, haven't you?"

Everyone fell silent. Gossip provided by the bucketful.

"If you would but accompany me to the flower stall, we might discuss the matter." His voice was a shade testier. "I know Miss Charlotte's intended, Sir Joseph, would value my knowledgeable opinion, and these flowers I have in mind are conveniently in bloom."

"What flowers aren't?" she had the inclination to add, but with much fortitude held her tongue or Charlotte would never forgive her. To now refuse his arm would create more talk than it was worth, while to accept would also damn her to the category of a fallen woman. She snapped her periwinkle skirts, a maneuver designed to let the other women know she was not attending this tête-à-tête for the pleasure of his company, and accepting the offer of his arm, excused herself from the company of Fernsby Ladies Literati.

She walked side by side with John, her hand resting in the muscular crook of his arm; sandalwood inflamed her senses so she had to busy herself with adjusting her hat and neatening her sash and skirts with her free hand. Any discussion with the man was nigh impossible. She could not be one second with him without wanting to... Slap him? Kiss him? Her daydreams ran the gamut of how she might respond to John Wylde—annoying in the extreme when she needed to concentrate on Howard. She cut him a quick glance, noting today his cheek contained the barest hint of dark stubble, so it would be rough and soft at the same time, disturbing when she wanted...

"I must speak with you," he said, his voice sounding as if he'd drunk and smoked too much, which by rights should revolt her instead of vibrating south of her waist. No doubt some drunken orgy.

They reached the flower stall, where she smiled at the owner and, pretending to admire the blooms, whispered to John, "If you sought me out about the young boy's drawings and your suppositions about blackmail, I will not be drawn. This is my life, and I will not have you dally with it before you disappear on your voyage."

"Correct. It is your life, and we must talk," he whispered back with far more urgency and subterfuge than she liked. "In the dell by the brook at the wooden bridge, in half an hour. There have been developments."

"Developments?" She swallowed. Her heart plummeted.

"Make some excuse to your daughter and whoever else has come with you."

"Might I remind you the last time we met I demanded you refrain from *all* further investigation."

"*This* time the development sought me, and you are

going to have to trust me until we can talk."

She blinked. Adjusted her shoulders. Trust him? She should argue it out, but yet again, he knew more than he said. Damn him to hell! Her heart started beating erraticly. She wanted to drop her reticule and fold herself up on the ground under a table of honey pots. God knew what trouble he would cause for Charlotte, for herself, for Howard, for his own personal safety, for everyone. Could he not see her family were a dysfunctional mess? And what did he mean she had to trust him? Of course she could never trust him!

"Have you been gallivanting around—"

"Shh," he said under his breath through those perfect white teeth. "You're attracting attention. Can't you for once just do as I say? I am trying to help you."

That was the trouble. She crossed her arms. She needed to put a stop to this once and for all, even if it meant revealing Howard's physical abuse. John would not pursue this adventure with such spirit if he learned she would be the one to wear the black and blue marks of his enquiries.

"Very well. I will meet you privately. I have some issues I would also like to discuss," she agreed. "Charlotte and Joseph are entertaining some friends with recounts of his Grand Tour. I doubt Charlotte has given me a thought. Aunt Bess stayed at home."

"Your father?" His eyes skirted the fair.

"He's trying to source Dr. James's Powder for the cook. The concoction is so out of date, he'll be gone for hours."

"Remember. Half an hour." And he had turned, striding away with little more than the slightest of limps. Damn him.

81

****

She waited, as promised by the wooden bridge, a full ten minutes before the requested time.

Tapping her shoe against a wooden step, the compensation to John's high-handed manner included his not having a wife, although it would have neither stopped nor altered her feelings if he were married. Despite the situation she now found herself embroiled, the beauty about John was that she always felt as if she had discovered the man.

Of course, there contained the senselessness of it all. She had the vision, but could not act—action was left to the ministrations of other females. A bevy of them.

What did it matter now anyway? John was going to sail away. He always did, and she had already organized herself and Aunt Bess to return back up north after Charlotte's wedding. In four days, everyone would be separating forever. Except for Howard.

Hell, what was going on? She bit her lip. What-if questions dogged her these days. What if Howard was leaving her? What if Howard planned to leave the military? What if Howard planned to commit her into some asylum? What if it was her funeral Howard organized? Nothing was beyond the man.

And worse, what if her feelings for John were resurfacing stronger than she'd allowed? She touched her wrist.

Just then, John's uneven tread sounded on the path. She lifted her head as he strode through the dappled shadows. Lord above, but he was handsome.

"Thank God you're here," he said as if he had been running, which was ridiculous because the man couldn't outrun a snail. "Come. Sit."

Anne perched herself on the old log he indicated.

"I have disturbing news," he said when she was comfortable.

Anne shifted, straightening her skirts, determined to keep her head in the conversation rather than on his physique or her skittish nerves.

"Two days ago, I had a visitor."

"Was it Howard?"

He frowned. "No. It wasn't Dankworth. Have you told him I made enquiries in London on your behalf?"

"I would never breach our confidence, and anyway, he hasn't been at Graystone. I have no idea of his whereabouts." She watched a shaft of sunlight dapple across his cheek.

He nodded. "Anne, it was the word blackmail that disturbed you when we spoke, wasn't it?"

She lifted her chin. "Blackmail implies dirty secrets. Family or military secrets. You stated at the beginning you did not wish to become embroiled, and you were right, of course. It doesn't concern you."

"It concerns me."

She gave a heavy sigh. "John, you must desist. I was wrong to involve you." She held up her hand. "It appears Howard is involved in a military matter, and he will deeply resent our involvement if he ever discovers it. Howard's regiment are loyal and will take care of their own. It is no matter for civilians."

"Annie." He lifted his hat and dragged his hand through his hair. "I might remind you, someone followed you, concealing their intent to make pictures of you. Those same pictures were handed to a person in London. You had no confidant except myself because your loving husband"—he spat the words—"never cared nor was even present, and as much as I dislike having to tell you, the subject of this conversation is indeed a family matter. Now, about Dankworth. I need to know everything about him."

Her heart gathered pace. "I have asked you, politely, to let it be, John. We are a few days from Charlotte's wedding. I'll look into whatever is amiss once the wedding is done. You have aided me enormously. Now at least, I know not to ask Howard about finances, especially if there's a possibility blackmail is involved. I even think the note with the obscure reference to Howard's funeral might have been some sort of military code used by someone blackmailing the regiment. Not everyone is as convinced of Howard's capacity for command as the press or king would have us believe. He does occasionally strike trouble within the ranks."

John didn't even react to this information. Instead he repeated, "What can you tell me of Dankworth?"

She sat up straighter and looked away, wishing she had a fan. "I believe I have already told you more than I should."

"Annie, I know Dankworth is a gambler. The worst sort of gambler."

The rake was quite the speechmaker. All this chest-beating valor when she sought to dampen his spirits. It was like struggling with an enthusiastic puppy over a piece of knitting.

"Did you know Major General Dankworth was a gambler?" he said again.

"Of course I knew. I'm his wife."

"You might have told me."

"Tell you?" she repeated, as she stared at him. "Hell, John, all military wives live with their husband's vices, and you know it as well as me. Just walk through Margate! I didn't speak, have never spoken of it, because I sought to protect my husband's honor. Look at your own father!"

She expected John to abuse her, to recoil, but instead he took a measured step away. He clasped his hands behind his back. "Annie—"

"Don't call me Annie. You have no right, and you know nothing about wedded bliss, John. You love your injury and adventure and whores." She flicked her hand in his direction.

"He has been violent toward you, hasn't he?"

Her body went to stone. This was her secret to tell, not John's arrogance to say outright, in broad daylight, as if her shame and humiliation were a bloody general topic of discussion.

"Before you take any more abuse from your husband, there is something you ought to know."

She could not breathe. The blood stilled in her veins. She did not want to hear anything John had to say and began to make a move to leave.

He gave her a long assessing look. "You are not Major General Howard Dankworth's wife."

"Oh, dear God."

"You are not Dankworth's wife."

"You are lacking reason." She stood, dusting her gloved hands over her periwinkle skirts. "Major General Howard Dankworth is his name. He is a living breathing person. For God's sake, this conversation is ridiculous even for you! I can't stoop this low."

"I don't dispute the man exists, just that you were

never married."

She raked her eyes over him. "I don't know what misapprehensions you are under. However, I am Lady Howard Dankworth. Now, I want to go back to the May Day celebrations before people speculate where we are. I've already caused enough trouble for Charlotte. I do not wish to add more grievances by being seen talking to a rake and rogue in the woods. I can hear the pipe and tabor have started playing so the Morris Dancers will soon—"

"Anne, three days ago I had a visitor. Captain Barton. He drank too much, and no, I did not pump him for information. It was more than freely given, which in itself is worrying."

"Oh, and let me guess. This Captain Barton claimed my husband had lost to him at a game, and I have lost my house or some such other deplorable outcome. I will admit it has happened before, and I've no doubt it will happen again. You do not need to feel any pity for me."

"Annie, Captain Barton claimed you were never Major General Howard Dankworth's wife, in law."

"Lies."

"Captain Barton requested a picture of you because of a conversation he overheard while in India, where your husband was also stationed at the time."

"This conversation has gone far enough. I am sorry for whatever deplorable tale Captain Barton has spun you in his drunken state—"

"Between your husband and a third party, a document was shown which subsequently came into Captain Barton's possession." He drew from his coat pocket a piece of vellum. "I have here your marriage certificate."

"It proves I'm married. Although I am not sure how it came to be in Barton's possession. Stolen, most likely, and how it ever fell into your hands, I don't know." She turned her shoulder to him.

"I paid for it." His eyes were dark. "And yes, it proves your marriage. Of sorts."

She took a step back.

He opened the document so she could see it. "It proves you were married at St. Enid's Church, here in England."

She glared at him.

"On the 11th day of December."

"I know when I was married, John."

"By the good Reverend Sykes. Below is your signature, and Dankworth's."

"Yes, yes, yes, yes!" She threw up her hands, heart beating loud enough to shake the ferns on the forest floor. "This is absurd!"

"Anne, St. Enid's Church does not exist. St. Enid does not exist, has never even been a saint. I fear I must ask, have you been a willing participant in this duplicity, or are you as innocent as you appear—as I would like to believe?"

"John. This is obscene. I know I was married. For pity's sake, I suspect you've suffered too much sun, or perhaps too much pain from your leg. Perhaps the leech has extracted too much blood and left your thoughts in some strange pattern, or some pirate—"

"Annie, I am sorry. I had to make sure—"

"No. What you suggest is preposterous!" She stamped her foot. "Enough. If you are referring to the banns, we did not go through the procedure because

Howard obtained a special license from the Archbishop of Canterbury."

"In a church that doesn't exist? Have you seen the license for yourself?"

She gathered her skirts and shook her head, heat leaving her face, then flushing it. "It's a spelling error or something. Anyway, I don't care about church names. I've tired of this discussion. I am sorry you need to fool yourself with these lies. It is sad a man like you, so respectable and honorable, should be bound up in this despicable subterfuge because you so crave an adventure, and I am sorry I approached you when you do not have the presence of mind to be able to conduct any investigation with impartiality. You need to depart on your voyage to Botany Bay."

"Annie—"

"Don't call me Annie as if you care or I mean something to you! I am the one in charge. This is my life, and I am ordering you to desist."

"What reason would I have to lie?" He placed his hand on her arm. "And now I have satisfied myself you are innocent of any grander scheme, what reason for any of this? I do care. Somebody has tried to blackmail me about this marriage for a sum which beggars belief. The pictures of you were to be used in the blackmail. If I know of this marriage sham, then others will too. The truth will come out."

She looked at his hand, at the misplaced warmth and stupid empathy. This boyish enthusiasm was winning in a youth, but in a man, it repelled her. He had been too long at sea. His reasoning had been affected by scurvy or something.

"How were pictures to be used in blackmail, John?

Nothing makes sense. Yet you've paid money? No. No. You have every reason to lie. You hate me. You hate Howard. You hate the military. You hate my father. You hate Charlotte and our family. You want to see me hurt. You shunned me, and then three days ago you tried to seduce me! My senses are spinning with your reasoning!"

"Annie." He dropped his stick and grabbed her by the shoulders. "Whatever might or might not have been between us, I would not wish this lie upon you. Upon any woman."

"No." She threw him off, stepping away. "No. We are in the middle of a wood, and it's the first of May. There are ants crawling over the stump and a mushroom by that…by that bark…and…No." Her shoulders slumped. "No. It is England and daytime and our cook is poorly. I am a wife, and the world has to go on like it did before. I slapped your face and—" She buried her face in her hands. "Oh dear God."

****

Just when he thought she would walk off and never speak to him again, her fury and hatred ran so deep their relationship would never be salvaged, her shoulders wracked with sobs.

He wrapped his arm around her narrow body, not sure if she believed him, unsure whether anyone could ever soothe her again, but he proved a wicked sympathizer, for the revelation of Dankworth's lie gave him pause to consider his own. That while he comforted the woman in his arms, in truth, he rode on waves of joy. Even a slim prospect of her freedom from the marriage bond was a sweet temptation. Such a prize. An opportunity. Another chance. His juices hummed, his groin ached, for she might yet be his.

For a whole day, he had sat on this information, attempting to cool his blood, but now here—he ran hotter.

Oh, but what price her freedom. The humming in his blood quietened to a sluggish boom.

Because the devil exacts a price.

He had had more time to assimilate the facts than poor sweet Annie. He knew it was criminals who harbor secrets for years, deceiving those closest to them. Dankworth was a criminal—he never doubted it, but there were other considerations. Some women, bruised and battered, still loved their husbands. Did she? Unhappy wives were his mainstay, and Anne fitted every criterion, yet she never complained about Dankworth. Indeed, only mentioned his gambling when pushed. Even in her accusations of Dankworth embroiled in some unscrupulous activity, her tone contained no judgment but pleaded for aid to protect the reputation of her child.

His self-seeking flirtation when she had sought integrity and assistance, sent his body shivering.

But he was wicked still, for he held her small body to his own, fitting her into him with a well-remembered snugness, as if they were children and some upset worried her. Now, however, an evil had cracked beneath the surface of her life, like a whale with cruel intent, rising from the deep to overturn their craft.

So he let her cry, while he could.

"Why would he do such a thing?" she asked. "Why pretend at marriage for all these years? It makes no sense. And what now of poor sweet Charlotte? The wedding? Oh, John…" She burst into a fresh round of sobs.

"We will discover the truth."

"Why?" She dropped her hands, staring at him, wet eyelashes clumping in dark long strands, moisture shimmering down her cheeks. "Why treat me like this? I have been faithful, I swear I have been faithful."

"Of course." John ran his hand down her back. Even in her deepest shock, she hadn't claimed to love Dankworth. Even in her sadness, he drew consolation. She had been faithful. He cursed himself for questioning it while wishing for one sweet taste of those red lips.

Fool to talk of this out here by the bridge. An oaf at every turn.

"I can't believe he would do this to me!" Her voice grew. "He is a decorated hero, knighted by the king. Why compromise everything he worked for yet reveal all to some third party? Some stranger in India! And others! Why would he do this? Why say such things about me? Me? I supported him. I have been a good wife. A devoted wife."

"We will discover the truth."

"Oh John, I wish I'd never read the letter! All my marriage, I never intruded in Howard's life, but with Charlotte's wedding, I gained nerve. I have done a wicked thing to question my husband's actions. You were right. I am just a woman in his household. I should have listened and done as he ordered. Ignorance is better than this awful knowledge." And then she turned and buried her face in his chest, so he had to hold and comfort her and draw her close, holding her tight. The enemy in friend's clothing, exploding such a longing in his breast, he wanted to yell to the world his joyousness. "I don't believe it," she repeated.

A bitter emptiness and rage at the convoluted mess they called their lives overwhelmed him. His urge was to howl at Dankworth and the heavens and even the ants on the stump for their quiet, relentless movement toward one objective without care for his universe, Annie's universe.

But he placed his hands on her shoulders. "Come. We will go somewhere private where you can collect yourself. The truth will always out."

She sobbed, shaking her head. "I can't go home. Charlotte, Father…" She started crying again as he guided her to his waiting carriage.

****

She woke cozied in an oak-paneled room in a wide bed with a pale pink comforter and linen sheets which were fresh, white, and crisp, on a soft mattress smelling of lavender, in a room where everything looked out of place, but as it should be. A dream? It must be, for a candle guttered low, overflowing its holder, wax stalactites cascading onto the bedside table. Her periwinkle dress placed over the back of a chair, a fire glowing and crackling in the hearth with bits of ash fallen by the grate. A bunch of wildflowers sat on a table, one flower stem from the group angling out and downwards.

She sat up. John. She had fallen asleep some time ago, had received news that turned her world into a nightmare—shaken her to the core. Howard. How long had she been here? A small parting in the pink drapes showed darkness. Night? She looked down. She was wearing her chemise. Someone had undressed her? The last vestiges of sleep dissolved as she flew from beneath the covers and grabbing a wool blanket from the foot of the bed, wrapped it around her shoulders so as to find a maid, somebody, anybody.

Running barefoot down the wide polished stairs, she called softly into an empty slumbering house. In the main hall, yellow light seeped out from under a closed door. She knocked and entered at a rush.

It was a large library, and John sat in a chair by the hearth, firelight dancing red and yellow shadows around the room, caving the outer areas in eerie solid darkness. She stood barefoot, heart pounding, panting, while he sprawled, relaxed, shirtsleeves rolled to the elbow, revealing the muscled contours of his arm. This wasn't the time to notice such things.

He smiled and stood, flexing his leg, as if he had been sitting in the same position for hours and needed to stretch. "I hope you don't mind." His voice sounded thick, his gaze raking her with mingled worry and relief. "We left you sleeping. You were so distraught we dared not wake you."

She took a few steps, breathing in the rich deep smell of beeswax and wood smoke, the warm fireplace glowing below the mantel, the old hunting dog by his chair shifting, and all the books looming on the walls, forming a snug guard around her. Home. No. She had no home, had never known a home. At least, no place as welcoming as this.

"Charlotte will be worried," she said.

"I took it upon myself to send a note to Graystone stating you would be staying at widow Woollie's." He shot her an uncertain smile.

Widow Woollie had been an invention of their childhood, when they wanted to escape and meet without the knowledge of adults, a forbidden game that kept their friendship safe from her father. She had not expected him to remember, and the heat flushed her cheeks that he had. "Thank you. I could not face them."

"Please, sit." He indicated the chair opposite. "I expected you would wake soon. You might not be hungry. However, I had a meal prepared. Sukie kept it warm until you were ready." From a small rosewood- and brass-inlaid table, he lifted a silver cloche, revealing a pie filling the room with its rich buttery aroma.

Her stomach growled. "I am not dressed. I don't want the staff to talk. If you will give me a minute to change."

"The staff are asleep, and they are used to women. They will say nothing."

"For God's sake, John. I am not one of your women."

"Never." He recoiled. "It was not my intention to suggest anything of the sort. Merely, you have had a trying time, and I often have people—friends—from London to stay. Anyway, it's past midnight, and my staff are discreet. No one will ever know you ate dinner in your chemise and a blanket." Again he indicated the seat opposite him. "Eat if you can, while it is hot."

Her stomach rumbled louder. She took a step toward the plate, pulling the blanket tight. "Well, if you promise the staff won't find out." She took up the plate and sat, pausing to give him one last penetrating stare. "You'll have to tell the servants you ate this. I was never in this room with you."

He gave a perfunctory nod. She drove her fork through the papery gold crust into the rich brown juices.

"While I'm eating, you can tell me how I come to be in my chemise? I wouldn't put it past you to take unfair advantage—"

"Heavens, Annie! What opinion you must have of me." Firelight sparked in his dark eyes. He sighed and shifted in his chair, frowning. "I don't know why you must persist with this vulgar notion of me."

"I saw you with those two women. The day I first came here. It's worse than a Persian harem."

His face flushed. "Those two doxy whores." He rubbed his face. "They meant nothing. I have a reputation to uphold."

"Which is what worries me."

He shifted in his seat. "Sukie put you to bed and wanted to see you comfortable. You were inconsolable. Maggie suggested giving you a dose of her sleeping draught to assist your nerves, but then, perhaps Maggie's Scottish nerves are stouter. It took effect quicker than anticipated. Maggie and Sukie have been worried about you. We thought perhaps you might sleep through the night and made this pie in case you woke. I would never take advantage of you, and you should know better than to even suggest such a thing."

Anne placed the empty plate on the table. That John tried to defend himself somehow made her feel better, safer. Which was a ridiculous notion because no woman in England would feel secure in the company of this rake. She laid the fork in the center of the plate, the action reminding her of her father, so she leaned the fork at an angle. Who was she to cast judgment against John's whores, when she'd not been any better in her youth? "I am eating to fuel my anger."

He leaned forward, his voice softer. "I am relieved

you have not folded. Do you feel up to a discussion?"

Anne nodded, her stomach warm and full in contrast to her presence of mind. "I keep turning it all over. I don't want to believe you, and yet, I think what you say may be true."

"I did not dare hope you would believe me."

She looked at him then, his eyes clear with curiosity and concern, sitting forward, eager for what she might say. It made her heart leap, to have it replaced with the horrid prospect of her future, her waters chilling despite the warm room and her satisfied stomach.

Had Howard lied to her? The notion didn't have as much impact as it should since no one, not even John, could ever guess the truth she had kept from her daughter. She sifted through the history of her wedding and Howard's deceit making sense of her life, which sometimes made no sense at all. "I believe you because parts of my wedding day were at odds. I always knew it was different. It was certainly not the ceremony of a young girl's dreams." She hesitated. "On some level, I expected things to be untraditional because it was so quick. However, in other ways…"

"What was odd?" he prompted.

She looked to the fire, flooded by a barrage of words she'd never spoken to another living soul. How she longed to pour it all out and couldn't. "I was married late at night. Rather unusual in itself, and I didn't know the church or the vicar. You say it was St. Enid's."

"Did you express your concern?"

She shook her head.

"Where was the church?" He probed, letting the

earlier question fall.

"I don't know for sure." She looked up at him. Questions about the church were significant. She could focus on them. "It was night."

"You've no idea at all? Anything."

She took a deep breath, wanting to weep for the girl she had once been. Innocent. Alone. Afraid. She gathered herself, forced herself to answer as the stronger woman she'd become. "Some years ago, I was travelling with Howard to Canterbury, and we stopped at a small tavern in Barfrestone. Whilst he issued orders to some underlings, I stretched my legs and happened to walk by the church. It looked familiar. When we returned to our carriage, I asked him whether it was where we had been married, and he looked unsettled. He asked me why I thought it was, and I told him I remembered the stone doorway."

"What was Dankworth's response?"

"He said I was a hen-brained woman, a fool, and later he would make me pay for my curiosity."

The room was quiet. John took up the fire iron beside his chair and stabbed a half burned log till it sparked. "What reason did they give you at the time for having the wedding at night and at a church which wasn't your own?" His voice was quite with coiled fury.

"No explanations were ever given." She threw off the hot blanket and walked to the fire, drawn to the yellow flame destroying the log in leaping blue tipped tongues. "None of it matters now. It was a church. A lifetime of marriage, believing I was Lady Howard Dankworth, covering for his gambling and drinking, making good his debts, when all the time it might have been a lie. It felt like a lie, even while I lived it."

The dancing flames hypnotized her, and John's gentle questions gave her relief. For the first time, someone was listening.

"I have been everything Howard asked of me. I kept his house; I accompanied him on his excursions to dinners and parties. I played the hostess and kept the secrets of a hero."

He gave a deep sigh. "I'm sorry, Annie. I find this conversation disturbing. I need a brandy. Will you join me?"

"Thank you."

He stood and went to the decanters, fancying he might need the drink more than her. After the disclosure of Dankworth's violence, he had wanted to pour the alcohol down his throat, smash the bottle against the wall and so armed, walk till he found Dankworth and exacted retribution. Bastards who hit women were worth stomping on.

Instead he poured the balloons and brought hers over to her.

Firelight caught the liquid, the crystal in her palm, her fingers long and fine, cupping the glass. Her fingers and hand cupping him. Could he not keep his thoughts away from her body for one minute? This was so damned inappropriate.

Although why pretend? She'd seen him with those women. She was under no illusion as to the type of scoundrel he was. He sat and crossed his legs, cleared his throat, and tried to concentrate on anything but her hands. "Perhaps we should make a toast. Although I can't think of anything that would be appropriate under the circumstances."

Annie took a large swig from her glass, then coughed. "This is all rather tawdry, isn't it? My family's reputation is tarnished in a way I could never imagine. Perhaps our toast should be to nightmares."

He wanted to take her, have her long fine arms encircle his waist while he kissed himself into her dreams. She deserved better than Dankworth—but did she deserve a rake and rogue?

At least it was within his power to make her forget all this pain and humiliation with one kiss…If he had a chance…

"No. I still can't believe this is happening." She shook her head. "There was no use Howard pretending a marriage, no point in it at all. I was already down."

He covered the tenting in his lap, thankful for the dim light; she aided his subterfuge by turning her back on him, facing the fire, so he could breathe again. She had not told him the full story of her marriage, and on some level he didn't expect her to divulge it. She had a right to privacy. Except blackmail and lies relied on privacy for their survival.

By now the brandy would be warming her, making her breath sweet and hot. He frowned at the intrusive observation and straightened his shoulders.

"Why were you already down? You were getting married. The one reason I can think of is if you were already pregnant." He kept his voice emotionless, Stating the fact.

Her back tensed. Perhaps he pushed too far.

"Yes. I was pregnant." She stared at the fire.

An insane jealousy came up from his stomach and grabbed him. He had suspected it when she began speaking, yet to hear her admit it, shook him. Twenty years ago he'd been protecting her virtue, too damned naive to see Dankworth was not so scrupulous. "Fuck." He mouthed the word so she wouldn't hear.

He wiped his hand across his eyes. He was supposed to be supporting her. He downed his brandy. "I suppose your father sanctioned the marriage. Dankworth being one of the regiment, it would have all been amicable."

"Very," she agreed, then turned to face him. "There is a lot, it seems, we don't understand about each other's lives. For example, where is Captain Barton? The man who instigated this?"

The shock of her pregnancy still ravaged his body, but he was not so shaken he could not see when the topic of conversation had been swapped from her, to him. She did not want to talk about the pregnancy. Neither did he.

"Barton returned to London on Wednesday."

Firelight drew into shadow the outline of her body under the fine chemise, the gap between her legs, the wider hips and narrow waist. He swallowed, the provocativeness of her stance made all the more alluring because she was unaware. He had been going to ask something important, but other parts of him created a greater urgency and he wasn't sure he could speak.

"Why did he need my picture? I don't understand." She frowned, her humor sour and insistent, discordant with the beauty of her body. "I don't know where to begin. There are so many facets, yet you seem to know everything and you sit there questioning me, but you haven't told me the details of this visit with this gambling blackmailer called Captain Barton. If he is indeed a captain."

He cleared his throat, sweat beading on his forehead. "Sit down, and we will discuss it."

"I am not sitting down," she snapped. "Don't order me around like a wife. If you think I am doing another man's bidding ever again, you are wrong! I need to know what was said by this Barton man, and I want to know now."

John had never seen a more distressed and angry woman in all his life. She bewitched him. The transparent chemise, her pink lips parted in shock and accusation, dark cascading hair, the darker shadow at the juncture of her thighs promising delights, the fluttering glow of the firelight, and the brandy, all having an intoxicating effect, which was more seductive than if she'd been before him naked. He ached, stirred, and moistened. She was made by God to be ravished, here. Now. She had every right to take her anger out on him. He welcomed her fury, absorbing all the torment and frustration because where she was weak, he was strong, and all the pain she threw at him would not be enough to blot out those years. He swallowed. Her lips would taste of brandy, the gentle curve of her pendulous breasts cupped in his hands, lifting her nightdress to access the bounty. He should seduce her now. Right this minute. Take her soft and gentle…

"Are you going to tell me?"

"Yes. Right. Well. Mmm. So."

"Oh my God." She moved away from the fireplace to stand in front of him. "Is it so hard?"

"Pardon?"

"I am not asking for much here." She lowered her

face so it was mere inches from his. "Just for answers about my life!"

As she spoke, a lock of hair fell over her shoulder, the tip of the strands brushed across his bare arm to excruciating sensitivity, causing the hairs to rise, tingling into his armpits and across his torso. His head spun. Her warm brandy-scented breath fanned his cheek. The world began to drift out of focus. "Yes. Sorry. It must be the late hour."

"I am keeping you awake?"

"Yes. I mean no. I mean my leg is throbbing." And he dug his heel into the floor until pain shot up into his knee, through his thigh, though it did not stem the tide of fucking sexual urgency ripping through his shaft and balls. She was killing him! "I meant my brain is attempting to process too many pieces of this plot. Please have a seat, and I'll explain."

She dropped into the chair opposite and crossed her legs. He was safe, for the moment. He let his heel release, blood pounding through him, centering on his knee, which engorged his buckskins, providing a nauseous distraction from his shaft. Blood and wounds—she had him swelling in places no man ought.

"Your husband." He swallowed. "Your supposed husband was gambling on cockfights in India. Barton was present and saw Howard leave with another man, ostensibly to finalize a bet, but Barton is astute. He knew there was something else afoot." John ran on, not daring to pause for breath. "Barton listened to Dankworth's conversation and overheard Dankworth admit his marriage was a hoax. Dankworth showed the other man papers as proof of the deceit, but the officer did not accept Dankworth's wager. Barton saw his opportunity to make some money with blackmail but knew he would need the sham document first, so that night after he'd got Dankworth drunk, he crept into Dankworth's room and removed the paper. Stole it. Dankworth didn't even have it under lock and key, thinking the paper would be useless to all except those who knew the truth, and even those weren't interested. Except Barton."

"By now, Howard would know the marriage certificate is stolen."

"Yes."

"He'll be alert to me knowing."

"I doubt it. The certificate was stolen in India, and anyway, I fancy Dankworth is too arrogant to suspect you would have any knowledge of the marriage hoax. Not after all this time. Added to this, the document is worthless except to those who are deceitful enough to try and profit from it. Your loyalty to him as his good wife puts you above suspicion."

"But it doesn't explain my pictures." She leaned forward.

He glimpsed the valley between her breasts. Her lips were plump, her cheeks flushed. She was too upset to realize the neckline was low. Oh, dear heaven and earth, she tested him beyond reason. "No. No. Well, as it turns out, the pictures were another avenue Barton might want to progress. Remember, he is a man of opportunity." He told his heart to slow as he talked. "Barton first planned to blackmail Charlotte's in-laws with the scurrilous truth about Charlotte's illegitimacy because you had never been lawfully married. This was his plan when he learned of the wedding, but everything changed after I showed up at White's instead of the wigmaker from Margate. He came to Fernsby and spoke to me. I showed interest, and Barton needed money. I am far wealthier than Charlotte's intended in-laws, so I became the mark."

"So if you hadn't intervened, the threat could— would have spread through society, the family, Charlotte's family?" She whispered the horror.

"The pictures were ordered," he went on, careful to avoid gazing at her breasts, "because Barton was calculating what avenue of blackmail would benefit him best. He had numerous ideas. He told me he had contemplated blackmailing your father or, if this proved useless, then to abduct you and exact a ransom. It also crossed his mind to abduct you and sell you off, marry you to some rich eccentric. Even marry you himself if all else failed. Since the certificate is forged, he had many avenues to pursue, only limited by his unscrupulous imagination."

"How did he manage to entice young Turner into the deception?"

"Barton visited Margate to catch up with some of his regimental cronies. Turner displayed his nephew's art, and Barton seized the opportunity. The boy was told to make use of his charcoal as a gift to the bride. As I explained earlier, that is the extent of the child's involvement. The child and uncle are innocent of the knowledge Barton was using the pictures in blackmail. They thought it was for a wedding gift, were honored young Joseph had been asked, but had their suspicions because mutual acquaintances later hinted Barton had a reputation for no good."

"So what does this Barton want now?" She stood. "We are mere days away from Charlotte's wedding.

Her plans can't be disturbed."

"Ah. No." He stood and came toward her, preventing her from standing in front of the fire, taking her by both elbows, his erection hardening. "Do not distress yourself. I have taken care of Barton."

"This is supposed to calm me? The man is a criminal. A bounder who would wreck lives. He knows things that will damage Charlotte if it becomes common knowledge."

"Annie, please." He took a step toward her, wishing in that instant that he were naive about women, for in all his experience, of which there had been so much, no female was as soft, supple, or right as Annie. He was the true bounder in this scenario, not Barton, for it was John who celebrated breaking her life apart.

"I explained to Barton, Charlotte was about to marry, a society event which Major General Dankworth would be attending. I suggested it would be more than Barton's life was worth to attempt to coerce Charlotte's intended in-laws before the wedding with a forged document, as the Chichesters would no doubt go straight to Dankworth. Dankworth would shoot Barton on the spot. Barton agreed. This is why he blackmailed me. I've paid. He'll be silent."

"Why would you do this? And why would Barton stop at extorting money from you?"

He ran his hands over the fabric, up and down her slender arms as small and fragile as a bird's, the fabric of her chemise bunching under his hands, lifting and sliding across her skin. He looked down onto the top of her head, her dark curls catching the warm glow of the firelight. One hair floated up, tickled his chin, swayed in his breath.

"I did it for Charlotte," he lied. Dear God, what she would say if she knew the truth, that he admitted to Barton he loved Annie since they were children? Good money was paid, not for a blackmailer's silence, but his confidence. "I paid Barton to leave well alone, and in any case, Barton isn't interested in the certificate. To have any value, the document has to be proved as a forgery, which Barton has no interest in pursuing. It requires work, and believe me, he is the type of man who detests having to toil at anything." He drew a deep breath of her scent.

"I will repay you."

"Please." He watched her wide pupils caught in the firelight, glittering down into fathomless depths, tears pooling below her lids. "Annie"—his voice was gruffer than he intended—"the money is but a trifle. I know you have little reason to trust me, but I give you my pledge, I will discover the truth."

"This is not a truth I want to hear." She closed her eyes, burying her head against his breast, rubbing into him, her hair mussing on his chest, driving him to a fever. "Howard is dangerous," she said, her voice rumbled down into his groin. "There are other things, secrets which should remain undisturbed. Oh, I have felt it and ignored my suspicions, never daring to ask."

"Annie." He lifted her chin to meet his gaze. "I am used to dangerous men who take opportunities, and secrets which have been held a lifetime."

He lowered his mouth to meet hers.

Chapter Eight

So he was supposed to be more experienced, more practiced after all the women he'd taken to his bed. What happened? He sank into her and lost his soul. He plundered her lips and slipped beneath the surface of logic, down into the watery depths of craving darkness. If she had been the ocean, he would have never come up for air, would have died in her warm arms. He teased himself into her wet brandy-flavored mouth, and her tongue flickered back its velvet response, a tickling. She moaned and billions of air bubbles swam through his body, finding their way to the surface through his blood, cascading up his spine and down into his groin.

All thought stopped, yet below the surface, a primal instinct raged at his loss. Why had he run away from this? Why had he gone adventuring when the purest, most lovely of creatures existed here in England? He drew her closer, a shiver wracking his body sending him into the heavens, dragging him into a frenzy of time and life wasted while this sweet everything pressed herself into him, beneath his guiding fingertips.

She went to pull away, but he followed her with his lips drawing her closer, winding his arm around her waist and bending her to him like seaweed flowing in a current, pushing her against the length of his hard body, imprinting himself into her soft curves and flesh, feeling her bond. Her nipples hardened to tight buds beneath the chemise. He groaned into her mouth, the deep sound reverberating into her soul. Twenty years— one drop.

When she broke away a second time, he knew to stop. Even through the fog of lust, he could reason he had been right years ago to pause, and maybe to have sent her away because now it was almost impossible to pull apart. Back then, as a frustrated youth, she would have had no say in the matter. Back then, a young boy's lust stirred uncontrolled. He would have taken both their lives, shipwrecked any future they might have had. For the first time, he realized he had been right to run away to sea.

He swallowed, giving her time to gather her wits and call him every name a rake and rogue deserved.

"You are dangerous." Her eyes glittered bright, her tone tremulous so he knew she was affected. Her hair curled and tossed around her face as she surfaced from the depths, yet he could not remember putting his hand through those soft tresses. He needed to feel her again, explore, and take more. Always lost opportunities.

"Fair comment."

She lifted her chin. "I have wondered what it would be like to kiss you, as a woman, and now I have, I find I am guilty of enjoying the sensations. I suppose it comes from your expertise."

A chill whipped across his bones. She presumed he had orchestrated the tide of emotion? He wiped a corner of his lip. Was she the calculating baggage he'd convinced himself she was all these years? To be so unaffected by their first kiss?

"Yes, it must be my expertise, for I tasted none in

yours," he bit out, hoping to hurt her, then the next moment cursing his flaming temper. Here he was again, hurt by her, reacting like a child.

He waited for her stormy reaction, yearning for the thunder and lightning conflict, for then he could take her in his arms again and show a display that would dampen all calculations.

But she straightened, picked up the fallen blanket, pulling it tight around her shoulders. "I have dreamed of this, John Wylde. Yet now I am here, I don't know what to do or say. The kiss makes me nervous. It changes everything, doesn't it?"

What did she mean? He shook his head. "I think we are both experienced enough to know the repercussions of a kiss. Do we need to analyze its meaning and purpose? Can't we savor the moment while it lasts?"

"I suppose you mean if my marriage is proven to be a counterfeit, nothing stops me kissing who I please."

No. He did not mean that. He raked his fingers through his hair. "Perhaps the question you need to be asking is, do you love your so-called husband?"

She shrugged, pretending at some artful nonchalance.

"Do you love Dankworth?"

"No. Yes. I don't know," she whispered. She glanced at him, then shrugged. "I hate him. Although sometimes I've glimpsed a different side to him. Especially toward Charlotte."

He was lost, rudderless, floating on some endless sea without bearings.

"John." Her gaze darted to him. "John, it crosses

my mind since the kiss, to wonder if you may have devised this ridiculous untruth about my marriage status so you could take me to your bed."

His erection ebbed. "What would be my purpose in devising such a plot?"

"To ruin my marriage."

"I would never deign to ruin a marriage. It is the most sacred of rites. Although, I am rogue enough to enjoy what fruits a woman offers and not care so much a thought for her husband."

She stared up at him, as if the weight of the question settled on her small shoulders, not his. "The kiss is complicated."

"No. The kiss is the easiest part. It's your marriage which is complicated."

"A complication delivered by a blackmailer." Her voice was too concise. "A common criminal. Why would I trust him? The document might be a fraud. My marriage might be legitimate."

"I never said I trusted Captain Barton. However, I do know how we will proceed. I want to talk to you about searching the church records, wherever you think you have been married. This will show the truth and provide us with incontrovertible proof because you will have signed the marriage register, and the minister will hold the special license there."

"But I do not know for certain what church I was married in."

"We know it wasn't St Enid's. We should start at Barfrestone." He turned away, resting his arm on the mantel, assaulted by a sudden vision of her nipples by firelight, where he could taste them, feel the warm pearl slide beneath his tongue.

"I do not know whether St. Enid is a saint or not," she was saying. "I must settle this in my own mind, and then, when I am satisfied, I will decide how to proceed if the marriage is a hoax."

"Annie, this was not a hoax, so much as a malicious deception." He turned and strode as best he could toward her. "It was a deliberate deceit perpetrated over many years. Whatever the reason for this situation you now find yourself in, we must act." Which started with lifting her gown.

"Kissing. Is this your intended strategy against Howard?" Her forefinger ran along the back of the chair. "Tarnish my reputation? Cuckold my husband? Ruin my husband's brilliant career? Destroy our family? Blacken our name?"

"No. It is not my intention." Yet even as he spoke, he knew it for a lie—but his body spoke where his tongue could not, so he spread his hands wide, revealing his tenting erection, giving her proof of how deep he desired her, how hard he pulsed for her, how hot she turned him.

But her gaze didn't travel in that direction. Instead, she studied her forefinger.

What the hell! What in God's name was he supposed to do now? Of course he wanted to ruin her husband's career, destroy the family, blacken Dankworth's name! Did she think he was a saint? He scratched his head, trying to form words in his mind that might make sense. He stood before her— vulnerable—while she studied seams in the upholstery?

"Annie, I wish I had staged all this about your husband, for then it would be a matter of bowing after the performance and taking you straight to my bed."

His breath steamed at the thought. "However, your marital dilemma is not my amusement." Fuck, he was a poor liar. He took a deeper breath, raking his hands through his hair. "My strategy in the kiss, my dear Annie, was to…" He paused. If he admitted he'd kissed her because he craved her, she'd know him to be an insensitive dolt who'd made use of her distress. If he said he lost all sense and reason in her presence, she'd question his self-control—and he couldn't have her questioning his control when she needed to trust him to discover the truth about Dankworth. Dear God, his mind stretched for ideas while the lower half of his body didn't give a damn about reason. His shaft already pointed to the target. "My strategy in the kiss was to complete a youthful curiosity." He grabbed at the lie.

"Youthful curiosity," she echoed, drawing back. "I hoped the kiss meant something for the future, yet all the while you were concentrated on reliving the past?"

"Dammit, woman, you are twisting everything! I want—no, hoped for a future too. I just wasn't sure, I mean, I am trying my best, but I can't follow the conversation when you wrap your arguments and words around me!"

"The way I have had my pledge of 'I do' twisted?" she shot back, standing upright, pulling the blanket across her breasts in tight fists. "You don't even know the meaning of how one's life might be twisted. When I left you on the old drystone wall, my life changed forever. Meanwhile you've been the rake, travelling the seas without responsibility or regard for others except yourself. Even tonight, when I am at my lowest, you kiss me. Your kiss was as self-seeking as any man I've ever met."

He reeled, not from her words—he deserved it all. He reeled at how he dismissed the hurt and fraud perpetrated on her. How deep the damage went. She was right of course. He had behaved like a snake, plundering her soft voluptuous body, tasting her when she was vulnerable, blaming youth, enjoying a straining hard erection, wanting her visual approval of his lust! Her words were naïve, yet perhaps her experience eclipsed even his own.

He had to believe her marriage to Dankworth was loveless. His heart lifted, while shame slapped him down.

He stepped away, sitting back in his chair, his hands open on the armrests. "My sincerest apologies for my behavior. I believe this situation, as it has been revealed by this Captain Barton, whether it is true or false, has stirred us. We will begin by visiting the church where you believe you were married to check the register. I will be guided by you in all future dealings with this matter, and as a token of my good faith, I promise I will not kiss you again. Unless you ask. I am still rake enough to think of the flesh. You can't expect me to go from sinner to saint over the course of an evening, can you?"

She stilled.

By his reasoning, handing her the power had its advantages, gave her self-assurance in the face of an uncertain future. He wasn't in the slightest bit confident she had the expertise to wield it, but it was a risk he had to take to spur her to action. If she accepted his offer, then at least they were rowing in unison.

"What of New Holland?"

"It will keep."

She looked at him, then—"We start at Barfrestone. After Charlotte's wedding."

First step. "I will be guided by your judgment Annie. However, I must add a word of caution. I'm not convinced we can wait till after Charlotte's wedding."

"Why not?"

"Dankworth has the advantage. Every minute matters. I have already made some preliminary enquiries, and the archbishop is—"

"My priority is my daughter," she interrupted.

"Your marriage status is vital. You may be living a lie."

"You are so naïve, John."

He didn't disagree. He had never been married, so perhaps it was fair comment. He didn't want to push her away in his desire to help, and he didn't want to bully her the way Dankworth had, but time was of the essence. He frowned. Perhaps this was the compromise he needed to make. He would do it, even if it risked a frenzy after this blasted wedding. He hoped precious Charlotte appreciated the extent of Anne's devotion. Unfortunately, he'd heard rumors to the contrary. By all accounts, Charlotte was a brat.

"I have a favor to ask," she said.

He waited.

"Could you please accompany me to Graystone, this morning? Charlotte and Aunt Bess will not take my word about widow Woollie so close to the wedding. I will need added weight. From a man. They will not question you."

"You are not going back. You will be putting yourself in harm's way of Dankworth."

"I can and I will. Not to return will compromise

Charlotte, and anyway, Howard's not home, but in any case, he will not risk bruising me before the wedding. The hero protects his reputation at all costs. I am safe for the minute."

His blood boiled to the rafters. "Annie, it worries me to hear you talk like this. I have grave misgivings about letting you return. You must not."

Her disbelief was clear. "This is my decision."

"You should stay here at Elfleet Hall under my protection."

"I won't." She turned her back on him.

He studied her, aware something else simmered, some hard-edged unspoken worry influenced her, and he could not fathom from where it came except she seemed to be under some cloud, of her own or Dankworth's or even her father's making. Everything was becoming more complicated. The woman was swamped, and he could not reach her.

She kept her back to him, the tension around her shoulders increased. "Tell me, John, did you ever consider the consequences of your affairs on the lives of your mistresses? Weren't your romancing and bedroom antics a manipulation by flattery?"

His skin prickled. He shifted in his chair. Perhaps her problem was him. Regretting he'd ever taken any woman to his bed, he resigned himself to answering her, even though it was the sort of conversation he reserved for late nights on the deck with his men. "Annie"—he searched for ways to adjust his phrasing—"I have met many women who sought me out for fleeting happiness. Seeking pleasure is the way of all flesh. A release. Lust. I never lied there would be a relationship beyond the sheets."

She gave a bitter laugh. "Do you know, Howard tells me the same? He too has never pretended at more than he can give. He gives nothing."

Every fiber in his body shriveled. His leg caught fire, flames consuming him in searing agony. The breath rushed out of him, making him gulp as he struggled to stand, for she wounded deadlier than any lead shot. "The servants will be rising soon. You've had a shock and need rest before I take you to Graystone. I'll escort you to your room."

Chapter Nine

Saturday, May 2

The carriage rocked her back to Graystone—an awful prospect but for the company of a handsome man whose outstretched legs commanded space in the small confines of the cabin. Hands clasped in lap, with an arrogant cut about his jaw, his gaze lingered outside, roving over distant trees or a grassy verge, no doubt cogitating strategies against Howard.

Pretending to observe the countryside, she sneaked a closer inspection. Damn, but her heart raced at the presence of him. How many women counted in his number? And why concern herself with John's lovers? Perhaps it was because, at last, she could be one of them? What a delicious notion. Her tongue ran across her scorched, bruised lips.

"Annie, whilst we agreed not to deal with this matter till after the wedding, you are going into danger. I must remind you, when you return to Graystone, do not reveal our findings to anyone, especially Dankworth. If you need me at any stage, send a message to Elfleet Hall, and I will be here at your side."

She sighed. "Thank you. For the first time, I don't feel so alone."

He leaned toward her, his breath fanning her cheek. "So you understand my position, it has been my experience that when there is a glimpse of some menace breaking on the surface, the corruption will go down deep. The evil is rising for some reason we know little about, and it must be harpooned, dispensed with. You want me to wait till after Charlotte's wedding, and against my better judgment, I have agreed, but once the ceremony is complete, the day after Charlotte is wed, I will arrive and take you from Graystone under my protection."

Anne moved away, cramping herself into the corner of the carriage, pulling herself straighter with the strap near her head. She didn't want him whispering to her when she needed to claim distance, or she might be tempted to kiss him yet again.

"Please give me some credit for thinking the matter through instead of dismissing my interest. After all, you agreed last night to be guided by me. Perhaps I do not need your protection."

He looked at her as if considering a distasteful idea, although he said reasonably enough, "Very well. Indulge me with your thoughts on the matter."

She let go of the strap and readjusted her shoulders, for in truth it would be a relief to discuss her schemes that had kept her awake all night after leaving his library.

"I will leave Graystone straight after the wedding, to go back north." She clutched her hands in her lap and turned better to see him. "Once there, I will prudently question Howard. If I discover this situation is but a fake marriage story and Howard is merely guilty of talking drunken gambling tales in India, then I will put the matter to rest." He stared at her. She had been correct in assuming John had not anticipated this.

Emboldened, she continued. "If the marriage is in reality a counterfeit, then I will threaten to dishonor him, announcing the scandal to the papers if he does not agree to my demands." John remained quiet. Her spirits lifted. "I may be able to convince him to proceed with a separation and maybe a divorce. He might say he wants us to continue as before, but I cannot countenance living a marriage which is a lie once I know the truth, although I may need to wait till Charlotte settles in her new life before I create a social storm. Whatever eventuality, I hold the power, and he won't be able to discredit me by calling me insane or having me deported."

John was quiet for a heartbeat.

"Have you lost your mind?" he exploded, coming toward her across the seat, the warm strength of his thigh pressing against hers, their shoulders touching, the rustle of her skirts from his advance, the junction between her legs melting at his proximity. "Anne, the man has continued a sham marriage with you for years, he is violent, and you wish to negotiate! Do you believe you are in any position to give voice to your demands! No! You are not prudently questioning anyone unless you have protection, and the more you speak the more I know I am right to assert my involvement as a necessity. You have been under his abuse too long to think logically."

Anne's heart galloped as she clutched her breast. How he had ever got a reputation as a rake, adventurer, and rogue? She never expected any man would care so much about her, and yet here he sat, offering to protect a woman who wasn't even his wife. She should lean over and steal another kiss at those delicious plump lips, which had explored her with dizzying intrusion. "Thank you."

"Annie," he said in an exasperated tone, but already they were at Graystone, back at her cold hard old life that was as bleak as the gray stone foundations.

The cane he held clattered to the floor of the carriage. While he bent to retrieve it, his hand shot beneath her skirts, grabbing her ankle. She was shocked by the hot grip where she had never been touched by another human. A flame shot into her groin scorching her hot and moist, paralyzing her from all movement.

He whispered, "You go nowhere without my protection."

His rough voice went through her. She stared into his eyes, as his forefinger drew a slow line up her calf and probed the soft skin in the fold behind her knee. A frisson shimmered down her spine at his audacity.

The door catch clicked open.

"Ah, there is my cane." He brought up the stick as the footman opened the door.

"My darling Anne!" Aunt Bess wafted down the stairs in a puff of purple feathers and silk to greet them as they exited the carriage.

Anne turned in a daze, heart banging in her chest, the touch of John's hand, burning behind her knee. "Aunt Bess!" She threw herself into the open arms of the one person in the world she called friend.

"You have been a naughty girl, staying away overnight, but I watched the carriage coming up the drive and knew it would be you." Her eyes raked John with more than a twinkle. "So, where have you been? Or should I not ask."

John bowed and kissed the older woman's

extended hand. "A pleasure to meet you again, Miss Belet. However, before we are drawn into further conversation, allow me the opportunity to tell you I remember with fondness your sister, Anne's mother. I never knew my own mother, but had she lived, I always hoped she would be like Lady Gastrell-Smythe."

Anne turned to John, the sunny day brightened, and a gentle breeze ruffled through his hair like a spectral hand. Was it her mother's spirit come from heaven to bestow a sacred, beneficent approval on John Wylde? She didn't think anyone but herself and her aunt remembered her beautiful mother.

Bess melted, clasping her hands to her feathered bosom. "Oh, but in life she was a heart-warming motherly soul, wasn't she? Anne has inherited all her mother's natural beauty and generosity of spirit." She gave Anne's cheek a lingering pat. "But aren't you a charming neighbor to remember my sister when all I ever hear from my brother-in-law is how your families are feuding. You must have been a young boy when Felicity passed on."

"Thirteen, I recall."

"Just a lad. Wasn't her funeral a spectacular event? Black horses at a slow trot, black carriage, black feathers on the hearse. Simply wonderful. Did you taste the mourning biscuits? They are out of fashion now, but I loved them. I arranged it all. What a shame some fashions disappear, forgotten."

John inclined his head. "I could not attend. I was boarding at school."

"Ah well, it was many years ago now." She smiled at him through dull gray glassy eyes. "I am sure the village will remember the funeral, as I am also sure they will remember most of the goings-on at Graystone." She inclined her head toward the manor. "This household has provided more than its share of gossip over the years. I've no doubt my eccentric militarized brother-in-law has supported most of it."

John coughed into his fist, while Anne imagined what fodder the gossips reveled.

"Come. Don't disappoint me, your lordship, by feigning discretion!" Bess goaded. "We have all read of your wicked reputation for adventure. Surely simple words won't deter you?" Bess took him by the arm. "It is always the same at Graystone, isn't it, Anne? My brother-in-law puts everyone in a mood, but despite his obtuseness, I would love for you to join us for an elderberry wine on the terrace. It is a small group, but we would be honored by your company…and I made the wine. A family recipe."

"Thank you, Miss Belet, I would be honored. I should warn you, however, my presence risks raising the general's ire."

"But wouldn't that be the point of his lordship staying?" Bess smiled.

"Indeed it would." John smiled in reply.

Gathering her skirts and steadying herself with one hand on the stone balustrading, Bess reached for John's arm as she climbed the stairs.

Anne tutted. Yes, she wanted John's assistance while explaining her overnight absence to her father and Charlotte, but she had enough conflict without these two renegades making more for their own diversion. Her knee still tingled, John's kiss bruised her lips, she'd been awake all night, her marriage was questionable and—

"What in the name of all that is right is this man doing on my property!" the general exploded as the group entered the house, Bess teetering past with John in her grasp.

Bess sniffed. "Your neighbor has gone to considerable trouble to bring your daughter home from her overnight stay, so I've invited the earl for drinks on the terrace."

The general's face went purple. He turned to his daughter. "Where were you last night, Anne? Charlotte has been beside herself as to what trouble you've been causing around the district. Leaving the May Day celebrations without a by-your-leave, returning home this morning, delivered by a rake! And as for you"—he turned to John, his purple complexion contrasting with the white spittle forming at the corners of his mouth— "I warned you before. I want you off!"

"Reginald," Bess said with increased volume. "You need your hearing checked. I have invited the earl for drinks on the terrace."

"There is nothing wrong with my hearing, you old bat. I forbid it. I forbid this man in my house! I forbid him sitting on my terrace sipping drinks! I forbid it, do you hear me?"

Bess turned her back on the general, and said, "My lord, would you accompany me to the terrace?" Then, smiling up at John, added, "Major General Howard Dankworth is waiting for us."

Anne felt, rather than heard, John stop, which was strange because it happened about the same time her heart collapsed and she lost the use of her senses. Howard. She wished to crawl under the hall table or hide crouched behind the umbrella stand. As her blood pounded, the rhythm pushing through her ears and veins, she hoped the shock had not registered on her face, but perhaps it did, for when her aunt's face came into focus, Bess was watching her with alert curiosity.

"Howard is here already?" Anne ventured, her voice echoing in the cavernous hall.

"Yes, dear. Wasn't due till this evening, but for the first time in living memory, he arrived earlier than expected. Last night."

Anne looked at John who stared at her, his eyes searching hers, his blue arctic gaze cold yet warm, enveloping her in a sweet security of strength, support, and secrets which belonged to them. In a heartbeat, Bess pulled on his arm, urging him toward the doors leading onto the terrace. He resisted. Anne gave an imperceptible nod. His eyes lowered, bowing to her wishes, then he moved away in Bess's tow.

Anne joined them on the terrace a full thirty seconds later, cast in time spans of a thousand years.

Major General Howard Dankworth approached her first. Her husband, yet not her husband. A stranger whom she had seen a thousand million times, yet never seen at all. Caricatures of this national hero portrayed him as tall and commanding, wearing his tricorn, looking down on his troops, yet in life he was her height and ordinary. The sort of man you'd assume performed a heroic act in the preparation of his toilet for the way his hair was puffed and styled with maximum loftiness.

"Anne." Howard strode across the terrace to peck the air beside her ear, then withdrew to return again with a glass. He was never demonstrative. Something was wrong. John's presence? No. His bored expression said he concentrated on other matters, a half smile, but never a true engagement.

She accepted the drink.

"Isn't this adorable!" Bess clapped her hands. "Allow me to perform the introductions. The Earl of Rochester, this is Baronet, Major General Sir Howard Dankworth."

John stretched out his hand. "We've met a few times over the years but never had an opportunity to speak."

Dankworth gripped John's fingers, one sharp shake, arms dropped, and several steps backwards. "Have we? Yes. Perhaps. Before India."

The handshake, the off-hand remark, all dirtied John, for he was the one person innocent of the foulness of this party. John's presence burning bright with truth and nobility, the kiss of last night, his touch behind her knee, his lips on her wrist, all points of contact stamped her so her waters shivered and ran in his vicinity. Howard? Here was the person she could not drag her eyes from, the wolf in sheep's clothing circling his prey with languid steps.

She knew Howard well because he was a younger version of her father, but unlike Howard, her father didn't need the protection of a sheepskin. Her father controlled the pack with vicious snapping violence which Bess, the old matriarch, managed to retaliate with effect.

"When was it decreed that a man was not master in his own home? In fact—"

"Reginald, don't behave like a bore," Bess barked. "We have in our company Sir Howard, your famous son-in-law, decorated and knighted for his services to the expansion of the kingdom, and also at Graystone, the earl, who is likewise a knighted entrepreneur who has made shipping and mercantile success from the same expansion. An English seaman and a soldier in our midst. Gentleman, I can see this national prosperity continuing well into the next century with you both at the helm as examples of the enlightened man. Our kings have done us proud."

"Bunkum!" Hands clasped behind his back, the general planted his feet wide apart, a sweat forming on his upper lip. "This earl is nothing more than a wastrel who has made cash from the king's resources which included blasted tea, a woman's drink, and then has the impudence to argue abolishing slavery, which is the order of society and has been since the age of time."

"Reginald, don't talk politics in mixed company unless you want me to air my views, which would be in complete support of Lord Rochester, and furthermore, you stand to be corrected. The earl is your rich neighbor who exports agricultural equipment and is involved in the barricades, or so I've heard. You're no slouch, are you, your lordship?" Bess passed John a crystal glass of elderberry wine with a wink.

"Then he can afford to move to London and visit Lloyd's Coffee House. Leave me in peace. Why you feel inclined to visit Graystone defies logic. If it's because of your injury, then I suggest you entertain yourself at the blasted reading circle rather than at my home!"

"Well, he won't want to stay in this backwater now you've insulted him, will he?" Bess said.

The general's face filled with blood. "I'll remind you, sister-in-law, you are also a guest in my home."

"Only until this wedding is over, brother-in-law, and then Anne, Howard, and I will be gone back north. Thank heavens." Bess took a sip of wine.

"Correction, Miss Belet," Howard said. "Anne and I will be staying at Graystone the week following the wedding."

"But our arrangement was to go back north the day after the wedding, Sir Howard. Anne and I discussed this months ago. We've made arrangements to leave." Bess shifted in her seat, clearly displeased. "I certainly don't want to impose on my brother-in-law's indecent hospitality a moment longer than I need. No. If you have business to complete and wish to stay on, then I'll organize to visit the Hotham the Hatter after the wedding. The sea air will do me good. Anne, you'll accompany me, won't you, dear?"

"Anne stays here with me," Howard said. At Bess's obvious surprise, he added, "There's a function in Margate a few days after the wedding. Anne must attend."

Anne glanced at John, who sipped his wine with a concentration far beyond the demands of the task.

"Don't let my sister-in-law's meddling interfere with your plans, Howard," the general growled, pleased at the opportunity of putting his sister-in-law in her place. "You are in charge of your wife. You know where she needs to be."

Bess glared. "We speak of Anne. Not a platoon."

"Both need firm management, sister-in-law."

Howard said, "We will discuss details after our guest has departed."

The general looked as if he would argue this too, but he was stopped by Dankworth, who changed the direction of the conversation. "Does your lordship gamble?"

John shook his head. "No."

Dankworth shrugged. "I took you for a club man."

The general snorted in obvious enjoyment at the ridicule. Bess humphed with disdain, although John remained silent, so the bait fell flat.

Howard found a different interest. Managing to exclude John with a turn of his shoulders, he said, "I intend to travel to Margate this afternoon. There's some dice on. I was thinking I'd leave soon."

"But you've just arrived!" the general erupted. "Surely you can resist the temptation of gambling in Margate for a few nights? We don't want to see you in the Gaoler's Coach when we need you to escort the bride down the aisle the day after tomorrow!"

"No fear, General. With your good name and reputation, the coach I enter will be the one I procure myself."

The general sucked his teeth. "I'll hold you to that. In the meantime, you can make yourself useful and pick me up a copy of the *Chronicle*."

"It would be my pleasure." Dankworth gave his superior a small bow.

Bess humphed and raised her eyes to the sky. "I always think there is nothing as insincere as ingratiating humility. We all know the words pleasure and General have never been uttered in the same br—"

"Mother!" Charlotte bounded onto the terrace. "Where have you been? It was mean of you not to be home after May Day, when you knew I would need your help with placing the embroidered roses on my gloves. The seamstress had arrived, and you know

Joseph and I are so particular about style. Oh!" She came up short. "My lord. I didn't expect to see you here. Father, Grandfather, Aunt Bess. Are we having a gathering?"

"Impromptu," Bess said.

"If you had told me, I could have asked Joseph." Charlotte indicated to the staff she wanted to be served a drink.

Bess's feathers rippled while Anne's scalp squeezed and tightened around her temples.

"Father, I am so pleased you're home," Charlotte went on as she lifted her glass from the server. "I cannot believe it, to see you standing here adding a touch of distinction to the gathering."

"Not for long, dear." Howard gave a shallow smile. "I have some business in Margate this evening. While I'm there, I'll hire a bathing machine and wash off the dust before your wedding."

"But Father, I was hoping we could have some time." Charlotte gave her foot a little stamp. "Joseph is desperate to speak with you about his prospects. You promised."

Howard's lips constricted. If John hadn't been present, Anne might have allowed Howard to answer Charlotte's insistence, but the bride was too temperamental for comfort and this gathering contained enough unstable participants.

"My apologies for staying away last night, Charlotte darling," Anne intervened with a calmness she did not feel. "I didn't mean to get waylaid with widow Woollie and upset you. The earl brought me home in his carriage."

The bride-to-be was undeterred. "Father, you

promised you would speak to Joseph. The servants can draw you a bath here."

Dankworth gulped back his drink and kept his gaze distant.

"Father, did you hear what I said? Need I remind you this is my wedding, and my father and mother should be with me, not gallivanting around the district?"

"For once I rather think I see the girl's point," Aunt Bess said, then turned to Anne. "So tell us about this widow. You knew her when you were a child, didn't you? Have we been introduced?"

"She's as old as Methuselah." It was the general who replied, his gruff loud voice making everyone jump. "I saw her once, at St. Ursula's years ago. Looked like an ex-pugilist. She needed a shave. I trust she hasn't been invited to the wedding."

"No," Charlotte said. "I don't even know the woman. How is she connected?"

John cleared his throat. "The good widow is my charwoman's aunt. Not connected, except she makes a delicious barley soup."

Charlotte's nose scrunched.

John shot a glance at Anne as much to say *How does the general think he knows this fictitious widow?* She gave her shoulder a slight shrug. She had no idea except every person on the terrace was party to a pretense of some sort, each contriving a lie others believed or doubted.

Anne cleared her throat. "Father, widow Woollie is overcoming an attack of gout and asked me to play cribbage."

"I was having trouble with my wedding." Charlotte

pouted.

"I wasn't having any trouble at all until all these guests arrived," the general brooded.

"Grandfather, you better not cause a disturbance at my wedding."

The general turned to her. "How dare you preach to me in my own house! I tolerate it from my sister-in-law, but you, Granddaughter, are having this wedding at St. Ursula's because of my piety. Your mother and father may have spoiled you to a fault, but do not think I am naïve of your self-interested tactics. The one good thing to come out of this wedding will be if you give me a grandson, and you better not dally. It is the reason I'm suffering to have everyone here."

"How dare you say such despicable things!" Charlotte stamped her foot.

"Anne," the general continued, undeterred, "you have done an abysmal task raising this rude, ungrateful, impudent chit of a girl! That I get no peace in my own house! Inviting neighbors who I hate! The fault is all yours, and I will be pleased to be rid of the lot of you. The day after the wedding, I want you all gone. Even you, Howard. Every last blinking rude one of you!" So saying, he marched inside, banging the door behind him.

"We aren't going, Anne." Howard contradicted the general before the noise of the slammed door had subsided. "Your father can demand what he likes. I have business, which takes priority over an old man's routine. You will stay here until I come and take you to Margate."

Anne's head imploded as she nodded dumbly. How she longed to take a peek at John, to reassure herself of his support, but she couldn't risk tipping Howard to his plan.

Bess snuggled into her chair.

Charlotte's cheeks were blotched red. "Thank heaven I'm marrying Joseph. I've had enough of this deranged family. If you'll excuse me, I need to write a note to Joseph. Oh, and my lord, I haven't invited you to the wedding, not because I would not enjoy your company and influence, but I am limiting the guests." She attempted a cute smile. "You will have to visit us once we are married, although I believe you will be at sea by then. You don't mind if I dash, do you, Father darling?"

Howard nodded her to go.

As Charlotte left the terrace, Anne wilted, a headache threatening to squash her skull. "I might also take my leave and make use of the opportunity to freshen after spending the night away." She needed to crawl beneath the covers of her bed, settle her head on a pillow to await blessed sleep.

"Yes, dear, go ahead. You must be exhausted after tending to a sick old widow." Bess smiled.

"Goodbye, Lady Anne." John gave a small bow.

"My lord, thank you for your kind offer of a vehicle. I trust my family has not tested you too far." She tried to sound sincere, struggled with an insane desire to run, then following her instinct, turned on her heel, and left.

John watched Anne leave. Her skirt swished with a dancing movement around her dainty ankles even while her shoulders sagged. There was a lot to be said for his gallery of portraits. At least she had the presence of mind not to glance at him when Howard talked of her staying on. God, but she was magnificent.

He turned his attention to Dankworth, who was topping up his drink and saying to no one in particular, "I want to look at the vegetable patch before I start the trip to Margate."

Bess and John said nothing as Dankworth, without a glance, left by way of the garden.

John watched Dankworth's short slender target of a back. Damn the yellow-livered bastard's eyes.

Bess broke into his thoughts, patting the seat beside her. "I fear the general's outburst dampened everyone's spirits, and I was so hoping for a pleasant chat."

John reasoned he should be taking his leave, but the idea of Anne remaining vulnerable and alone in this deranged family, as Charlotte called it, made him reluctant to go.

He sat beside Miss Belet, relieved at indulging the eccentric old aunt after all the other impetuous tempers in the family. "It is a beautiful day though, isn't it, Miss Belet? Although the wind is picking up. We will have a storm later."

"I despise discussing weather. May I be so bold as to come to the point, my lord?"

"I would encourage it, Miss Belet." He took a sip of wine, savoring the liberal dose of gin.

"You like Anne, don't you?"

The liquid paused in his throat. Hot and cold.

He turned to the older woman whose gray rheumy eyes held an unnerving observant quality. He continued to swallow. "Yes. She is a clever woman."

"And beautiful."

"Oh, yes. Beautiful. One can't deny it."

"I live near her, you know, up past London. We

visit each other whenever we can. Every few days."

Strange how he'd never envisioned Anne having a confidant other than himself, and yet she had a life in the intervening years. How little he knew. He turned toward Miss Belet and nodded, encouraging her to continue.

"She has a veritable list of suitors who do not care she is married. Anne does not give a crumb about them. Yet you"—she pointed a bony finger at his chest—"you she communicates with across the terrace with the smallest of shrugs. Not even her husband has this advantage."

A rush of pleasure tremored through him.

"You are right, my lord. I see the understanding in your eyes. Howard doesn't wish to have any advantage over Anne. This last month or so it has become worse."

John tried to appear relaxed, at ease, in control, unflappable, composed, self-possessed. Tried not to show his heart beat with the secret knowledge he'd kissed her already, tasted her soft lips, and experienced her warm breasts crushed against him. How he thrilled learning Howard sought no advantage.

"If you might take the advice of an older woman, the kitchen garden is around the other side of the house. You can follow the outside wall. I believe visiting the vegetable patch is Howard's way of taking leave for a pipe. He knows nothing of gardening."

"Are you suggesting I speak with the major general?"

"Yes."

"Miss Belet, I have no reason."

"You do, my lord." She leaned closer. "Charlotte's wedding has compelled some undercurrents to move.

You are a seafaring man. With all your ships and sailors and money, you are used to authority and understand my meaning."

"I'm not sure I do."

Bess plucked at a loose feather on her purple wrap. "I adore gardening, but sometimes a seedling will not grow because the soil is infertile. Diseased. No matter how much water or love we give the plant, it refuses to revive. Then it must be pulled out and the land left fallow until it restores some condition, before we can plant again. Sometimes the soil will never recover. Do you wish me to continue with this analogy?"

"I'd prefer it if you would make your point clear."

"It is my opinion Howard intends seeking a divorce," Bess whispered.

John stopped himself pulling away in surprise. There was more to old Aunt Bess than purple feathers. "Why would you think this?"

"Howard has been more distant. More distant than normal. Distracted with her and everyone. I think the gay divorcee would be a role Anne would suit, new ground so to speak, but she is old-fashioned and too trusting for her own good. This will sound impertinent, but could I impose on you to make an enquiry of Howard—a short conversation should be all it will take—just to ascertain the direction of his thoughts? You see it would be less of a shock to the poor girl if she were alerted in advance that trouble brewed. She protects Charlotte with her life, and if there is some lurking situation, it is best she is warned. You will find her a capable woman who can circumvent troubles and situations involving Howard, so long as she is given fair warning. The truth is, I have tried talking to Howard.

However, he is not capable of talking sensibly with women. You, my lord, are the man to do it."

If there were no damned marriage, divorce would be impossible! Yet, he was shamefully reminded of Anne's words when she first came to him asking for assistance. He had turned her away, and now the aunt made a similar request. He couldn't go against Anne's express wish that the matter rest until after the wedding, could he?

He considered the distant tree line of Rutherford's Wood, where a line of thick luminous clouds banked high above the green treetops, soaring into the blue. For all its majesty, the air was growing thick, humid, and oppressive—hot for the second day of spring. He would not compromise Annie's safety or hard-won trust by being indiscreet again. "I will speak to the major general after the wedding, when I have time to assess the situation."

Bess sat forward, placing her hand on his knee with a slight squeeze. "Your lordship, you will not have the luxury. The man is never at home as it is."

"With all due respect, Miss Belet, I have my reasons for not wishing to speak."

Bess sat back and crossed her arms.

"I will speak with him as and when I see fit, Miss Belet."

Bess shrugged with a certain coolness. "I am reminding you, my lord, Howard has the nature of a gambler and drinker. If you care about Anne, then I believe you should act. Now. Like a champion, rather than waiting like an insipid fool until poor Anne collapses with the shock of it all."

Something had the old woman in a fluster. She was

manipulating him to her will every way she could. "Why is it you are so insistent, Miss Belet, about a relationship which is none of our affair?"

"Anne is my niece, and it hasn't been an easy time for her, not that she'd ever suggest otherwise. Anne is too loyal to Howard. When she was young, she had such a fair and giving heart, she enjoyed life, only now I watch it ebb away. Charlotte has been the glue in the marriage. They gave their daughter every advantage, too much I believe. Truth be told, it is the one area I would agree with the general, though I'd trust you not to repeat it." She tapped his arm. "You see, Anne always wanted to raise an independent girl, and her wish has eventuated with Charlotte about to leave to make her own home. There is the problem."

"How?"

"Anne has no happiness, apart from her daughter. Left with Howard, he will destroy her. The General killed my sister with his arrogance and cruelty. I am scared the same fate awaits Anne. The men in this military family are all the same. You must help her. Please."

How could he resist such a plea?

He stared into his glass. Dankworth enjoying years of a lie had hampered John from having the one woman he'd ever wanted. The pain of absence and loss shot through his heart, his world shriveling to a small black hole. He looked away and shifted in his chair.

Confronting Dankworth in the kitchen garden about life's illusions was not edifying. Yet Bess did have sound reasoning for haste. Dankworth had been in Graystone a day before he organized to visit Margate, and there would be no opportunity to discuss anything with him the day after next, when the wedding was due to take place. After the wedding posed its own problems, with the general's orders to leave, Dankworths insistence Anne stay, and his own plans to take Annie away from Dankworth and Graystone altogether.

His finger tapped his empty glass. Annie's mother had been too gentle for the men in this house. He put down his glass and took up his cane. He must act.

"I believe you are correct, Miss Belet. I will speak to Dankworth immediately. Till we meet again." He bowed.

Bess smiled.

Chapter Ten

John followed the hard brick contours of Graystone Manor, coming to an archway that led back toward the house, into a large high-walled kitchen garden. There, on an upturned pot, tucked into one of the far corners beneath an old apricot tree, sat the famous hero, Major General Howard Dankworth. Eyes closed, arms folded, head tilted back, sucking on his pipe.

"Major General." He strode up to the man, careful to cast his shadow over the officer.

Dankworth opened his eyes a slit, took in John, and closed his eyes again. "Well, well, well." He gave a long pull on his pipe, the pungent sweet smoke hanging in the motionless air. "The famous rake and adventurer, no other than John Wylde, whose name lives up to his nature, so they say." He gave a deep sigh of satisfaction. "I last saw you at the opera some four or five years ago, wasn't it? Passed you on the stairs. Yes. I remember you had Lady Withington on your arm. Was she good in bed? Most accounts suggest she bucks like a horse and responds best to a good tethering."

John was used to such talk on his ships. He ignored it then, and now. "Do you mind if I join you, Sir Howard? I wanted to speak with you. In private."

"Why would that be? Don't tell me we've been sharing a whore and you have some infernal disease."

John had been concentrating on sitting upon

another upturned pot, but now he paused. "Sharing a whore?"

Dankworth's heavy lids opened, revealing a clear golden gaze. "Anne." Dankworth closed his eyes and tilted his head back to rest against the bricks behind. "Why else would a notorious rake be wanting to talk to me? I am no fool. Cowards like you fight with their cocks. They seek approval and a gentleman's agreement before they engage. Don't bother getting comfortable. You already have my best wishes to fuck her. Just wait till she gets back home, up north, before you thrust."

An immediate tingling drained John's blood into the pit of his stomach. The kitchen garden imprisoned him, the air growing heavy with the relentless sun beating on his black jacket. He needed to see the clouds banking above Rutherford's Wood, have the cool wind on his face, be anywhere in the world, in fact, than in this cloistered atmosphere, conversing with a fool with an overblown sense of his own importance.

"I am not here seeking permission to bed Anne." John kept his tone measured.

Dankworth's head shot forward. He ripped the pipe from his mouth. "To hell you aren't! You've come in here thinking I'm going to give you access to the whore, and you have the balls to order it of me. I'm nobody's fool, Rochester. I watched you on the terrace with your little furtive glances." He laughed without humor, his eyes alight with speculation. "You want to fuck her? Go ahead. It'll be a departure from what you're used to. Tell me, do you like to take your women from behind? That's the way Mrs. Dankworth enjoys it."

John stretched his hand on the top of his walking stick, watching the tendons and veins around his knuckles rise. "Major." The word caught in John's throat. "I have come here to speak with you about your marriage."

"You aren't the first, you know." Dankworth snorted. "Not by a long shot." He started laughing, the insincere bark ricocheting off the bricks. "Do you have any idea how I hate men like you? Conceited, arrogant dandies who make their money on the blood of soldiers who give their lives for the cause and love of their nation? I despise men like you who think they can purchase the country, who believe they are so good with all their women and powdered wigs and travel by coach. What do you know of the dangers of war? The death and constant drudge of wagons in mud and midges and low rations? You know fuck-all, dearie, except about the weight of your purse and the plumpness of your feather bed. You'd show women your pistol and let them play with it like a toy. Oh yes. I bet you let all the women play with the muzzle. Show them what a big man you are. I bet you read all those rags too—encourage the editors to write stories about your bravery. Go ahead with my blessing, soft cock."

Bitter bile rose to the back of John's throat. "I have not come here to barter over Anne like a common whore."

"Fuck you and your damned indignation!" Dankworth leaned forward. "Look at me, Mr. Dandy Sleep-With-The-Women Wylde, and tell me you're not itching to take me on, that I haven't irritated you so violently you want to punch me here and now. You wish. Within hours, I could galvanize half the country's troops, and you'd be routed out and killed. I'd have you and all your friends who are lolling around all year in their velvet gentleman's clubs getting fat from my victories, killed. Dead. Over a stupid bitch whore with the brain of a hen."

The flash of heat through John's body seared across his brain, making his head hurt, his breath fast and boiling. He bolted forward at twice the speed of Dankworth, the pain in his knee shooting up as if the devil himself had entered his being and commandeered his body for his own. He welcomed the fire.

"Look at me, Dankworth, and see me, for I would plunge this nation into civil war over the honor of a woman. Wars have been started over less. I have manpower, ships, and gold at my disposal, more than you could ever guess. Dare me to do it, Major. You take your instructions from the king. I take my orders from no one."

Dankworth stared at him, then gave a long sigh, and closing his eyes, let his head fall back against the wall. He waved his hand in the air. "Perhaps you aren't as intimidated as the others, but beneath your black merchant's garb, you're a soft cock with a full pocket. The whore has grabbed you and is leading you around like a lapdog on a lead. I don't give a shit about any of you."

John stood. "Major, I give due warning. I am about to call you out."

"Don't believe me?" He opened his eyes a fraction. "I've been trying to tell you, but you don't seem to hear. Take a look at Charlotte. There's the proof. Any fool can see the girl has none of my features. She has fair hair and blue eyes. The girl is all her mother and some other's gonads. I'm not dueling with you over Anne's virtue—when there was none in the first place. There is no dispute, and you armed with your cock and walking stick. Fuck Anne blind for all I care. Other bastards have. You want to ask me about my marriage? Find out all about it from my wife. You'll discover for yourself she's a boring little bitch."

The air in John's throat froze despite the bricks and heat and quiet garden solitude. For the first time in this whole twisted conversation, he knew Dankworth spoke the truth. Charlotte had nothing of the look of Howard Dankworth.

But this was an English country garden, the essence of dignity and noblesse. Danger came at sea, not on land when the sun was warm and the apricot tree was laden with sweet ripening blossoms, and bees buzzed lazily.

"Shock you?" Dankworth laughed and closed his eyes again. "I can see by your face your testes have shriveled up into your gut. You didn't even see it, did you?"

Pure unadulterated spitting lava exploded white hot in John's veins. He grabbed his pistol, pointing it at Dankworth's sealed eyelids.

A sudden clatter erupted from behind the trellis. "Oh, my apologies, sir, my lord," a girl said, kneeling to pick up a pewter bowl that had fallen to the flags, though she kept her gaze transfixed on John's firearm. "I-I was just coming to collect some rhubarb, for dinner, before the storm. I didn't realize anyone was here."

Howard with his eyes still closed—the sleeping serpent. A bully who'd abused his Annie.

143

One small lead pellet through closed eyes was too virtuous an end for this bastard. The place to take down this smug hero was before the nation and with multitudes of unforgiving pain and humiliation.

"Don't apologize," John told the maid. "Thank you." He motioned her to be quiet and leave. "I was about finished with this discussion."

Dankworth's closed lids didn't flicker. "Running to the breast?"

The girl took small steps away, her shock transferred to Dankworth at the comment.

"I'm not running anywhere," John said. "We've both agreed I'll be staying around." He nodded to the retreating maid, stuffed his gun into his belt, and then limped out of the garden, into the refreshing windy turbulence of a promised storm.

Wind pushing at his back, his spirit in a maelstrom, he strode around to the front of Graystone into the hall, signaled the butler, and asked for a piece of paper and a quill. He scribbled a note to Anne in handwriting he didn't recognize as his own, ordering her to visit widow Woollie that evening. He folded the letter twice, instructing the butler to deliver it into Lady Anne's hands, when Lady Anne was in her own company. He hated leaving her in Graystone—this pit of horrors. His consolation was Dankworth would soon be on his way to Margate.

For a man with a limp, John fled down the steps of Graystone, into his waiting coach, and banged the roof with his walking stick to get moving. His mouth was dry. His knee screamed as if dragged across the ocean floor. Some terrible evil had been stumbled upon.

But what?

Chapter Eleven

He arrived back at Elfleet Hall a few hours before the threatening storm broke. Racing around his house with staff, closing shutters, shouting orders, the normality of man against nature safer than man against man. For the first time in his life, John had been mere moments away from killing someone not in the protection of his men and property. For pleasure.

As the rain drizzled, he eased into a chair, lifting his foot onto a stool for a much needed rest. The desire to kill quenched him like a bittersweet elixir, making him as vile as the man he sought to eradicate. Fuck, but he hated these moments of personal insight, for he wished to kill and make it sweet. Dankworth knew no mercy or restraint—he lived to take life, and John would meet Dankworth on equal terms.

His gaze lifted to the weapons on his walls as he rubbed his knee. Constant small cramps from overuse and standing too long had swelled the joint to the size of a pudding. He had sat amongst many warriors, had experience enough of such men and the strife they could harvest, didn't want to face another foe, but he must. He'd assumed Annie weak and changed, but in the face of Dankworth's anger, she had shown more strength than any woman should own.

The shuttered windows rattled fierce, while a musky dampness permeated the air like cold spilled blood.

Anne should be with him at Elfleet Hall, standing before the fire, warming her vulnerable sweet body. The Earl of Rochester was the one man in England who could save her now. Who else from the aristocracy or military would believe the insanity of her husband?

Donovan knocked and entered. "My lord, while you were predisposed this morning, a message came from your man of business, Master Cox, which I took the liberty of leaving on your desk for your attention. There has been a fortuitous opportunity for rescheduling our departure to next week."

"What's that you say?" John turned his attention from the fire. "Next week? I can't do it. Get a message to Cox, will you?"

"Saying what, my lord?"

John shook his head, clearing the last vestiges of her curves and violets. "Tell Cox to keep *Siren Song* in preparedness. When I leave, it will be on a moment's notice."

"My lord."

Donovan bowed and went to leave, but John stopped him. "Donovan, after recent events, I've been thinking about, well, I wanted to take this opportunity to thank you. For all your help these last months. I haven't been an easy patient, I think."

Donovan bowed. "The staff have noticed your increased energy these last few days, my lord. We are all praying for a speedy recovery. Might I hazard to suggest it is since the women have ceased their visits?"

"No. It's because I am rid of the damned leech. Donovan…" John paused. "We are of around the same age. Have you ever considered settling? I mean, in your case, it would be entering the sacrament of marriage."

"Yes, my lord."

John blinked. "Where is she then? Or do you intend to marry the church, become a minister, and save a congregation, rather than just my worthless soul?"

"A woman, my lord."

"Why is it you've never spoken of her before? What is her name, you old devil! After all these years together, I can't believe I am hearing about her now, and here I was thinking my manservant a saint!"

"Beth, my lord. Small pox."

John's breath left his body. How could he have been such a fool? The big man with fumbling hands had a gentle soul. "I am sorry. I had no idea. Wait for me while I stand"—he braced his arms on the chair—"for I wish to take you firm by the shoulder. It would be a comfort to us both."

Donovan stepped forward, laying his hand on John's shoulder instead, stilling him. "I appreciate your concern, my lord, but do not disturb yourself. Now you be seated. It was a dim and distant time ago, and I do not fret so anymore. Beth is up there singing with the angels. She tells me she's happy, and one day I'll be with her."

"Yes. Yes. Of course." John moved back into his seat. "Thank you, Donovan. For your honesty. Beth, you say? Next time I'm in a church, I will say a prayer, for her. If you like. I mean, if you think your God would listen to me. I am not shriven."

Donovan's pockmarked countenance barely changed, yet somehow the room became warmer. It was as if the man had given John a large flashing smile. "I've never met a sinner yet whom the good Lord would not receive into his flock."

John shifted. "I have met a few, but thank you."

After Donovan left the room, John stared at the fire. The dour Scot possessed feelings. Donovan never had a second chance at love with Beth, yet somehow destiny had put Annie in John's path. He would not lose her again.

Dankworth's wickedness stood in his way, but today had proved honor was never held so close by the hand, as it was in the heart.

And he was a warrior.

He sat back in his chair till the pistol dug into his spine.

It was twilight before a timid knock sounded at the door. John called the staff, demanding why nobody had spotted the arrival of Lady Anne. But it was a maid, the same woman who had been collecting rhubarb, who entered his hall shaking cascades of water from her coat.

"Where is Lady Anne?" he demanded. "What's happened to her? Is she all right? Tell me."

"She's fine, my lord. She hasn't been able to get away, my lord."

"Come in and tell me what is happening. Sadie, get the girl a huckaback before she catches her death."

The maid shuffled in and took the linen Sadie offered, using it to rub dry her wet hair and arms, while telling John the message she had been given to repeat. "Lady Anne does not understand why you wish to see her. However, she says if you find yourself needing to speak with her, perhaps you could bring your carriage to the second bend on the drive and wait there until she can see herself free to leave once everyone is abed. She wanted you to understand the general is in a terrible mood, my lord, and if you visit the house it will put him in a vile temper. She begs you not to risk it. Also, Major Dankworth cancelled his trip to Margate."

John scowled, fists balling at his sides. "Are you Lady Anne's personal maid?"

"Oh, yes, my lord. I have been with Lady Anne these past three years. I should have mentioned at the start, my lord." She gave him a bashful glance. "Lady Anne told me to tell you, only I forgot in my hurry. I am sorry, my lord. She trusts me, my lord."

"Forget your apologies. Donovan! Prepare the coach immediately! What was your name again?"

"Jenny, my lord. Sorry, my lord."

"It's all right, Jenny, I won't bite your head off."

"Very good, my lord." Her look was skeptical.

If she knew the black murderous rage he had in his heart, she would run and never stop. "Jenny"—he softened his tone—"I'm going to take you back to Graystone now, but this is what I will do. I will park the carriage behind the stand of silver birches on your left as you come up the drive, not on the second bend as Lady Anne suggested. I will wait there for however long it takes Lady Anne to leave the house. You must tell her I do not care how long I must wait, but it is imperative we speak. Because the night is stormy and dark, I will have Donovan here wait at the arched gateway into the kitchen garden. When Anne is ready to meet me, Donovan will escort her to the coach."

"Very good, my lord." She gave a quick glance and nervous smile with a nod to the impassive Donovan.

"Let us go, and Jenny, not a word to anyone."

Half an hour later, from his hiding place in the

darkened coach, through the constant rain, he could see Graystone's lights flickering, people moving before windows, curtains parting then being drawn together to darkness. He stared long and hard at those windows. Even a glimpse of what he presumed would be Dankworth's silhouette would have driven him to insanity. Blood and wounds, he hated waiting, restrained in a vehicle while some quarter of a mile across the landscape, his beautiful Annie was plagued by God knew what insults and abuse, keeping quiet for her own protection.

The nerves in his knee screamed in a cramp as if caught between the bones, the pain bringing a fine sweat. He breathed, imagining the carriage door opening, her head bent to climb into his premises. Dear God, his mood went from torture to lust in a heartbeat. His erection hard and instant. The ache in his groin impossible to control. He could not be kept waiting much longer.

Chapter Twelve

Anne stood before the drawing room window staring into the wet night. Somewhere out there, John waited under the cover of darkness and foul weather. She wished she were by his side, her cheek pressed against his warm chest.

"All this chilly rain harkens back to winter," Anne observed, "and just when I felt spring and summer was on its way. Mother Nature must want to remind us of what we have left behind."

Bess snorted. "Forget the weather. I tell you, I like the man Wylde. He is rather a gorgeous example of the contemporary man, don't you think?"

Anne left the window to sit beside her aunt. Dinner had been a culinary ordeal of watery pea soup, Howard's morose silence, and the general's voluble rants, which ranged from concern for Cook's health to threats on John Wylde's life. Charlotte had escaped, having dinner with Joseph's family instead, leaving Anne and Bess to each other's company while the men took their cigars and port. Every bang of some door deep within the house had her jump, fearing Howard and her father might return to the drawing room in their eagerness to torment her.

"The earl is rather handsome. He always was," Anne agreed with a quick glance at her aunt, gauging a reaction to this disclosure.

"He likes you." Bess crossed her ankles, her eyes alight. "In fact, Anne, I was thinking earlier today, he would be the perfect man for you to enjoy a torrid affair with."

"Well…" Anne raised her eyes to the ceiling as her heart came up into her throat and strangled further words. She was used to Bess's outspokenness, but hadn't prepared for this.

"You know I have never approved of Howard." The older woman warmed to her subject. "He might be your husband and the rest of the world might hail him as a legend, but I hold an altogether different opinion, which I have enumerated on several occasions over the years, and now Charlotte is about to make a life of her own, I feel I have a duty to see you thinking of yourself, Anne. What are your needs? Do you want to continue being cosseted away in your house up north waiting for Howard to come back from his next campaign?" The blue eyes pinned Anne. "I fancy the earl knows there is more to life, and before you object, I will remind you extra-marital affairs are not as frowned upon as they once were. In young girls they are because there is the threat of pregnancy, but this will not apply to you."

Anne scratched the side of her nose, studying one of the pictures above the harpsichord. It was a large oil where the lifeless black eyes of a leveret, its neck broken and head lolling, stared at her. Ever since her mother's passing, the still-life had taken on a menacing significance.

Bess crossed her arms. "To be honest, dear, one woman to another, I've never known how you've shared Howard's bed. I've told you this before. He is like a woman the way he thrives on gossip. It isn't tasteful. He wants to know every detail. Army, strategy, it's all he ever talks…"

As Bess continued, Anne turned away from the painting and Bess's monologue—both were wearing. She went to the harpsichord. Lifting the lid, she propped it open with the lid stick, which she found resting on the top string. How long till the string broke? Graystone was perishing with neglect.

Like her.

She let her finger slide over the smooth ebony plate of C-major, without pressing deep enough to cause a sound. How does one confide in an aunt, "My husband is unable to perform in the bedroom in any capacity whatsoever?" Anne couldn't. Bess would blame her the way Howard did. A man like John with a reputation as a rake and whose lovemaking skills were superior would never guess the national hero couldn't maintain an erection—he was a man yet a boy—and she, the married woman, had little more experience in lovemaking than a virgin. It would be easier on her if she lied, told everyone Howard enjoyed a love that could not be named. Yes. That outcome would be more acceptable than the truth, even for Bess

While Bess took a breath, Anne pressed down middle C. The note soon lost its sound. Every moment spent with John was fraught with a yearning to touch his body and be touched, yet why was John responsive to her kiss when Howard said she was so unattractive? And how could she ever admit to John there was no physical connection between herself and Howard at all? Howard did nothing to inspire her loyalty with regard to intimacy. There was no reason to keep the secret of his underperformance, and yet this personal information was too shameful to divulge. His secret had become hers by default. Or perhaps she didn't know how to tell the truth anymore. She couldn't even tell Aunt Bess, the words dying on her lips like the harpsichord sound.

Lacking dynamic was her trouble.

"Give me a man like John Wylde any day," Bess continued. "He can be discreet, has experience and knowhow in conducting affairs with regard. Plus, you know him. I doubt whether Howard would even care who you slept with, dear. He barely glances at you, and I know I shouldn't say this, but if your poor mother were here, she'd be agreeing with me. Give me a merchant over a military man any day."

Perhaps Bess wouldn't be so shocked if Anne were to tell her Howard came home a decorated hero, not because of his superior military strategy or tenacity for life, but rather stupid luck. He'd told her often enough when they were alone—threw it in her face to humiliate her and keep her in his lie. She paused and frowned. Perhaps she'd been keeping too many of Howard's secrets over the years: Their nonexistent love, his excessive gambling, his ill luck on the battlefield, and everything else.

But there was one area where Howard excelled. Anne turned to her Aunt. "For all your criticism of Howard, Aunt Bess, he does have a soft spot for Charlotte."

"She's his daughter!" Bess baulked. "One hopes he loves his daughter!"

Bess's words hit an unintended note. Anne looked away, perching herself on a chair further from her Aunt. She sat on her hands. So many secrets. Where one lie stopped and another started all seemed murky and unclear, except it made the discordant music of her life, without rhythm or purpose, floating on the ether.

Charlotte may not be Howard's daughter, but Anne had watched Howard once when Charlotte was a child, had seen him pat the top of Charlotte's head while she played and hummed with a doll he had brought back from the Americas. It was the closest Anne had ever seen him be with anyone. A simple pat, full of tenderness, everything a father should give to his daughter.

Charlotte adored the man, and Anne wouldn't break the bond by revealing the truth.

"All these military men are the same." Bess grimaced. "Look at your father! He wanted a son, ensuring the hereditary line and so forth, and you being a daughter is worth naught as far as he's concerned. Couldn't even be bothered thinking out a nice name for you on your birth except plain Anne. It's stunting for everyone concerned, including your poor mother who blamed herself for not providing a male heir. Disgusting—all those lost babes, not one of them going to full term—although I blame your father for this also. Is it any wonder I never married?"

In a sudden rush of affection for her aunt, Anne crossed the room to sit beside her and take her hand.

"I spoke to Lord Rochester today," Bess continued, her voice small, like a young girl. "After you went upstairs to rest."

"Oh yes?"

"I told the earl he should speak with Howard."

Anne took a second look at her innocent aunt.

"Ohh, Anne, let us not pretend once Charlotte is wed, Howard won't be off. He doesn't care for you."

Bess looked at her niece, her voice softening. "I did my family duty by asking Lord Rochester to see which way the tide turned. Howard won't answer me. He despises me, but today, John approached him, and while I have yet to hear his report, I am quietly confident Howard might press you for a divorce."

Anne blinked and withdrew her hand. So this was why John needed to speak with her. Had something awful happened? Had John been indiscreet? He had disregarded her wishes not to speak to Howard till after the wedding, which was worrying.

"Are you annoyed with me?"

"Yes. A little. Aunt Bess, if you wanted to know about the status of my marriage, pray, it is I who should venture to query my husband. This is a private family matter. John does not possess the skill."

"Oh, Anne, sometimes you can be so naïve. Howard treats all women like French clay on the sole of his boot. I see the way he dismisses you, and it's becoming worse the closer we get to Charlotte's wedding. Howard respects men in his corp. I would have asked your father to speak with Howard, except I could be sure he would deny me also. Damned military men. Although of course Lord Rochester rose to the occasion with all the necessary skills. The man is a true adventurer. I called to his blood."

It seemed a number of people felt duty bound to interfere in her life as if she weren't even there. She stopped. Except, she hadn't been there, had she?

"Aunt, you did wrong. I did not want the earl speaking with Howard. Howard is too erratic of late."

"Of course you didn't. You never would, but someone has to stand up to Howard, and there aren't many men who can."

Anne came closer to her aunt. Some knowledge lurked behind those old eyes. "What is it you know and fear, Aunt? Tell me. I order it. You aren't just concerned about a possible divorce, are you? It goes deeper."

The older woman looked away, her fingers fiddling in her lap. "Don't pummel me so, Anne. I know nothing." Bess's fingers slowed. "My love, something about him is not right. It scares me. I can feel it, like the soul of your mother is standing over me, directing me. Charlotte has been a halter to Howard, but with her gone, I fear for you. In all these years, I have never asked you to break the confidentiality of your marriage, I never would, but even I can see the earl might be a man who could offer you some armor in the coming months, if Howard becomes too intolerable. Do not misunderstand me, the earl was most chivalrous, as if he felt the same way himself. I found it endearing, and I am sure you would too, if you gave him but a chance."

Anne looked to the windows. What had passed between her husband and her lover?

****

It was well after two before Anne could slip through the darkened house to the kitchen, across the cold floor, and out into the blustery night. She drew her coat tight around her shoulders, cool rain feathering her face. She picked her way through the walled garden to the arch where Donovan waited, nodding to the man, then followed his hulking form as they crossed the wet and muddy grounds.

Yet despite the trials of the meeting, stepping into the coach gave a fearful delight at the secret rendezvous. "Father was so late to bed, I've had the very devil of a time getting out." She shrugged her arms out of her damp coat, making sure her dress wouldn't get wet, watching John while he lit a candle in one of the sconces.

"Oh," he said, which came out as more of a groan.

"Are you all right?" The candle spluttered into life, reflecting a deep warmth in his gaze, which raked over her. The cabin closed around them. The booming of her heart vibrated the air. God, but he was powerful; the back of her knees ached for his touch, and more. She swallowed.

He couldn't help it. He grabbed her by the shoulders and drew her to his mouth. No finesse, no foreplay, no introductions or sweet whispers, no seduction. Her mouth was hot and cold from the rain and soft and moist, and when the tip of her tongue flickered against his, the exhilarating lightness sent him shooting high above the stormy clouds, up into the stars in the heavens. Her succulent mouth responded deeper, and she weakened into him till he might collapse. Fumbling with her buttons, drawing her dress down from her shoulders, exposing a breast, and with a chain of kisses down the arch of her slippery wet smooth neck, he took the warm softness of her hardened nipple in his mouth, her skin, the sweet taste of her driving him insane, the catch of her breath and groan, arching her back with shocked pleasure like a wave swelling and rising to meet him. This gave him unholy solace, a balm to Dankworth's cruelty, and he made to strip her of her clothes and have her hot naked body quivering next to his in tides of—

"Stop, stop," she said, her voice coming to him

from afar, her nipple pulled from his mouth, adjusting her clothes, covering the sweetest heaven. He went to take her again, but she put out her hand. "Stop." Her breath rasped. The light in her eyes was wild, her pupils dilated in the candlelight with black fathomless depths. He moved again. "No," she said, firmer, though he knew her senses were reeling. She was desperate for him, wild for him…

She ran her hand down her long, white, soft neck as if smoothing where his stubbled cheek had roughed her. "No." Her hand went out again to his chest.

This time he drew back, cursing, panting for air.

"Did you order me here to kiss me?" she asked, her voice and tone tremulous as if she couldn't believe what had happened, but even still, might be favorable to it.

"I… It was something else. I lost my head."

"Yes."

He watched the way her hand had steadied. She lied. She loved that he'd dragged her down into the depths of desire and tumbled her.

"I should kiss you whenever the opportunity presents, I'm thinking. Your desire is written in your face, on your body, on your scent."

She stilled, though her breathing still rasped around him. The air tasted sweet, as if she had eaten rhubarb pie and used it as perfume. "I know you spoke to Howard," she whispered, straightening her skirt, then resting her hand on her breast where his mouth had been as if to capture the sensation.

"He was annoyed with me then?"

"No. Why would he be? Anyway, I thought we'd agreed not to say anything to Howard until after the wedding?" Her pupils, he noticed, were still wide and dark and seductive. It was some small consolation he'd had her nipple in his mouth.

"My apologies." He told the arch in her eyebrows, which were set by long dark lashes fluttering with lethal effect. She was wasted on every man, except him. "Your aunt made it clear Dankworth would be leaving too soon after the wedding, and it might be best to talk to him now. I agreed. Miss Belet is under the misapprehension that Dankworth will seek a divorce."

"You told Aunt Bess and Howard you suspect the marriage is a fraud?"

He sat up straighter, adjusting his knee and jacket, adjusting his erection, thankful once again their meetings had dim lighting. "I said nothing of what I discovered to anyone." Might he kiss her again?

"John, I, we, must stop. Your kisses are becoming more frequent and, I fear, more persistent. I enjoyed one, or two"—she swallowed—"but we cannot afford to be distracted when the wedding is so close. Not when I find I am becoming too attracted to you. Not for any relationship, of course, but as a man."

He wasn't sure what to make of the last part of the comment, but at least they were in agreement on the most important aspect. Those kisses were damned enjoyable. "I am a man." He reached out as if to brush her cheek, but instead brushed his hand across her breast. She gasped and moaned, a kitten's purr. "I would love to pleasure you, Anne. I want to seduce you here and now in this carriage, as we speak, I can see you're ready. Don't resist me. I can offer you comfort."

She squirmed in her seat. "What was said between you men that so stirred your passions?"

"The topic of our conversation was Charlotte." He nuzzled into the soft curves of her neck, where strands of hair were tipped with drops of rain.

"Charlotte?" Her hands pressed on his chest, forcing him away, forcing him to look at her. "Why would Howard talk to you about Charlotte?"

He sat back. How much simpler the world would be if women would just make love while they spoke, then his actions might calm her spirit. But no. His fearless Annie did not want words softened. He sighed. "He told me Charlotte isn't his daughter. He is gracious walking her down the aisle tomorrow, don't you think?"

He didn't know what to expect when he admitted the topic of their conversation. He supposed, like most women, he expected tears, or a slap. Hopefully, she would dissolve into a complete wailing breakdown where he could come to her aid and comfort her with kisses to her neck and lower. Annie did none of those things. She sat. He wasn't altogether certain she even blinked. It was as though time had stopped, but for the gutting of the candle throwing shadows and the gentle rain drumming overhead. Not a good sign.

"Annie?"

She shook her head. "He's never told anyone the truth before today."

"He wouldn't want the world knowing anything which would damage his reputation in the sack."

She turned to him, her eyes were dark and lost and soulless. The heat had all but gone. "His reputation?" she repeated. "He doesn't care about his reputation; he never has. It is I who had the child. It is me whose reputation he protects. Oh, but this is bad, for it proves he doesn't even seek to offer me protection anymore." Her eyes grew large. "Please, John, please say you aren't angry at this news. Howard, my father, and I have never told another living soul. We agreed to keep the secret for Charlotte's sake."

He pulled back. "Why would I be angry? You had a baby and that's that, unless it has bought you pain. No. That doesn't sound right. I am saying it means little to me whether you had one child or five, but you enjoyed being a mother. My concern is for the future, not the past, for I can change naught which has gone. For either of us. Neither my life, nor yours has been saintly."

She nodded.

He had no idea why she nodded, but her soft gentle voice, the way her hands played in her lap when she was nervous, intoxicated him. Yet he looked away, his body ripping in small shreds for all the unhappiness and uncertainty she must have endured. He had refused to make love to her, and some bastard had made use of the opportunity. Annie had been a willing accomplice in the act, but the bottom of his soul screamed he was the person who had done wrong to her.

"I can appreciate that at the moment it is Charlotte who requires your attention."

"What do you mean?"

"You must tell Charlotte Howard is not her father. It will be difficult for her to accept, but she will." He reached out and held her hand.

"I beg your pardon?"

He glanced with irritation at the cabin roof where the rain pounded heavier when it should have quieted for their conversation.

"John, I'm not revealing anything to Charlotte of this matter."

"You must."

"No." She pulled her hand from his grip. "Charlotte adores Howard, believes him to be her father, and is proud and supportive of his feats and fame. It would upset her. I can't speak to her of this the day before her wedding!"

John shuffled in his seat, ostensibly moving his leg, in reality needing time. "Don't you believe Charlotte has a right to know who her real father is?"

"No! Howard has been in her life from her birth and has been good to her. What is the use of upsetting her? She does not ever need to know the truth. I am protecting her from humiliation which was my silly fault and had nothing to do with her."

"Lady Charlotte has an unassailable right to know the truth about her parentage. Every person has the right. You can't make this decision for her."

Anne turned to him, her hands spread wide, shaking her head. "What of orphans or children who are adopted? They don't know their natural parents. The real parents are the ones who look after the children, give them a bed at night, and feed them, not the person who happened to sow the seed during a fit of passion with no afterthought, no ownership, or sense of duty to the poor pregnant female."

"Don't you think Charlotte has the right to make this decision?"

"I am the one who gave birth to her. I will decide what is best for our family. That is my role as her mother. Anyway, telling Charlotte the truth now would only alert Howard. It may put her in danger of some sort. I won't risk it."

John looked toward the window, wishing the confounded rain would stop so he could open the shutters and get some air. He had not considered the notion of Charlotte being in danger, but Anne was correct. He wiped his hand across his brow. "So where is Lady Charlotte's father now? Why can't he support Charlotte down the aisle?"

"Charlotte's natural father died. Before Charlotte was born."

The rain pounded.

John rubbed his hands on his knees and shook his head. How could he have her sweet-tasting warm nipple in his mouth one minute, and then be so at odds with the woman the next?

"I am sorry, Annie. I can't sit here and comprehend Dankworth dictating family relationships. Lady Charlotte may have other blood relations who would care about her and want to be by her side on this special occasion, and what about when she has a family herself?"

"She won't ever know, and you have no concern to tell her."

John massaged his forehead, the rain coming in large drops pounding the carriage. "Correct. I don't have any concern to tell her. It is your duty. I may not agree with your decision, but I have no intention of breaking your confidence."

Anne closed her eyes giving John the opportunity to scrutinize the long neck and soft skin. What went on in her head? What thoughts spun there? For the woman in his carriage now did not bear much of a resemblance to the woman he once knew. In her kisses she was every bit the same, in her looks and manner, it was the same, but her thoughts? Those had changed. Perhaps too much time had lapsed for them to ever recover. Who was Charlotte's real father? And did it matter when Howard was the lucky bastard with a doting wife, loving child, national fame, fortune, and success—the smug bugger claimed all of it—and was worthy of none.

He looked away, the rain pounding his nerves. Next time he found Anne's nipple in his mouth, it would be with nothing between them except naked truth, for there would be a next time. She needed ravishing, was begging for it. She needed to learn that in bed, where she wanted to be, there were no secrets, and John was the man to instruct her.

"When you go back to the manor, I want you to lock your bedroom door." He leaned forward, taking the pistol from his belt. "Here. Take this."

"Excuse me!" She stared at the weapon.

"For your protection."

"No! I do not shoot anymore."

"Annie, he is dangerous. Take it. I would have given it to you earlier if I had known he was staying on at Graystone tonight."

She pressed herself into the corner of the carriage, staring at the pistol, then back at him. "I don't understand you! I come to meet you and you're ordering me how to relate to my daughter, and now my husband—"

"Not your husband."

"The point is, I don't need armaments or your advice on the security of my bedroom door!" Her voice grew louder above the rain. "For heaven's sake, this evening's danger has come from you, not Howard!"

"You have tonight and tomorrow night remaining under your father's roof, but then, I am getting you out and taking you into my care."

"Spoken like a blasted military evacuation!"

"You don't have any choice or control in the matter. I will collect you the day after Charlotte's wedding. I have made plans already, a place where you will be safe and can remain hidden while we investigate Dankworth's motives for this fraud."

"I always have a choice." Her voice shook.

"No, Annie. Take this tale to anybody else in the whole of England and see how far you get. Will they even believe you? Dankworth is a national hero—you are nothing." His voice grew louder. "By my reckoning, you'll be in Bedlam within a day of Charlotte's wedding. Dankworth's anger is unjustified—which you maintained from the very beginning, but which I only recognized today. More fool me. Some plan is afoot, and I'll not have you stay in proximity to the man. Unfortunately, we can't even count on your father to assist."

She pushed her arms into the sleeves of her coat and put out her hand to open the carriage door, but he reached past her and banged it shut in her face, holding the handle fast so she couldn't escape.

"How dare you!"

"No. You won't run away again. I warn you, Dankworth is mine. I am the one person who has the means and money at their disposal to discover the truth. Dankworth will come for me."

"What makes you believe Howard cares a fig for you? You are nothing but a merchant chasing skirts!

No. You're as bad as Howard. Worse, because you kiss me like it means something. Now let me go."

She struggled, trying to rip his hand from the coach door, but it was useless. He stared at her, his mind on the cusp of an idea.

"I won't let you out of this carriage until we are agreed. I help you with Dankworth, you follow my plans for the future, and in return—"

"What? What else can I give that I haven't already given every day for the last twenty years, and longer?"

He studied her, wanted her, lusted after her, but in return, her expression spoke of anger and bitter disappointment. "You tell me what you want in return. It is an agreement."

She was still. Hadn't expected him to allow her any currency. He swallowed and glanced away. Could he be admirable? He'd never cared in the past, but now, somehow it mattered. He needed her to ask something from him, any little thing, which he could fulfill, which would bind her closer to him and test his respect and commitment. In another age he might have kneeled at her feet, offering himself as her knight, pledging to honor and protect her life with his own. He would sooner die to keep her from Dankworth's harm, than return to the reckless life he'd once held so dear.

"What I want…" she said, and he looked back up at her, his arm across her body, holding closed her escape, brushing against her warm belly. "I want you to be guided by my knowledge of Howard, for I am an authority on the man whether you like it or not, and I also want…" Her voice faltered.

He waited for his quest.

"I want you to know I am a bad woman. The worst.

Your expectations should be minimal. I cannot stand for you to think highly of me. I am a rogue."

"You are bad?" he whispered.

"Yes."

"I believe I am convinced." Not.

"Be careful of this promise, give it due consideration, for it may not be as easy a bargain as you think."

"Anne Gastrell-Smythe. I am not scared, though no bargain with you was ever easy, and for an adventurer and rogue like myself, there lies the attraction."

She gave a sad smile. "I thought it might be the case." Removing his hand from the door, she blew out the candle, then stepped into the wet night.

John sat in the dark and scratched his head.

What in hell had he agreed to?

Chapter Thirteen

Monday, May 4

He stood beside good old Stephen Jones, Dearly Departed and in Loving Memory, waiting for the wedding procession to file out of St. Ursula's. Old Stephen had done well by him many years ago, when Anne's bargains were simpler pleasures of sweets and petticoats. Once, in this spot, she'd lifted the flouncy white frills of her skirt above her dimpled knee to show him the pale skin on her soft white thigh where blue veins threaded a maze. He'd watched, spellbound, the juice pounding through him like it had never pounded through Stephen Jones. She had him in that moment, had him craving more. Had him fearing less.

His gaze searched the endless sky. Perfect day for a wedding. Warm, a faint cooler breeze filtering through the trees, enough of a stir to make any feathered hats flutter, carrying laughter and perfume.

Charlotte's marriage might be beginning. Annie's, however, was dead except, unlike poor Stephen Jones, it wasn't buried. Yet he was the gravedigger, tired and sore shouldered, grubby shovel in hand, shifting the dirt Dankworth had amassed with his rotten lies.

The courage she had shown in the awful pretense of a marriage with Dankworth ate at his innards and kept him awake late into the night. The day before, he had sent a message to the young Joseph Turner commissioning the boy to paint Annie as an avenging angel—for that was how she appeared. Her tenacity, her loyalty, made his life of debauchery pale into insignificance. When this hell was over, no matter the outcome, he would give it to her as a gift, so she would be reminded of her own power to change the world. She needed at least that. Fuck, she showed up his own cowardice in every turn of her head, in every smile, in every breath she took. One bullet to the knee and he had crumbled, yet she maintained her gentle elegance despite Dankworth's hammering fists. His experience of this life was nothing compared to her.

As the bells pealed, his muscles became alert, his eyesight keener. Within minutes, they erupted from the church in a streaming riot of color, merriment, and congratulations. The new wife, Charlotte, smiled and laughed with guests. The new husband, Joseph, held his chest forward, full of proud responsibility…

And then came Anne.

God, but she took his breath away and made him weak at the knees. She was an indomitable goddess…

She talked to someone, stepping onto the path, laughing, dark wisps of curls around her face, her eyes sparkling, in a dress of deep pink, a color he had never seen her wear before, but it showed her figure and breasts and narrow waist to advantage, and a slight breeze pulled the skirt dancing about her ankles and small slippered feet. She looked as if she hadn't a worry on this glorious day. His blood exploded, his breath squeezed. He preferred her barefoot, pink toes peeping from behind her chemise, before the fire in his library, ordering him to answer her questions, with her hair tumbling around her shoulders and her eyes sparkling with charm and devilry—looking as if she owned the world and wanted a goddamned explanation.

Then came the devil. John's bones froze, analyzing every movement, committing the gestures of a fiend to memory for later dissection. Dankworth, calm, resplendent, courteous. Not a fraction of discomfort. Indeed, the man smiled. All best wishes and effusive handshakes to guests and relatives, gleaming in his long-skirted coat with epaulettes, hair smug and high, tricorn hat tucked under one arm, bowing from the hip.

John's stomach knotted. He could take no more, instead turning his attention to Annie. Watching her, his body mixed and churned like a squall.

He hoped to God she had locked her bedroom door because the idea of Dankworth laying one finger on her beautiful body…No, he couldn't even venture the notion of the man's mucky paws on her without wanting to interrupt the wedding to murder.

Then, as John stood there, watching them, thinking the worst for a bride and her father that had ever been considered in the history of time, Annie looked across at him. Straight at him. He nodded, the briefest, before Miss Belet's high hat of falcon feathers waved between them and Anne rejoined the crowd. Guests milling, boarding carriages, and away. Guests vanishing in cascades of laughter, vibrant colors, and felicitations. Village onlookers, stragglers, fading back into their houses.

All the excitement and celebration Annie would never know for herself.

While he kept company with Stephen Jones.

Weddings weren't for people like him either.

Chapter Fourteen

The day following the wedding, John set one of his men hidden on the road near Graystone to advise when Major General Dankworth departed the premises.

John arrived at Graystone in his curricle and pair fifteen minutes after Dankworth, saying he had come to collect Anne for an extended visit with widow Woollie.

His plans were set. He knew where he would hide Annie, knew how the investigation would proceed, had arranged food, stores, and transport—accommodating every contingency they might need, just as he would plan a voyage to some distant shore.

He kept busy because of one enormous shortfall. Himself.

Here he was, the legendary rake, about to spend private time with a woman for whom he had pent-up frustration, who believed she was bad and had no idea of her own innocence. To make matters worse, to gain her trust, he had passed control of the investigation to her who, he feared, might be so damaged by her past, she had no idea how to instigate a simple kiss let alone a complex dispassionate strategy for humiliating a national hero.

Complicated? He didn't want to linger on how knotty this situation presented. His body ordered him to take Annie to his bed and make love to her; his mind ordered him to respect her situation. Somehow he must conspire to turn Dankworth's life into a wretched hell—without implicating Annie, so that her reputation remained untarnished. Meanwhile, he must flirt with her so outrageously she would be driven to quench her desires with him or go insane.

It was the most unfortunate scheme he'd ever had the misfortune to develop.

On his arrival at Graystone, Annie kept her demeanor reserved, hands clasped before her, eyes downcast. Her reserve inflamed his desire further. As Anne's bags were hurriedly packed and carried into the curricle, she donned her hat, gloves, and coat with such liquid grace, he had to bark orders at her maid, who, he decided, would be staying on at Graystone in order to pass on information about Dankworth's movements.

The general, who had arrived in the hall at an inopportune time, bullied and yelled that he didn't give a fig where his daughter was going, only he didn't want her silly stupid maid staying on in his home. John had to point out Jenny might come in useful as a helper to the overworked scullery maids while Cook remained ill, to which the general grudgingly agreed, but then the general insisted on knowing how he might contact Anne when Cook's health improved, so the chit could go home. John told the general to make enquiries in the village, but if by any chance nobody in Fernsby knew where widow Woollie lived, then the general could go next door, to Lord Rochester's residence, and he would be reliably informed. The general shouted at the last part of the suggestion, making it clear he would prefer the bowels of hell than ask his merchant neighbor for directions.

John bowed his head. "As you wish."

The general, whose face was pulsating by this stage, glared bloodshot eyes at John, then marched out howling about another hundred years not being long enough.

Meanwhile, Miss Belet came downstairs wanting to chat about Charlotte's beautiful wedding. She was insistent John stay for some of her homemade elderberry wine on the terrace, but he wasn't to be drawn a second time. He stood in the hallway waiting for Annie to finish organizing her trunks, as immovable as a carved wooden black boy. He did enquire when Miss Belet would be leaving to visit Hotham the Hatter, which she advised would be immediately, and then she ventured to enquire whether she should return by way of Fernsby and collect Anne, so they could make the journey north together, but John was obtuse about finalizing any future travel arrangements, blaming widow Woollie as indecisive about her health, which set a glimmer in Bess's eye.

Once Bess saw they were alone, Annie having gone upstairs, she enquired how John's talk with Howard went in the kitchen garden some days earlier.

"It went," John replied.

"As bad as that," Miss Belet conceded.

"Worse."

"Oh."

It was all in the intonation of the Oh. Miss Belet was the sort of woman who reveled in tidbits of information but would be mortified if she ever learned the extended version of the chat. Better for her to think Annie on the cusp of divorce than never having been married. Dear, but she was the most intelligent confidant who didn't require words. Extremely dangerous of course, which was why he adored her.

"Well, at least Anne has widow Woollie."

His composure slipped a fraction. Too intelligent perhaps?

Miss Belet smiled.

John struggled to maintain his wooden countenance.

Miss Belet patted his arm, wished him well, and then tripped upstairs like a young girl.

With the first gigging of the reins in the curricle, Anne wasn't as discreet as her aunt. "I think widow Woollie has made a ham fist of herself, the way she commandeers my time. We need to make some other arrangement. Howard will be livid when he arrives home to find me gone. He'll personally search every cottage and barn in Fernsby, so I hope you prove my trust in you is well placed. By the by, where are we going?"

"As a renowned rake, I have a love chamber I use to bring ladies who required discretion."

Her back went rigid. He shot her a sideways glance and, pleased with the effect, continued, "It is a little cottage which had fallen into disuse. I believe the place has been there for many hundreds of years. There is a stream nearby, so I always wondered if it might have started life as a hermit's residence."

"So it is dilapidated?" Her tone spoke volumes of disapproval.

He chuckled, and with a quick glance over his other shoulder to compose himself, spurred on the horses. "Don't fret. It was dilapidated, but after my father passed away, I had the cottage rebuilt to my specification and design. It is small and unknown except to a few of my trusted staff who will not breathe a word of its existence, even if Dankworth threatens them with a gun. I believe it will provide the ideal location to control our investigation and cosset you away from society while we figure the depth of Dankworth's deception. It's named Hermit's Peace."

Anne clasped her hands in her lap and looked out over the fields. Apart from the fact that Howard would easily find a cottage, the idea of sleeping in John's love chamber put her waters in a spin.

She longed to have him beneath her fingertips, his hard body pressed against hers, his lips roving over her skin…Except she hadn't the expertise to wield the responsibilities he appeared to believe her capable. Then she had gone and insisted she was bad? Dear God, what had she done?

By the time they turned down a disused track, her fears bubbled to the surface, popped, and remained in an excruciating frothy confusion. In their youth, it hadn't gone well for them. What made them think anything could be different now, when their lives were more complicated? Anyway, John may not have any thoughts beyond undressing her. It wasn't as if he had made any promises, and he was a rake. Howard, on the other hand, would be furious at her.

Her white knuckles clutched her reticule, on the cusp of ordering John to turn the gig around and take her back, when the road dipped and curved into a shady dingle, where a thatched cottage nestled into a hillside. Discreet, and the most picturesque escape she had ever seen.

It crossed her mind that as an aid to seduction, this would work well on any number of women she knew.

Damn him.

Her spirits spiraled.

Yet as they alighted and brought in cases and food parcels, Anne couldn't be more in awe of her rescuer. For the first time, she glimpsed the essence of the man. An adventurer eager for unknown distant savage shores, who retreated to this romantic spot?

What she found in his love chamber confused her further. She stood in a simple wide room without dividers. To the right was a mahogany tester bed, ahead a small sink with a faucet and open pantry, and another mysterious recessed door, while to the left sat a wooden table with two chairs, and either side of a wide inglenook were two plump wingbacks. The area was bathed in light as on three sides, tall windows with wooden seats and cushions looked over the gentle sloping dell through the lacy trunks of fresh-leafed silver birch strung with honeysuckle where birds trilled a spring chorus. At the bottom of the incline ran a gurgling brook green and lush with ferns.

Her head swiveled back. One bed.

She looked at John planting their trunks inside the door. When he noticed the direction of her gaze, he placed his hands on his hips and smiled.

She humphed, imagining any number of women walking naked through his love nest. She squeezed her eyes closed to dismiss the vision, then reaching up to withdraw her hatpin, glancing at the furnishings, placing her hat on the table with feigned cool disinterest.

In truth, she didn't want him noticing her delight. The materials and colors invited her to fall back onto the bed and wallow in the stunning array of rich luscious fabrics, textured and patterned styles that were atypical of reserved Georgian design. It was a riotous confusion of sumptuous exotic luxury from around the world. The perfect place for a tryst…

Something about this wasn't right. She checked again. A well-stocked pantry, bookshelves covering the wall… She turned to him.

"What?" he asked.

"You don't bring women here."

"How could you deduce such a thing? You've not been here two minutes!"

She waved her hand toward the shelves. "A true romantic would have volumes of love poems and stands of feathers and perfumed linen, not books about shipping architecture!"

"Yes, yes. You are correct, damn your eyes. I enjoyed teasing you. I alone enjoy the peaceful solitude of Hermit's Peace. Only Donovan knows of its existence. I had him prepare it for us."

"I can see why you keep it a secret." Her heart skipped and sang while noting the thick feather eiderdown would soon have the imprint of her body. She wished she could tell him she wanted to be bad this instant. "I promise not to tell a soul."

"Oh well, I suppose you can tell the world, so long as you don't reveal the coordinates, and you must include the most outrageous lies—of mythical proportions. No doubt I can trust you to supply the imaginative details with one small correction. Feathers are fine but incense rather than perfume, if you don't mind."

A cloud of happiness floated over her heart. "John, it's beautiful! You designed this yourself? The windows are magnificent."

He went straight to the windows running his finger over a small part of the leadlight caming. "After being on a ship, I love seeing as far as the eye can travel, so I increased the size of the glass pieces and made them rectangular instead of diamond. The increased size makes them more fragile. However, I was able to source a thicker gauge of glass."

"It is the expanse of the glass. There are no supports between each section so it runs out into the dell."

"Yes, it was important. I wanted to convey the feeling of being on the bridge, so the house parts the landscape the way a prow slices through water."

"It is masterful. You must have had the plan of it in your mind even when you were young. Look. I have something to show you." Turning away, she opened her luggage, bringing forth a small ship whittled from a leftover piece of oak from the local mill.

"After all these years." He took the toy, running his thumb thoughtfully over the knots and grain.

"Do you remember? You gave it to me after Mother died. You told me to put it near my bed, and if I was ever upset by any little thing, I could put my troubles in the boat at night, and it would sail away with my worries, so my dreams would be free. Then, in the morning, the boat would be back empty, so I could start the day anew. I've always kept it. This whittled ship and your Hermit's Peace—they are alike, don't you think?"

He stared at the toy in his large hands, turning it over, squeezing it as if testing the strength of his workmanship all those years ago.

"You are a fine craftsman and imaginative designer."

His concentration remained on the boat.

He was so quiet she bit her lip and cursed, wishing she'd left the toy in her trunk. He'd dismiss her as childish and living in the past. However, with great care, he placed the boat in a prominent position on the ledge beneath the window-frame. "This gift was for you, Annie, but I suggest we leave it here as a reminder of the journey we are undertaking, that when this madness is over, perhaps we can start the day anew."

"I like that notion." She smiled.

He shook his head, clearly saddened. "Unfortunately, by coming to Hermit's Peace, by spiriting you away in the manner I have, we are entering stormy waters. Dankworth will know us as his declared enemy, and there is still so much we must discuss, strategize and plan."

"Oh, I know, I know." She attempted to sound serious, to have her countenance match the task ahead, but she couldn't contain her pleasure at the escape; it wanted to spill out despite John's obvious worry. "John, I do understand our need for haste, but first, I must go down to the brook. I can't think at all when I long to explore the beautiful dell and the house and stream. Charlotte was only married yesterday, and now the fuss is over and I am free of Graystone and Howard, I need some peace for myself." She drew a cross over her heart. "However, I promise I will put my mind to discussion after a few hours rest. Please."

He looked too erect, too formal. "Dankworth is dangerous, and we are gazing at toys. I can't put your safety in jeopardy by being selfish. We have to discover proof of Dankworth's duplicity, or what he plans for this coming week for you. If he plans to trump up charges of some sort, it might already be too late. He will have arrived in Margate even as we speak."

She went up to him, laying her hand on his arm. The tension disappeared from his shoulders, although the all-too-familiar heat penetrated her fingers. She pulled her hand away. "John, please, a few hours. I have never been to a place as beautiful as this. I don't know what horrors the future will bring, so indulge me with this short time to enjoy myself, and then I will settle."

He frowned and shook his head, as if he would disagree, but instead he said, "You deserve it. Let us go."

Anne laughed and rubbed her hands.

Four hours later, she woke on a rug in dappled sunlight. Water gurgled, butterflies wandered, and the sun's warmth had seeped deep into her bones as the trills of blackbirds piped into the clear air. Was this how life should be?

She looked for the man, her childhood friend, spying him sitting on the edge of the stream with a fishing line jiggling. She smiled. He might have been a boy.

Relaxed, on his haunches, the fabric of his breeches pulled across muscular thighs. He'd removed his jacket, shirt open at the collar, the white material taut across powerful shoulders, habitual firearm tucked into the back of his belt. Safe for the first time with a man whose sleeves rolled up to his elbows and whose look searched thoughtfully into the running stream. A man who wasn't dressed to perfection or glittering like a jewel but was rough and uncut. Perhaps the full import of their maturity had not made itself clear until now, when he sat as a boy. True, he'd kissed her, but had it merely satisfied a childhood curiosity? Had she responded as a true woman might? She swallowed and shifted, remembering the moist warmth of his mouth and the hardness of his body pressed heavy against hers, the gentle loving caress of his lips against her wrist and nipple.

She turned away, resting her head in the crook of her arm, allowing the dappled sunlight from the leaves overhead to play against her closed lids. A man could live here for years in contemplation of the wonders of God and nature. Admittedly, after a time it would be lonely. Anne swallowed as the tingling returned.

Rolling onto her side, she propped up on an elbow, thankful John had thought to spread a blanket, and they had made a lunch of torn bread, hunks of cheese, and ratafia drunk straight from the bottle. Two hours ago, the simple luncheon had seemed like an innocent picnic. Now, looking at the remains of the feast and John, it seemed loaded with danger.

She wanted him to keep fishing so as to indulge her fantasies, but her movement must have alerted him. He looked over. She thrilled at the observation but pretended to cover her mouth from a yawn.

"Sleepy head," he said with a slow twisting smile. "I've let you rest long. We must begin our work."

She sat up, adjusted the bodice of her dress, and tidied her hair. The tingling gained favor with the slightest movement.

"The wedding and its preparations have exhausted you, no doubt." He put the fishing rod by the stream, then came over, his shadow falling close.

She blinked up at him, his body in profile, dark against the afternoon sun, and shielded her eyes, better to see. He sat and leaned back, legs stretched out, resting on his elbows, his groin level with her knees. On the top of his collar, a small curl lay against his neck. Might she twist the honey brown hair around her forefinger? She cleared her throat and sat up straighter. "I've been exhausted for years. Strangely, I feel very awake at this moment. I see you still enjoy fishing."

"I fished and caught nothing—never do in these inland streams—but I managed to contemplate the direction of our enquiries."

"Would you believe I was likewise cogitating?"

He smiled wicked at her. "Were you?"

His frost blue eyes pinned her, the lashes, curled high and pitch black, were the sort of lashes women would die for but men were born with. The devil take him. Although she didn't want the devil to take him, not when he belonged to her.

Did he belong to her? Did he belong to any woman?

"We need to agree on how we will proceed to control it because I'll need your assistance," he said.

She took a deep breath, not altogether sure what he said made any sense. However, he seemed to be waiting for a reply. "I need to discover the truth, so I will do whatever I can," she answered.

He nodded, so she must have given him the response he expected.

"I want us to start by checking the register of the church or chapel where you were married, but this means finding the place. How do you feel about a trip tomorrow? If you aren't up to it, you can stay here and I'll go on alone."

She had never seen a man stretched out on a rug, casually dressed. It was a provocative sight with the fabric resting against his manhood, not outlining it as such but tantalizing and close. "I'll stay by your side all the time. You make me feel safe." She swallowed, wanting to draw her finger from the bottom of his chin down across his chest to the buckle on his belt.

He brushed at an ant on the rug. "If the marriage is proved to be legitimate, then we can do naught. It will be a matter for the king if you want a divorce, but I doubt Howard will make it simple."

Reality was awful. "Charlotte kept us together."

"I'd lay a wager, and you know I am not a betting man, that Charlotte's marriage is the catalyst for this whole situation—whatever it entails."

"John, I was thinking, if the marriage is a fraud, it is without precedent. Any social standing I have will be in tatters. The ton will be laughing. They had already relegated me to a backwater person of little interest— and I was hoping it would stay so. I do not want to become a public spectacle."

"I believe the ton would be shaken to their boots before they would laugh. A national hero, decorated by the king, knighted, a worthy gentleman who controls an army and has a personal life that is less than perfect? Such a fraud would unsettle, especially with rumors of growing unrest in Paris surfacing daily. No. My concern is whether you are married, for if this is the case, I don't believe Dankworth will ever grant you a divorce."

"We have enough information about his activities:

gambling, blackmail, fraud, or otherwise, to pressure him."

He sighed. "Anne, let me warn you, nobody pressures Dankworth."

When he sighed, his shirt fabric wrinkled and she glimpsed a section of his stomach, flat, covered in a smattering of fine dark hair. Dear heaven, the heat was affecting her…

"Are you feeling all right?" he asked, his eyes alert. He sat up, and the view of his skin disappeared.

"Fine." She licked her lips and looked down at her hands, fiddling in her lap, suppressing the rush of desire firing through her belly.

The fine dark hair on his arms reminded her of the glimpse of his stomach, the muscles in his forearm flexing, reaching to pick a piece of grass. The sappy blade broke. She swallowed. Lord, but it was hot. She fanned her cheeks with her hand and tried to concentrate.

"Why would Howard go to so much trouble to mastermind a fake wedding? We could have married by law or gone to Gretna Green."

He looked toward the stream, and she studied the outline of his thighs. She cleared her throat and waved her hand a little harder. He appeared to have found his morals, while she didn't care a fig for discussing her ridiculous marriage. Why had she insisted on being bad!

Of course her reaction was due to the heat. She was no good in the bedroom. Howard had told her this a hundred times. She had no ability whatsoever to pleasure a man. John told her the same on the drystone wall. Some women she knew possessed this appeal, but without the dress and high bosom, she wasn't one of them. Anyway, in this sultry afternoon sunshine, John proved a lot of man to handle. She could not imagine him submissive, the notion bringing a new flush of heat and moisture to her loins.

He picked at the rug. "I wonder whether Howard didn't have the time for the journey to Gretna Green. Or perhaps he thought to call the marriage as false a few days after marrying you. Perhaps he planned to put you in a bad light, tarnish your reputation by bringing the fraud into the open, so no man would ever have you. Did he hate you so much?"

She stopped and considered the notion.

"No. I don't believe he hated me. Hate is too strong a word. More he wasn't interested, oh, but that doesn't sound right either. I think Howard wanted me the way a person wants to add a vase or plate to their collection, to have it placed just so. On show. He had already asked for my hand in marriage twice before and was refused, so I can't believe he hated me. I believed he liked me. At the start."

John sat forward. "You refused Howard before?"

"Well, Father did."

"I didn't know."

She shrugged. "It isn't important. It was common for officers to make requests for my hand. Father always refused."

"Common?" He sat up further. "How many offers of marriage did you have? You were underage, for God's sake! Anyway, as far as I was concerned, you were going to marry me! You can't tell me the regiment is so fixated on women!"

"Of course the regiment are fixated on women,

they think of little else!" She paused, then searched his face to make certain she had heard correct. "Did you think you were going to marry me?"

He looked away. "When we were young. I thought all sorts of things."

She wasn't sure how to take that admission. "The marriage proposals weren't important. It was never me the men were after. They wanted a promotion, and by marrying the general's daughter, they believed they would get it. Did you want to marry me?"

"You were seventeen with the most superior abundance of natural beauty ever to be had, and you think they wanted to marry you for promotion? How on earth did you get such an idea! One look and it's obvious you were a prize, but I had no idea I was in a queue. This tidbit has somersaulted my confidence."

"Well, you were a nineteen-year-old boy, and you had no choice in the matter. Father was determined my marriage would be arranged to an officer, and I can guarantee the avaricious Wyldes from next door, who snapped up Graystone land after the Dissolution, didn't qualify, even if you were a male. Father had no intention of ever joining our estates. Anyway, it isn't anything to do with my looks. Howard and Father were in the same regiment. Keep it all in the family is the way they think, and the regiment is a family." She shrugged. "Father intended for me to make a better match, which is why he turned down Howard, but then, when I became pregnant…"

"When you were pregnant, the rotten bastard saw his opportunity and jumped in to claim the prize."

"Oh, but no, John. You have it wrong."

"Wrong!" He sat forward. "Howard is a maniac on

a quest for power who will not stop at profiting from the distress of others. He married you for promotion!"

"No John. This is wrong."

"It's not wrong! The scoundrel wanted to marry the general's beautiful daughter for promotion. It's as clear as the sun in the sky what he was up to!"

"No. No. You don't understand. Howard was my savior."

He stared at her, open-mouthed, looking as if his brain had been separated from his skull and dumped in a pail of ice water. "Savior?"

"Father and I were thankful Howard offered marriage. Howard knew I was expecting. Howard was wonderful. I don't think many other men would have done the same—married a woman who was pregnant with another's child."

John stretched his neck forward and to the side, pursed his lips, rubbed his hand over his forehead, then drew back and sat there staring at her, jaw ticcing. "I am sorry, Anne. I cannot believe what I am hearing. I had one conversation with Major General bloody Howard Dankworth, and I know as sure as snakes crawl on their bellies and hiss with forked tongues Dankworth has done nothing, ever, out of the goodness of his heart, let alone marry a woman who was carrying somebody else's child. Impossible." He shook his head. "Impossible."

"So what's the purpose in making the marriage fake?"

John frowned. "Was it to convince your father?"

Anne considered the question, then shook her head. "Father was so furious about the pregnancy, he didn't even attend the wedding."

"Yet he gave his consent for you to marry."

"Yes, he had to. I was aged under twenty-one and pregnant. My predicament meant we needed the special license to marry quickly. In any case, all Father wanted was an heir. A grandson by whatever means answered his prayers."

John rubbed his chin, then reached for her.

For one insane moment, she thought he offered to pull her into an embrace, so he might wrap his strong arms around her and give her comfort. Instead he said, "Let me help you up. The sun is going down behind the hill, and we still need to prepare dinner."

The atmosphere in the glen was charged, the touch of his hand sending shivers bolting through her arm, likely to sizzle and dry everything in the vicinity.

When they entered the cottage, she wasn't sure what was supposed to happen next beyond both of them stripping and falling into his bed. Provided, of course she had the nerve, or hadn't put him off.

"I'll get a fire lit for some water," he said. "I've packed some vegetables and meat. Can you make a stew?"

She tried to remember. "I think I possess some basic skills."

"Good. Now. Regarding the sleeping arrangements…"

She imagined the silky colorful sheets and pillows cocooning them. "The bed looks comfortable."

He was quiet for minute, then—"Good. So I'll rig up the chairs and footstool before the fire. For myself."

"As you wish." Damnation.

"Good." He stood, hands on hips, studying her. "It won't be too…"

"What?"

"Cramped for you. Both of us sharing, as it were. The same room."

"No. I'll be fine. What about you? This is your usual domain. I'm the intruder."

"Yes. No. No. I'm fine. Too. I have control of it."

"Good."

"So are you fine to take control? Of the dinner. While I light the fire?"

"Meat, vegetables, water. What could be easier?" She rubbed her hands.

"Are you adding some herbs?"

"I can."

"What herbs do you use in your stews?"

She put her head to one side and mirrored his squinting gaze. "Lavender?"

He nodded. "I'll get the stew."

"Yes. It might be for the best. After all, I am competent at lighting fires."

John crossed his arms. "How about tonight I get dinner and light the fire. My indulgence. You can look at the books."

"You don't believe I can light a fire? I think this is going to be one of those times when we need proof, like the size of the charwoman's nipple."

He stared at her. "You won't ever let me forget it, will you? I was a thirteen-year-old boy, and I told the story to impress you."

"It was sweet and naïve. I never believed for one minute her nipple was as big as a sheep's knuckle bone."

"And on par with you lighting the fire?"

"No. I can light fires. Up north I do it all the time."

"What about the servants?"

"Jenny? I can't have her doing everything. The poor girl would fall in an exhausted heap."

"You don't have anyone else in the household?"

"Not recently."

He scowled. "Agreed. You light the fire. I'll make dinner."

At the end of the evening, they sat before the hearth, hunger satiated. Sexual awareness starving. Anne watched the leaping flames in the fireplace highlighting contours of his body, which had no right to be illuminated, unless one was able to sink into them as well. What would he do and say if she stood up and peeled off her own clothes, before taking off his? With her teeth.

"You've been quiet." He massaged a brandy balloon in his cupped hand. "Something on your mind?"

She propped her chin in her hand. "Nothing a good night won't fix."

"Pardon?"

"The bed. I've been sleeping fitfully at Father's because the mattress was musty, so I'm looking forward to being warm and comfortable."

He took a sip of brandy.

"I might retire now." She stirred. "Is there somewhere I can change? A screen?"

"You'll have to trust me not to look."

"Can I? I mean, I don't want any rumors circulating about the size of my nipples."

He took a bigger swig of brandy. "You forget I've tasted them. I can control myself. I'm the bloody master of control," he added under his breath.

She suppressed a smile and, taking a candle, went to the other side of the room to change into her nightdress, hoping he would turn around, for she didn't know how she would get his attention otherwise. Being bad was more difficult than allowed. He must take the first step, otherwise it might end up as before, with him refusing her. Dammit, but men were complicated animals.

True to his word, he didn't turn around. Damn him.

"Good night," she called from under the covers.

"Good night."

She watched the side of his face catching the glimmer from the flames, his legs outstretched before the hearth. Safe, for the first time in her life.

Happy.

Wanton.

She snuggled down, pulling the sheets high.

When her breathing became regular, John looked over his shoulder. Her dark hair spread on the pillow like she was underwater; her face, for the first time, relaxed. She looked warm, happy, and soft.

He took a swig of rum. The air sizzled with her sexual provocation, but she refrained from using her bargaining tool, which had a vague nagging worry surfacing. What if she wasn't attracted to him? What if, now they were together, she didn't feel passion? What if he had been too arrogant in his assumption she would be led to seduce him? She had walked away all those years ago without a backward glance, perhaps she felt nothing for him. Not that he could blame her. He had had more than his fair share of women the world over and yet—this woman was special. She knew him better than he knew himself.

No. This wouldn't be a short rapid seduction of Anne. This beauty was worth waiting twenty years and twenty more, whatever it would take. He wanted to keep her precious. He mustn't risk rushing.

Damn, but his leg was aching fit to scream.

Chapter Fifteen

Wednesday, May 6

The next morning, they were away early, and it proved fine weather. John said he slept well, but he lied. She woke during the night to him mumbling with unsettled edginess. Something or someone haunted his dreams. He didn't linger in her company over breakfast either, instead went about, head down, organizing the day. He rarely spoke, but when he did, seemed preoccupied with discussing the condition of one of his horses. Anne felt sympathetic, but only because while he talked, she had an opportunity to study him, and discovered the study of John to be a pleasant pastime.

She had also enjoyed the worst night of her life having woken frequently, in part to John's sleep mumblings, and her own moans. She had a vague memory of calling out John's name in the throes of a dreamed embrace. At the heady moment when his lips trailed kisses down to her breast, they were interrupted by John ordering her back to sleep, which left her utterly despondent, but elated by whose bed she inhabited and his proximity.

By the time they set out, he was being efficient with the horse furniture, jangling metal and leather straps, so she didn't like to intrude, instead sat upright in the open carriage, skin tingling on the side closest to him, praying he would brush his arm against hers, or catch and tug the material of her skirt with his thigh. She dared to touch his arm once when she wished to draw his attention to a brown hawk wheeling high above the hills on a boisterous wind, but the contact lasted a moment before he brushed her away. This would not be a day for intimacy.

He told her the day was for business, his tone crisp and unyielding.

She had an idea that the church where she was wed might have been at Barfrestone, so after a brief discussion, it was agreed to go there first.

"You were married at night, which was the reason for the Archbishop's special license," he said, more to himself, as the horses found their rhythm.

"Perhaps, but at the time, I remember the reason given was because Howard was due to depart soon for India."

"Did he? Depart?" John kept his eyes on the road.

"Yes." God, these intrusive questions were uncomfortable. Every woman friend she'd ever talked to about her marriage looked askance when she revealed the details. John would be no different. Which brought her to another point. "John, you must promise me our enquiries will be discreet. I do not want the world knowing of this dilemma before I have all the facts myself. I cannot afford unnecessary risks such as you took trespassing on young Joseph Turner's property in Margate."

"In my defense, I didn't then appreciate the full import of this matter. It is different now I've met Dankworth for myself."

She hoped he meant it. When he was young and the

wind blew through his ears, he could be rather dashing and…

"How soon after you were married did Dankworth sail out?"

His voice was gentle and coaxing, but the edges were stilted, as if prying into marriage details wasn't pleasant for him. Awkward for them both.

"He left the next day to supervise preparations. Came and went regularly over the next few weeks. When he sailed out for good, I was six months pregnant with Charlotte."

"Not much time for the newlyweds." He gave the leather reins a shallow jiggle.

"As it happens, it might all be for the best." She made light of it.

"Yes."

He spoke one word, yet it carried an undertone of moral superiority. She had been naive, young, pregnant, and his judgment crawled into her mind like a beetle burrowing. "Being with Howard hasn't been all bad."

"Hasn't it?" He gave the reins two short snaps.

She looked across to the fields and gentle rolling hills, suddenly tired of the charade. Pretending to be a good wife exhausted her, but it wasn't until she was out here, away from her old life, where Howard grew distant by the day and John made her answer for her decisions and choices, that she realized how tiresome justifying the lies had become. Like a worn sandal, the leather straps frayed, the protection threatening to slip, and she, bent over, was focused on retying the bindings rather than experiencing the world around her. Out here, for the first time, she raised her head, finding John's strong arms encircling her, enticing her to let go of the lies and secrets once held dear.

The road ahead funneled into a dark tunnel of poplars. She turned toward John as they entered the speckle-filled path. The shadows, like John's embrace, wrapped her in a blanket.

"Blake was Charlotte's father."

John's head inclined her way though he kept his attention on the horses. "Another soldier?"

His voice reached her above the clopping hooves and squeaking carriage wheels.

"Blake was our stable boy."

John turned to her, his face still in shadow. "The same stable boy who serviced the maid, who you informed me all those years ago had apparently made the maid cry with joy because of his lovemaking expertise?"

"The same."

He snapped the reins as they erupted into hard sunlight. "So this stable boy, Blake, desired higher up the household female ladder."

"No. No. I made the advance toward him."

"Ahh."

"Don't say 'Ahh' with such a tone, John. You can never understand. I needed someone to—"

"You're wrong. I do understand. I am only angry I didn't understand it years ago." He gave a soft low command to the horses to go easy as they navigated a small stone bridge. "You forget how many women I have bedded. They all sought release. Every single one of them."

"And you gave it to them." She snapped her own reins, wishing they were in amongst the trees again where her shrewishness might be shadowed. His arrogant judgment wasn't helpful. Why did he have to make her so angry—couldn't he see she was trying to confide in him?

He shot her a roguish grin. "Oh yes. I gave it to them. Release, not love."

Splitting hairs. It didn't even make sense. John Wylde the rake. She would do well not to forget it. Damned impudence. She glanced away from the brook, across the solid ground. How many naked women had he had in his embrace and given this so-called release? Did he make them scream with joy?

"How did Blake die?" His voice came from a distance.

"He was murdered."

"Murder!"

"Before you ask, I don't know the details other than it was in Margate a month or so after I discovered I was expecting."

"I'm so sorry." He reached a hand to hers.

"Thank you," she whispered, although she wasn't thinking of poor Blake, rather she remembered two particular women, undressed, seeking release. She crossed her legs away from him. "It happened a long time ago." She shook away his hand of comfort.

"It won't upset you to discuss it then?"

"No. Blake and I had come to an understanding." Unlike you and me, she might have added.

"Yes. Good. I see. Tell me about this stable boy. Given your father's high ideals for an intended husband, he must have been furious at the turn of events with Blake set to make an honest woman of you, and then Blake dies?"

She shook her head. John pretended at being a

rogue, and yet his mind turned first to a woman's honor and principle. She wished she didn't have to break his noble image of her, but it had to be done. Bloody Howard and his treachery.

"Blake and I slept together twice when Blake wrote to me saying he was leaving Father's employ to make something of himself in America. We were never set to marry, and I would never have wanted it. Blake was, well, he had a massive—"

John egged on the horses. "I don't need the details."

"But you asked."

"I can guess."

"No, you could never guess." She leaned toward him. "Blake had a massive intellect. The boy was a poet who would have set the world ablaze with his words."

"Oh. Right. Yes, of course."

"What did you think I was going to say?"

"I thought…you know." He looked over his shoulder toward the fields.

"You thought I was going to say he had a massive bed, but no. We made Charlotte in the hayloft at Graystone, where I got a splinter in my bottom for the effort."

John tried to keep his face from becoming a study of absurd puzzlement. The impetuous voluptuous femme fatale sitting next to him talked euphemistically of splinters to explain lovemaking in which she had become pregnant? Where she had screamed for joy? He let the reins slacken and turned toward her. There was such coldness and detachment. Indeed she sat there, appearing to enjoy the scenery. How did an experienced woman speak of lovemaking, from which a child has been spawned, as if it were a mere irritation? He shook his head to clear the confusion. She couldn't have made love to Blake; it must have been sexual gratification, a release. She'd all but admitted to seeking out this stable boy because John wouldn't perform. Had she been so desperate and calculating?

He checked her again. She was soft, warm, and loving. Nothing about her suggested sexual manipulation and he had tasted her nipple—which he thought he had taken—but perhaps it was freely given, even orchestrated? Dear God, he was going insane. The woman squeezed him in her viper grip.

"Right. Right. So Annie, you never told Blake about the pregnancy, or should I say the splinter."

"Of course I told him! The splinter was embarrassing in the extreme. I had to ask one of the maids to extract it. Hurt for a few weeks afterwards, and I had a lot of trouble sitting. As to the pregnancy, I informed Blake as soon as I was sure, but he told me outright he had no interest in being tied down with a child when the world was at his feet."

There were so many aspects wrong with this comment. Where to start? He rubbed his cheek. "So did he have the world at his feet? This stable boy?"

She smiled, a shallow dimple appearing in her cheek. "If you had met him, John, you would understand. Blake was a free spirit. You couldn't imprison him with a mundane life of children and boring box hedge borders. Which makes his murder all so much worse. Blake was a man born to enrich the world, not to have it cut short."

John raked his hand through his hair. Blake was—disconcerting. "What do you know about Blake's murder?" He tried to refocus.

"Not very much except he secretly fled to Margate. He was waiting to get on a ship, had been guaranteed passage, when he was set upon and killed."

"Who was charged?"

"No one. I keep hoping one day someone will pay for the crime, but after all these years, it seems unlikely. Footpads were blamed at the time. I doubt they will ever be caught, which makes me furious to think they roam the countryside while a great mind has left the world poorer. The books and words Blake would have written."

"Yes. So if Blake had made his escape from your father's household secretly, how did you know about it?"

"He wrote to me. A beautiful letter too. I kept it, and can show it to you if you like. He was a young Shakespeare in the making. Such a way of making a woman feel—"

"Yes. So if Blake wrote to you and he loved words, perhaps he wrote to others too?"

"Well, at the inquest, his family said they had received a letter. There may have been others. Blake always said he wasn't the type to live his life mucking out a manger. I think he enjoyed having many new experiences, and he didn't care who knew, except Father. Blake hated working for my father."

"So it sounds as if this secret escape wasn't so secret, except from your father."

"Perhaps. I don't remember the details after all this time, and anyway, I was upset about falling pregnant. When I realized I was with child, I told Blake first, but of course by then he had already confided in me he planned to leave England. It took me a few hellish weeks to pick up the courage to tell Father about the pregnancy, and by then Blake was already in Margate waiting for a ship. Father was going to discover the truth at some point, so I was honest with him, and there was no question of giving up the baby. Father wanted Charlotte to be a boy, even if illegitimate, and with Blake over the other side of the world, it would provide an heir for Graystone. The perfect solution, as far as Father was concerned. By marrying me, Howard has been the savior of the family name, but then Howard was always so efficient at arranging our affairs. He made regimental adjutant in superior time. He was much younger than any of his peers. Quite the shooting star."

"Yes. Right." Fuck.

Talking about Blake's ghost gave her freedom, and yet with it came the realization there was a pattern to all the men in her life. None were dependable. None loved her. All put their own careers, needs, and wants first. She looked across at John. What was he hoping to earn by assisting her? An affair? A pining for adventure? A childhood love revisited? In truth, she was putting blind faith in this man who had yet to declare his interest. Once Howard was brought to account, John would leave her—he already had his ship waiting to sail for Botany Bay. She gave a deep sigh. The point of John's departure from her life cut deep. An awful hollowness rose from her stomach up into her chest and throat. John had left her when she was younger. Her mother died. Blake had left her. Her father had never loved her, and now Howard planned something vile. She was unlovable.

All her precious trust placed in a man who was a rake, a rogue, without a whit of dependability.

She looked across at him, drinking in the dark features, sinewy arms, and chiseled face. This man had kissed her, made her feel, for but a moment, as if she were the center of his universe. A blessed gift. Could she toss him aside once this ordeal came to an end? Could she ever return to her old life?

She turned away. Her body fizzled, some pit of anxiety tingling her fingers and arms. Other females might use John for their release, but she could not abandon herself like other women. A silly lovesick fool, she always seemed to be giving men more than they asked, and less than what they wanted. Even now, she'd involved herself with a man who had no interest in her beyond seduction and adventure. England was her world, not his. She turned to face him. He would leave and she would stay…

"We'll view the records when we arrive and check the vicar has kept the special license," he said. "A copy of the license must be somewhere. It won't prove the marriage took place, but at least it will show Dankworth obtained permission." He jiggled the reins, not bothering to glance at her.

"You will need me to describe the look of the vicar, and I'll also have to ascertain Barfrestone is the right church."

He nodded, but she wasn't sure he even listened. He was no different from Howard or her father. An emptiness overwhelmed her. How she wished to drain her body away and hide beneath the hedgerows—to disappear into nothingness where acute sensations could not find her, where pain and disappointment would pass her by.

"How long did you travel on your wedding night?" He broke into her thoughts.

"I don't know. It seemed like an age, a journey into hell. I was nervous." She babbled. "I remember the door because one of the witnesses, a soldier I didn't know, a friend of Howard's, held a lamp for me to enter, but when he stepped to the side to give me access, his lamp hit the post where there was a strange carving of a monkey. I worried he'd hurt his hand, and I didn't want any unpleasantness. The thought of blood on my wedding day seemed too horrible." She hugged herself. "The church wasn't well lit, and I concentrated on keeping my head down as a sign of repentance and respect, hardly daring to look up. I felt so embarrassed and ashamed before the vicar, such an inconvenience to Father and Howard and myself and the unborn child, I doubt I would have noticed if we were in a cathedral or cellar. It was the dead of night, in the depths of winter, and there had been a light fall. Although all churches have a presence, don't they? An atmosphere which is their own."

He prodded the horses keeping his gaze ahead. "The vicar provides me with holy water and a ceremony to launch my ships, but I'm not one for churches, Annie. Not since we grew up anyway."

She wasn't surprised. John was too principled to pretend. Not like her. She spent her life perfecting pretense.

They drew up outside the church and alighted. She longed to climb back into the carriage and take off down some other narrow road, but instead hardened her spirit and pushed aside the partly open gate. The overgrown path was much as she'd remembered from the day she'd walked past it, and there, on the doorway was the carving of a monkey.

She stepped through the arch, heat pricking behind her eyes. "This is the church." There was no reason to cry. No reason at all.

They turned as footsteps clipped toward them. "Welcome to the Church of St Nicholas. May I help you?" a man asked. He had a gentle face, wide brown eyes, and white thick hair. His soft enquiry, so normal, cleaved her younger self in two. Water flooded her vision. "Are you all right, dear? Can I bring you some water?"

"The lady is fine, thank you." John placed his hand under her elbow, thrusting a large crisp white handkerchief into her shaking grip. "She often cries when in church."

"Does she?"

John cleared his throat. "Yes, yes. It's the architecture. Crumbling like this." She glanced up at him. "She can't stand to see old buildings disintegrating. Upsets her all the time. History lost."

The man nodded. "I understand how you feel, my dear. There is an emotional connection with place and time. I, and many others through history, feel the same. This place was built in Saxon times." He spread his hands wide. "We do the best we can, but age will get us in the end."

"There." John smiled at her. "See, my dear? Didn't I say exactly those words when we drove up?"

Anne sniffed into her handkerchief.

"Is there something I can help you with, or are you passing through?" The man smiled. "I am most happy

205

to give you a tour if you wish. St Nicholas is the patron saint of sailors and children."

"How opportune. Actually, we came to view the marriage register, if it is available. We are cousins, researching our family."

"This must be divine providence." The man clapped his hands. "I have the last register on the altar. We've been considering taking it to the neighboring parish for safekeeping. Can I offer you my services? I am considered an authority on the district. What is the name?"

"Gastrell-Smythe or Dankworth."

The man frowned and scratched his head. "There's Smyle in the vicinity."

John looked doubtful. "Perhaps it might be simpler if I checked the register myself. We have been informed the young husband was an imbecile, so perhaps the spelling was incorrect. We may need to see the book for something to present itself."

Anne hoped her hiccough of shock would be mistaken for a sob through the handkerchief.

Soon they were standing before a great open book. They went through the register, running their finger down each line so as not to miss a detail, but there was no entry for Dankworth under the wedding date. Indeed the last entry was some ten years before her wedding, and anyway, Anne confirmed this wasn't the type of page she'd signed. The parish register was a mighty leather-bound tome, whereas she remembered one loose vellum page. They asked about the existence of the special licenses—where would they be kept so they could be viewed, but the man explained the vicar had kept all papers for a few years, then used them as tapers.

"Whereabouts is the last parish vicar and most current register, so we can make enquiries of a marriage which happened about twenty years ago?" John asked.

The man baulked. "My apologies. This has been a wasted visit. I might have saved you some time. The last vicar died some thirty years ago, but you can check his tombstone for the exact date. Reverend Forsyth, by the northern path, and you were looking at the last register."

They shared a significant look, then thanked the man for his help and turned to leave, but as they approached the door, John touched her arm, holding her back. "Before we return to the carriage, do you mind if I take a moment?"

"Is there something you have discovered?"

He shook his head, but didn't look at her. "I promised someone next time I was in church, I would say a prayer. You can wait in the carriage if you like."

"Nonsense. I will sit with you. If my marriage proves false as it seems, I will be desperate for the Lord's intervention."

Fifteen minutes later, they were back in the carriage, and as the church disappeared from view, it seemed her life also faded out of reality. The absence of her name on the register all but confirmed it. She had been lied to and manipulated like a marionette. Anne turned to John, her protector, no words wanting to form.

He covered her hand in his. The touch of him, warm, spread through her coldness. When he spoke, his tone was gentle. "Just because we found nothing here, doesn't mean our search will stop. If other vicars are as unconcerned with keeping their copies of the special license, then we could travel the country and not find proof. We need a change of plan. I will go to the archbishop myself and request a search of his register for the special license. It will mean I'll need to divulge our suspicions to him. However, I am acquainted with Moore. I believe it will be worthwhile."

Anne nodded. The possibility of Howard's duplicity being kept a secret from society grew bleaker by the minute. Once the archbishop was involved, it opened a circle of confidants beyond her control. Her stomach churned at how her future was about to change. Howard had robbed her identity when he pretended to marry her, and she would forever pay the price. "Will we go tomorrow?"

He spurred on the horses. "We go there now."

"To Lambeth Palace! John, I'm not prepared for such a trip!"

"No." He clasped her hand tighter. "Moore is in Canterbury. It will mean a long day on the road, but I have been reluctant to approach him until we had some thread to our enquiries. Yesterday, I sent one of my staff ahead to procure fresh horses and find us an inn for the night if needed."

"You are well prepared."

He dashed a smile in her direction even as he spurred the horses on. "I'm used to finding ports in a storm, and God knows, we are in a squall now. Donovan would tell me it was St. Nicholas keeping us safe."

She tried to reconcile the rake who slept with women on no more than a whim and opportunity, with the man beside her who formulated plans and strategies—enough to seek out the whereabouts of the proper authorities, organize fresh cattle, and who remembered to say a prayer. Somehow it did not tally. Rogues were never so thoughtful, were they?

As if reading her thoughts, he said, "I had hoped, for your sake, to keep this marriage problem secret, but I cannot make any promises at this point. Moore has already been in Canterbury for a week, which was why I wanted to start this investigation sooner, but be that as it may, I hope we can meet him before he leaves and question him in person. He can send a reply by courier once he has researched the license from Lambeth. It's a risk our enquiry might be made public, but we can't afford to act against Howard without confirmation, otherwise no one will give us a hearing. The wait from the archbishop should only hold us up a day or so, but it is imperative."

"Thank you, John. I don't know how I would do this without you. Indeed, I must ask—you have nothing to gain from this, why are you aiding me?"

He snapped the reins, considered her for a second, then whistled up the horses. "I hate Dankworth," he said as the wind whipped past their ears and the horses' manes fluttered. "I hate him for everything he has done to you."

She settled into her seat, wrapping her coat around her shoulders, a warmth stealing over her suddenly tired limbs. John made it seem, if only for a second, that she might be loveable, worthy of protection. The world was blessed and sweet, when someone cared.

They arrived in Canterbury in the late afternoon, tired and dusty. They soon learned Moore was at a dinner for one of his private charities. Anne wanted to accompany John, but he insisted she wait at a local inn whilst he spoke with Moore alone. He settled her into a private room, returning within the hour, well satisfied with his progress, having spoken with the archbishop, who returning to Lambeth Palace on the morrow, could promise all discretion and a speedy reply.

Despite the deepening shadows of the afternoon and the prospect of over a three-hour return journey to Hermit's Peace, John didn't want to stay in Canterbury overnight, fearing it would cause more of a delay. She also longed to get back to the bed she knew. With new horses and a full moon, Anne curled up on the seat under thick blankets for the long ride without thought of robbers or footpads. Nowhere was as safe as in the protection of John, her rogue. Her hero.

It was some time before they could enjoy a sleepy supper at Hermit's Peace. They were sitting before the windows with a glass of port, her muscles sore from the constant jolting of the carriage, staring at the dell bathed in moonlight.

"What troubles you most with this enterprise?" she asked.

"I wish I could say it was Dankworth, but in truth, it's you." He stared out over the silver trees, his fingers molded around the neck of the bottle of port he rested on his stomach, as if a glass were not enough to quench his thirst.

"Women have a habit of getting in the way." she agreed.

"No. No." He sat forward, placing the bottle on the ground, elbows resting on his knees. "I had not meant to confess this. However, I believe I must."

She waited.

"You were moaning and calling my name last

night." He paused, glanced at her, his face reddening. "The memory of it has driven me wild all day. I didn't sleep for listening to every rustle you made, every dream—far more profitable than the pirate stalking my nightmares, I assure you." He turned toward her. "You must find me a devious man."

She placed her glass on the table with a small chinking sound. "Yes and no. Tell me, do you wish to seduce me?"

His eyes answered her question.

A frisson of shocked delight ran down her spine.

"I always have," he said.

She stood. "I have given it much thought, and find I'm not averse to the suggestion."

He stood, then turned Anne by the shoulders so she faced him, and kept his hands there, the weight of him cupping her, heavy, like a yoke of warmth. His thumbs caressed circles on the front of her shoulders, stretching the soft fabric against her skin. Firelight flickered shadows. The wood crackled. Everywhere was deep blue midnight. Her breath hitched.

"We can't. Not like this," he said.

"Tonight is perfect!"

He shook his head and stepped back. "Anne, a seduction is no place for secrets or lies. Tell me, what happened between us at the drystone wall? Why did you leave and not come back? Tell me everything." His voice was rough and deep, rolling her.

She licked her lips, heart racing. "I had heard from the maid about Blake supposedly being a wonderful lover. Betsy said Blake made her scream with joy, and I wanted it for myself. I longed to be touched and loved, and I thought you would provide it. There was one day, when we were younger, when you asked to see my knee, and so I thought you would be accepting of the idea, that we shared a physical attraction. I know I was young, and it was silly to expect you to agree, and of course you were a true gentleman saying you wouldn't make love to me because you protected my virtue. But I was naïve. I was laying myself bare, giving myself completely, and I was angry that you apparently thought only of your honor."

"I protected your virtue." He dropped his hands and gave a deep sigh. "Annie, I need to admit the truth." He ran his hands through his hair, shaking his head. "I am no damned gentleman. I was a virgin, a nineteen-year-old boy, and that night you were so voluptuous and beautiful, I had no control of my functions. I saw you run across the field beneath the apple trees, in your white nightdress, barefoot, and when you ran to me and pressed yourself against me, breathing those shallow sweet breaths against my neck, I-I spent myself. We had not even shared a kiss. I wanted to use you to satiate my lust, but I was never good enough for you. There is the truth."

"But you…" She shook her head, confused. "You said I might hurt myself… You said I was artless in love. I was angry because I thought you blamed me."

"I was embarrassed, a young man who wanted to take what was before him and didn't have the expertise. As usual, I said the first thing that came into my stupid head." He took her hand, running his forefinger down the creases of her palm to the base of her thumb. It was calming and intimate with a soft tingling scratch where his hands had roughened from the sea. "I would have said anything that night, I would have talked till the sun broke because I was nervous, and you were a goddess—out of reach and too beautiful to violate. We agreed to explore each other, and I was susceptible to the stroke of your eyelash. Anne, if we had gone further I couldn't have vouched for my behavior. I would have become little better than an animal."

"I thought, all these years, you didn't like me."

"I adored you. I was shocked when I found out about the marriage and the pregnancy. It made me determined to be the best lover I could, but instead I drove you away. I was so hurt I created a void of ocean which neither you, nor any woman, could ever breach. I never wanted to be hurt like that again."

Her breath shallowed to a whisper. The rip through her core pained and stung like childbirth and desolation combined. All those nights crying herself to sleep, anxious, and they might have been together. All too late.

"All for naught," she whispered.

He tilted her chin up to meet his eyes. "No. We can't repeat our mistakes. We have learned a lesson, Anne. We must never give up on each other."

"You are here for revenge on Howard. You said so yourself!"

"Not revenge. You. I want you. The girl I remember filled with laughter and vibrancy, whose heart was untamed and wild, who would offer herself unconditionally to a young man who should have told her the truth."

He took her chin between his thumb and forefinger, the pressure and intimacy, close to her mouth. She closed her eyes, craving for his lips to press into hers and intrude upon her senses.

"What troubles me is after years of torment, I must spend another night with you when I crave to take you to bed, to show you how I've improved. I am a man. However"—his hand dropped—"I fear what Dankworth's plans might be. I cannot risk your reputation. We are years older, and I find myself again in this predicament where I must protect and respect your virtue."

She opened her eyes and stood. Dumb. What?

She wanted to order him to come to her, to strip her, to kiss her, to take her to his bed. Dear God, he was rejecting her again? She crossed her arms, holding herself tight. No. He wasn't rejecting her. He was finding his bloody principles!

What the hell was she supposed to do? She ached to feel his hands on her body, worse than any dream—this was reality!

"John, we are together and have time to fill while we wait for word from Moore," she whispered.

"Annie, no." He gazed deep into her eyes, drawing his thumb across her bottom lip. "I long to make love to you properly, and I can see you want this also, but if we make love and you are married, under law, we have just provided Dankworth with the bullet for your doom. You will be deported or sent to Bedlam according to his whim, and there will be little recourse I can take to help or protect you—indeed my reputation as a rake will blacken your good character. The sooner we discover what is going on, the better I can guard you from his threats. There are not many clues, but you are obviously a risk to Dankworth in some way, otherwise he would not have threatened you so severely. To understand why, I must sift through the anomalies in your life, and

Blake's death, you must warrant, is suspicious. Dankworth also spends more time in Margate than is justified. Margate is famous for its smuggling activities, and while it may be nothing, we can't leave any avenue unexplored." He let her face go and, turning away, crouched on his haunches to prepare the fire. "Tomorrow will be busy. We must leave early again." His voice echoed in the chimney, taking his words like smoke, up into the night sky. "We go to Margate."

He stirred the embers, sending a shoot of red sparks sputtering up the chimney. She might create her own red sparks of energy in his bed if she were given half a chance, but his back was hunched away from her, blocking her out.

"Margate," she echoed.

He swiveled toward her, still keeping on his haunches, a pinecone in his hand, which he was about to set on the fire, but he looked up with a studied, sad stillness. "I am sorry."

She looked away. He was right, of course. This whole situation would have been made tolerable if John Wylde, London's brightest ornament, an unscrupulous rogue and rake, were exactly as those rags portrayed him. Those editors knew nothing. She turned and stomped off to bed. The one principled rake in the whole of bloody England, and she had to share accommodation with him.

It was not fair.

Chapter Sixteen

Thursday, May 7

The following morning was similar to the previous, except loaded with a strained fatigue. She'd tossed and turned during the night, and Margate, a long dusty drive away, did not inspire her with energy. John was preoccupied with his horses, as usual. They stopped at his stables in Elfleet to change the pair, but then they were on the road again at a fast trot.

The weather this day was as bothered as her mood, a frolicking warm wind that kept chasing her and pulling at her dress and hair, drying her skin and lips, itching her eyes. Her proximity to John added to the boisterous atmosphere. The way he hunched in his seat seemed like a physical question posed exclusively for her, asking her why she didn't just reach across the distance between them and seduce him. She could. Easily. Howard had ensured she didn't have any sort of future, so she may as well make love to John and damn the consequences, be deported to Botany Bay for the pleasure of his touch. It was a price she was willingly prepared to pay. Yet she hesitated. Why? She turned her head away from the man. The answer was easier. A deep fear she would not be woman enough. Her eyes itched from the dry wind; salty tears were a secret balm.

As they came closer to the sea at Margate, a

blustering breeze cooled her but parched her throat and nose. John took them on a back route into the town, stopping at a small, well-appointed inn on one of the quieter streets, to refresh.

"I'll leave you here, while I start making my enquiries." He downed the last of his ale, placing the tankard on the table.

"I thought we were staying together today? Otherwise what is the use of my accompanying you?"

"I need to start on my own. I have contacts I can make enquiries of. One in particular might be of help, but he will not talk business with a woman present." He gave a nod to the owner, then turned to her adding under his breath, "I may need your assistance later."

"Wait." Anne tugged at his sleeve. He stilled. "Dankworth is my husband, and I was Blake's lover. Yesterday, I let you speak with Moore, but today I want to be involved. I have ideas we can pursue."

"Annie, my task is to protect you at all costs." He lowered his tone with a shooting glance to the other person in the room. "You are safe with me, but once we go out onto the streets of Margate, the town where we know Dankworth spends some of his time, you are in danger of recognition. I won't allow it. You are safe here. I know the owner well, and he will make sure you come to no harm. Also, you're forgetting I am a well-known merchant and have my own resources in the town that I can tap. It is why you wanted my assistance in the first place, remember?"

He was correct of course. Again. It was becoming an annoying habit. But this time she didn't like his reasoning. He hadn't asked her for suggestions. He had taken over, ignoring her, and he had an unstable history of acting without regard for discretion.

He gave a wry smile. "I have no idea how long I may be gone, but I've taken the opportunity of booking you a room for the day. Make yourself comfortable. Order whatever you like on my account. I'll return as soon as I am able." So saying, he stood and, donning his hat, left with a brief nod.

She watched him disappear out the door, her gaze narrowing. Wasn't this the position she had been relegated to her whole life, sitting pretty and waiting for a man to return from his travels? Keeping herself occupied cross-stitching little bookmarks? As if, after all this trouble, she could order food on his account! He treated her like a kept woman, which was possibly an unfair criticism, but it rankled at how her freedom continued to be curtailed by high-handed men.

If John had stopped to listen, she might have explained she knew Margate well enough to get around. Howard would never suspect her of being in the town, so the man had no reason to look, and if she were careful, which she would be, she could avoid an incident. Indeed, it seemed sensible that she should act on her own sources of information.

When the owner's daughter came to collect their dinner plates, Anne enquired on the whereabouts of a resident who might have kept copies of the newspaper over many years. She was handed the address of an old man in Broad Street who, once an editor, kept copies of the *Kentish Gazette*.

She scribbled a note for John, telling him where she would be, in case he made it back to the inn before her, then made her way down the narrow streets, her parasol keeping off the sun's heat and protecting her from recognition. A twinge of guilt for ignoring John's advice tugged at her, and yet, for the first time in her life, she was accountable to no man. Hadn't John said he wanted to see more of the free and uninhibited Anne from their youth? Perhaps it was the sea air invigorating her and the high circling gulls squawking and fluttering on a coastal breeze, but a sense of ownership crept over her soul and settled in her breast like liquid gold, pouring warm and treacle-like through her veins. This day belonged to her, and she would make of it exactly what she pleased. With any luck, she would be sitting back in the room when John returned, and he would be none the wiser of her expedition.

At the house, the old gentleman showed her the stack of papers. He didn't seem eager to help and commented a few times about women not having any regard for reading, their tongues wagged enough, but he kept out of her way when his wife screamed at him from deeper in the house, and soon Anne was able to find what she needed. She took the paper to a table before a window for better light and, pressing the paper out flat with her hand, ran her finger underneath each line of print, reading it half-aloud. With time her words became whispered with dawning horror.

During the evening of 3rd November 1769, the victim, Mr. Blake Hunter from Fernsby, was seen with a group of dragoons. They had all been drinking and left the King's Arms together in general high spirits. Mr. R, another patron of the same bar, left some half hour later and was passed by a youth with fair complexion, fair hair, and slender made, running in the opposite direction. Mr. R then walking across the Sands, came upon the victim who had been so badly beaten as to be *unrecognizable, gore, blood, and his brains on the sand. Upon calling for help and nobody knowing who the poor fellow was and a crowd gathering, he called Captain Dankworth, who happened to be passing with blood on him from a regularly occurring bleeding nose he'd acquired from the cold night air. Dankworth identified the body as that of Blake Hunter and called for assistance, even going out of his way to help the murdered victim even though he was ill himself. The coroner's report found Blake Hunter was bludgeoned to death with excessive force, possibly a cudgel, and robbery was committed upon his person being taken shirt, buckles, cloak, boots, and one very valuable gold lorgnette or quizzing glass which Mr. Hunter had been showing to great amusement and curiosity at the King's Arms just one hour prior. Captain Dankworth had shown extreme empathy, preserving good order at the scene.*

The article went on:

Young Mr. Blake Hunter had, at that time, been the past three weeks staying in Margate, awaiting transport to Bristol and thence onto America. He was said by his family to enjoy anything with literature and that he was kind and always trusting. There being no persons found to be guilty of this heinous robbery and murder but that it was robbery by a footpad gang or persons unknown, the matter was discharged. It is advised that all persons of Margate take particular attention when walking at night as this is not the first incident of gangs of footpads having come from London to prey on the innocent and who are particularly violent.

Bile rose in the back of her throat. Black dots flashed before her eyes; she was tired and cold and hot all at once. Howard never told her he had been the one to find Blake's body.

Her mouth went dry. What of the report of Howard's bleeding nose? She had never known Howard to bleed from the nose, let alone it be called a regular occurrence from cold night air.

The lorgnette sealed it. She slammed the paper shut and put her head in her hands, struggling for breath and to gain her vision. The world was falling upside down, taking her with it.

Blake had been murdered. Howard had done the deed. Why?

She needed John.

John would know what to do.

****

He sought information with the local Riding Officer, old Rutledge, who had a long memory and prodigious ability to notice nothing. John had the fortune of using Rutledge in the past, finding him a reliable source about shipping activities, both legal and otherwise on the Isle of Thanet, it being common knowledge Rutledge's meager salary was subsidized by the Isle's citizens who paid him to keep quiet about their smuggling. Even John admitted he had enjoyed the odd illegal tub of gin, and Rutledge likewise agreed with a sense of pride, that with all his staff, the Kentish coast was too big to protect.

John found the old man at their usual haunt and opened the conversation, buying a drink then putting a small stack of shillings on the table between them. "I'm making enquiries about the death of a boy many years past. Blake Hunter. You remember anything?"

Rutledge swept his hand across the table toward

the money. "I remember it was on Fort Green and never knew about the murder of a poor boy except it wasn't nobody's fault."

John placed another stack of coin. "Take as long as you need. Nothing at all come to mind?"

"I don't need no time. I never knew other than the famous Major General Dankworth finding the poor boy."

John paused. Dankworth found Blake? Anne hadn't told him. The information grew in value. He kept his gaze intent on Rutledge, then reached into his pocket and withdrew a money clip. He unfolded a note and placed it flat on the table where it wasn't in plain sight but was evident to his companion. He pushed it forward. "I didn't realize you knew Dankworth. He a friend of yours?"

Rutledge never even looked at the money. "I never knew a gentleman called Dankworth"—Rutledge spat on the floor—"except I knew a devil, damn his blood, though you not be hearing that from me, and I'd be telling you all this for free."

John placed another note on the table. "I would be most interested in knowing, Mr. Rutledge, why Major General Dankworth offends you."

"It might be my personal opinion, it might. Dankworth being a hero, a major general. The world knows he be an important man like no one else. My opinion ain't worth paying for."

John smiled. "Calm yourself, Rutledge. We have been friends many years. I am not about to abuse it." John steepled his hands before his face, watching the man. "What say you, Rutledge, if I inspire you to tell me what you know with a secret of my own?"

Rutledge's eyes narrowed.

"It has come to my attention—no details as to what quarter—that Dankworth might be less."

Rutledge was already nodding and smiling. "My lord, I never knew a military man, a major general no less, who concerned himself so much with smugglers who never had anything to smuggle. That strikes me as weird, that does. The rumors you heard might be true at that."

Smugglers. John put another note on the table. "You know about the smugglers, don't you? It's your job."

A fine sweat beaded on Rutledge's top lip. He nodded. "I be the Riding Officer, but I never heard Major Dankworth speaking, nor seen him down on the bay at high tide every few months that he didn't make it worth my while not to see him. Very generous is Major Dankworth, my lord, but I never heard him speak that I was certain he was damned, being the important man that he is. Dirty money it is at that. I don't like it one bit."

John leaned back into his seat. What to make of old Rutledge, he wasn't sure. He implied Dankworth was involved in smuggling, although the link seemed tenuous. Everybody on the Kentish coast was involved in smuggling in some form or another. John frowned. Except Dankworth didn't live on the Kentish coast. What had Rutledge heard? John shook his head and sat forward. The next note he held between his fingers, for if anyone was see the amount of money accumulating on the table, trouble would follow. It was equal to about three years' worth of Rutledge's annual salary—the undeclared portion. Now, however, John wanted value for his money, and he wouldn't be so pleasant to poor old Rutledge.

"Rutledge. It might be advantageous to tell me what you don't know, rather than a magistrate."

Rutledge swallowed, eyes darting left and right. He wiped his top lip with his arm and whispered, "I am a simple Riding Officer, my lord, and you'll be a good upstanding man, and I'll tell any magistrate. I never had no business with spies."

The whole world came to a stop.

"Spies," John echoed. He reached for his gin, emptied the cup. He leaned against the chair, his pistol pressing into his back, its pressure easing the fear that tingled down his spine.

Rutledge checked round him, pushed the money across the table, back at John. "I never wanted your money, my lord. I never wanted this day to come, but I knews it had to. Some day he would get caught with his smuggling nothing. I never saw no gin, no wool, nothing. Nothing but words. Nothing but words and I heard him one night too. Damn his blood, but he spoke better than the crew of the French vessel, and I heards him mention the dragoons and I knew. I knew."

John knew sweat was beading on his own brow, his heart beating loud over the talk in the inn. "Rutledge, you didn't confide this to anyone, did you?"

Rutledge shook his head. "I never. That man is too dangerous by half when the devil gets in him. Anyway, who's going to listen to an old Riding Officer when Dankworth be the king's favorite? Damn his blood. You keep your money, my lord. You just do what's right for England. I never was so good at this job, but I was never that bad either."

"Mention our conversation to no one. Understand?" He put all the money under his palm and pushed it across to his informant.

Rutledge nodded and in an instant had pocketed the cash. "For my wife and daughter." He took a final swig from his drink.

John strode out into the sunshine and windy air, certain of what he had to do next. If Dankworth was a French spy and also an English national hero, it meant he had been leaking secrets over many years. A more dangerous criminal John couldn't conceive. Marriage to Anne had hidden Dankworth's duplicity and given the spy access to one of the highest ranking military families, and Anne's father, the most upright of military men, had been the easiest to deceive.

The fallout for Anne and her family he couldn't guess, but for the moment, he needed to act.

What he sought to do would lead to naught if Dankworth were innocent, but if he were guilty…John found his steps taking him to one of the more notorious drinking places in Margate. If Dankworth were indeed a spy, John's action would be Dankworth's death warrant.

John's step didn't hesitate nor falter.

****

John ran toward Anne, reaching for her even as she fell into his arms. He caught her face in his hands, searching her eyes, demanding answers. What was she doing on the street? Walking in the open?

"You look terrible. Did Dankworth find you? Why are you not at the inn waiting as I instructed?"

"Please. I am so sorry. I haven't seen Howard, but we need to talk. I can't speak of it here."

He guided her back to the inn, asking her to keep her head down so none might see her distress and Dankworth, if he lurked in Margate, would not discover her.

At the inn's reception room, he ordered refreshments, made her sit and sip a cool ale while he tore bread and cheese, something for her to nibble. He tried to ask again, but she darted her eyes to the owner and shook her head, though she had to look away to stop the hot tears welling behind her eyes.

"What is wrong? What happened?" he asked, once they were alone.

"Please trust me. We can speak at Hermit's Peace, but not before. What I've discovered compromises me," she whispered.

"Annie, I asked you not to go out anywhere! Margate is dangerous for you."

"You have to trust me, John. I have ideas about discovering information. My idea worked. For all the horror it has caused me."

Jaw ticcing madly, he reached for her hand and whispered, "Give me three more hours, and then we leave. Can you wait?"

"Thank you," she whispered on a sob. He passed her a handkerchief, pressing it into her hand, then called for the innkeeper's wife to help her to the room, where she sat like a doll, waiting in anticipation of John's return. It took him over four hours to accomplish what he needed, and by the time he came to take her back to Hermit's Peace, her nerves were close to breaking.

After taking longer than anticipated to finish business in Margate, they arrived at Hermit's Peace near nightfall. He was desperate to know what had happened, and wanted to tell her of his findings while they were travelling, but every time he raised the subject, she shook her head, saying she could not risk breaking down into a wailing mess until she reached the privacy of Hermit's Peace. From her distress, it was obvious all was askew, and he feared she had learned the same as he, that Dankworth was a spy. Yet it was impossible she had made such a discovery. The information had been difficult and costly enough for him to unearth, let alone a woman. She wouldn't have had access to the contacts to gather such facts. Added to this, he didn't know how she would react to the news of what he had learned and couldn't guess at the misery she thought important now—for no revelation about Dankworth could eclipse the filth of his hard-won knowledge.

Blood and wounds, he wanted her to be spirited and independent, to see the old Anne return. He should have expected her to want to assist. Fuck. He would kill Dankworth with one bullet.

So he waited, speaking little on the trip home but keeping his hand pressed over hers for reassurance, which she accepted like a lifeline.

When he drew the curricle and pair into Hermit's Peace, the sky held a warm glow, but the air was brisk. The animals were tired. Even their furniture jingling sounded restrained and muffled. Anne went straight in doors. He needed to see to the horses, giving them a long draught at the cool stream and bedding them in their stalls with a generous provision of chaff. When he finished and came inside, it was late.

A lamp spluttered a yellow glow into the room where Anne had already boiled water for tea, a brew sitting on the table. She stirred boiling eggs for a late supper, but the room was peaceful for her presence, though she moved with a nervousness he had not seen before.

He pulled out a chair, its legs scraping loud on the oak floor.

"Hungry?" she asked, as if he had come in from a day in the fields, placing bread, a knife, and board on the table with a clatter.

"I am as hungry as a whale, and too tired to chew." He took up the knife and sawed through two thick slices, laying them flat for buttering.

"I have something revolting to reveal." She watched the eggs. "I needed the quiet here to be able to say the words. The road was too noisy and bumpy to speak of it. I am sorry, John. I could not tell you earlier. And now I am here, I wish I did not have to tell you at all."

He waited.

Her shoulders shook. She stood there sobbing.

He went to her, put a handkerchief into her hands, and guided her into his chest. Afterwards, when she eased, he put his hand beneath her chin and raised her tear-tracked face, wiping at the salty water of her suffering.

Her eyes bright yet bleak and empty as she stared up at him. "I met a man who had copies of the old *Kentish Gazette*," she whispered. "I wanted to search the paper to find what I could about Blake's death. I remember at the time one of the Fernsby Ladies was talking about an article. I had never seen it, but thought it was as good a place as any to start. I wanted you to know that I too have information I can contribute. I am capable of discovery."

He couldn't guess what Anne had exposed for he knew there would be no information about Dankworth's spying activities in any gazette. His stomach hollowed. He took her hand and pulled her toward the chair before the fire, making her sit, keeping her hand in his, while he perched on the arm of the other chair and waited for her to speak.

"The article explained Blake's death and stated Howard had been the first on the scene."

He ran his thumb in a slow circle across her wrist watching a delicate blue vein pulse.

"The article said Blake had the most gruesome death and Howard helped afterward, but Howard"—she gulped—"had a bleeding nose which was a regular occurrence." She looked up at him. "But John, Howard has never had a bleeding nose. The blood on Howard belonged to Blake. I know it." She dissolved. "Howard killed Blake, then lied about the blood. I didn't even know Howard had been present when Blake died! He never told me."

John left his perch, squatting beside her, putting his hand on her knee, which shook beneath the fabric of her skirts.

"Annie, dearest, I don't think you can make an assumption from a bleeding nose." But even as he said these words he knew she was correct. Anne never made accusations unless there was some basis in fact. Every moment in her company proved this.

"The article also mentioned a lorgnette."

"Lorgnette?"

She put her head in her hands and wept. "Howard always carries a gold lorgnette. He uses it everywhere.

Once, at the opera, I thought he was spying on other women, and we fought. Badly." She looked away, her fingers shredding his handkerchief. "The lorgnette was in the paper. Blake had one."

"You think it was Howard's?"

She nodded. "I think Howard gave it to Blake, so Blake thought it was his. Blake would love such a gift, but he would never have the money to purchase something so valuable. I think Howard gave it to him so he might rob him of it later. He murdered him, set Blake up, and murdered him. Howard would be capable of such a thing. We might never know the truth, but even the judge believed Howard's story. What hope have we of being believed? Nobody will ever take my word against Howard. Society loves him."

How was he supposed to admit he'd learned Dankworth might be a French spy when the man was a killer? She had every right to know the truth, and now was the moment to reveal all, yet he did not speak. He ran his hand across her bent neck. She was too delicate, had already experienced too many horrors. As her shoulders shook from sobs, the ramifications and predicament under which Dankworth's duplicity placed them, became clear. If Dankworth's sympathies were with the French as he suspected, Anne's life would be in danger if she knew any of it. Dankworth would not send her to Botany Bay or Bedlam—he'd kill her. In fact, the way to keep her safe was to not tell her about his discovery until he had proof. More importantly, it would serve Dankworth's plan very well if their developing relationship became public knowledge since then, both Anne and John's character would be disgraced, and their claims about Dankworth being a murderer or spy would be easily refuted. He longed to take this woman to his bed, to kiss away her fears, make love to her as he should, sweep away her problems in his strong arms, but he couldn't. Not until he had word from the archbishop that proved incontrovertibly her marriage was false.

He looked away, staring at the fire and steam rising from the heating water. He, who encouraged Annie to speak the truth about Charlotte's paternity, kept secrets himself—and the poor woman was better for knowing her husband was a murderer with not a shred of support from him, just as the daughter's life had always been safer for believing Dankworth was her true father.

This was the sludge, mire, and flotsam Dankworth heaped upon the innocents around him.

He drew her closer, holding her head to his chest. She lifted her face, her lips red and bruised, her cheeks flushed and wet, her eyes glistening and pleading.

"Please, John, kiss me."

He lowered his head toward hers. She was so upset she had not even asked him what he had discovered in Margate. There were a million reasons why kissing her was the worst deed in the world—she was at a disadvantage, he never kissed a woman in distress, Dankworth's shadow loomed. Oh, but he could not stop. Her lips were warm and soft and plump and drove him insane with their desire, hardening him in an instant. Dankworth be damned. Anne was in his arms, and it mattered not if she was married or free—she needed comfort.

The arm of the chair got in the way, so he drove his hand beneath her knees, catching the fabric of her dress and lifting her, their lips never breaking.

He placed her on the bed, laying her out on the rich flamboyantly colored spread, her pale skin and dark reflective eyes staring up at him, some small part of his brain registering the dark smudges beneath her eyes. She needed to sleep, and he should leave her there to snuggle into the bed. As her friend, he should advise her to put her worries in his wooden boat to dream away, and they could talk about the social dilemma a non-marriage might cause her in the morning.

But instead, the bed became an island of consolation and reassurance. She wound her fingers around his neck, up into his hair, and drew him toward her. He kissed her again, then stared at her, drawing his thumb across her wet cheeks, running his hand across her brow, smoothing the fine dark curls which bounced beneath his fingertips. She belonged to him. He would take away her pain.

Her fingertips traced his face too, drawn across the cut of his jaw and over his Adam's apple, her touch as fragile as a butterfly's wings making his heart leap.

It was the night of the drystone wall again. Here before him lay the woman of his dreams, exploring each other as they should have done. The sudden image sent his head reeling, swamping him as a young boy. This was the woman of his dreams; what if he couldn't fulfil her? She deserved better than him, a man of prudence and consistency. He went to draw away, but her fingers dug into his shirt.

"Don't go," she whispered, nay begged. "I want you, if you will stand to have me. Only you can drive away the horrors."

Her words tore him, and he fell upon her, kissing her with punishing force and heat, wanting to wash away her anguish and smother her in years of longing.

Her palm clutched his shirt, pushing it over his shoulders, and the cool air of the house and her insistence inflamed him like nothing else, so his fingers moved of their own volition to the drawstrings on her dress, releasing the small bow, and then the bow on the gauzy chemise. He drew the material aside exposing a fair rounded breast and rosy pink nipple, hardened with desire. He must taste her, draw her into his mouth.

She gave a small gasp and arched toward him as his tongue flickered across to the sweet tip. "Oh," she sighed. "I like the feel when you men do this."

He hesitated. He raised his head to see her face and her wide black eyes pinned him with an unhealthy curiosity. "Blake did this too."

"Blake?" He choked.

"He kissed me in the same manner. I didn't like to mention it before, in case you thought it might be a rake encounter you invented."

Blood and wounds! Was every one of their attempts at lovemaking to include comparisons to third bloody parties? And what did she think he was inventing? He sat up.

"What is it? Do you want to climb on me already?" Her breathlessness, lush mouth, and half naked exposure combined with the awful turn of phrase, made their lovemaking ugly, revolting.

"The eggs." He had no idea why he said it, just that he was grateful. "We forgot the eggs."

"Oh, yes." She lay on the bed, lifting her arms to run her hands across her forehead, setting her breasts moving.

With a control that ached, he got off the bed and

tramped to the fire, preferring to grab the hot pan with his bare hand and have the metal blister his skin to the bone than listen to Anne in his bed talking of other men's lovemaking. He could not fathom it! The first time they had tried to make love it had been the stable boy, and now years on, he was being compared to the bloody ghost!

Added to this, how could he forget the shadow of bloody Dankworth? Thank God she hadn't compared those lovemaking skills. He scowled. Dankworth was a cold bastard, not much finesse in that department, he'd wager. Wouldn't want to get his hair mussed. No doubt the bloody stable boy had dibs on Dankworth for technique—and when the hell did he start comparing the performance of the men she slept with?

He took a deep breath and strode across the room because he must be doing something with his energy. She had no idea what she was saying. She was distraught with the knowledge her so-called husband was a murderer.

He grabbed a linen cloth and pulled the eggs from the fire, leaving them on the hearth.

"Are you hungry?" she called.

He put his hands on his hips, refusing to turn around. Yes. Of course he was hungry. He had wanted to enjoy a sexual feast, but apparently he would prefer to stop now and peel the boiled egg instead! Wouldn't that be pleasant and cordial!

He shook his head. No, fuck it! There was no justification on this earth for a woman to say what she had. He looked back at her, lying on the bed, breasts spilling sideways, breasts that should be in his hands being mounded together where he could rest his head and float.

What was wrong with her? One minute she said the words a man longed to hear, the next she said the words he hated most.

Did she think he was such a jaded lover, mentioning other men's names was allowed?

But dammit, she wanted him; he could tell she wanted him, lusted after him, and needed him—that juicy clam between her thighs needed to be opened.

He clenched his jaw.

God, but she sounded like a nervous virgin. Yet this also was not true.

She had had a lover, a husband, and a child. Anne was no virgin.

He turned on his heel and looked at the eggs on the hearth. Then he turned back to the bed.

She was sitting up, had attempted to draw the edges of her chemise together but the edge of one pink nipple peeped out. She was all frills and tossed hair, and he wanted to ravish her.

"You don't like me anymore, do you? I've done wrong, haven't I?"

He cleared his throat. There was nothing for it but to say yes. He could stand here all night and not understand why she said what she did. The woman defied all reason.

"Why did you mention Blake's name?" he asked.

"So you would know I am experienced."

"Does it matter?"

She lifted a shoulder. The nipple came close to full disclosure, but she seemed unaware. He swallowed.

"I don't want you to be bored," she whispered. "I can't compete with those two women. I'm not good at being in a man's bed."

His eyebrows shot up to his hairline. Dear God and damn her blood! She was intimidated by him? This woman with all the wiles of a goddess doubted her own ability to even interest him? Had he not made himself plain?

Damn his own eyes. Nothing made sense! He wanted to swear, even wished Donovan, the big ugly brute, would interrupt them so he might extract himself from this disaster! He stood, hands on hips, mortified.

How the hell was he supposed to make love to the woman when she was so unsure of herself? And worse, if the marriage license proved valid—if the archbishop found the damned special license existed, he would never forgive himself; she would never forgive him for embroiling him in one of his sordid affairs!

She had no idea what she was doing by inviting him to her bed, while he had too much experience to ignore the fact once he lay with her, it would change them forever—he would never be the same, and he knew for certain, she wouldn't—he was too good a lover to have it otherwise. She didn't need a tawdry affair adding to her woes, and if she ever let it slip to a judge she had slept with John…

He rubbed his face. What the fuck was he doing?

"I have done something wrong already, haven't I? Please John, I don't want to force you. We don't have to do this. I understand Howard's too great a threat to risk making love."

There, she said it again, mentioning another man!

His nerves were so taut he grunted. His balls were so tight they were likely to explode between his thighs. His cock was telling him to part her legs and drive up hard past the nest of frills and claim her. His head was screaming not to go near her, and he wasn't even sure he was breathing. Things had gone from bad, to a whole lot worse.

"No." He grunted. "No. It's not you." God, but he was too old for this.

She sat up further, dark hair tumbling about her face, her chemise falling open. "John." She licked her lips, and he shuddered. "I can stay very very still."

His blood ran cold. Nausea swept him. He was an idiot, had underestimated everything: Dankworth, her experience, her marriage, her father, the whole bloody lot.

All she had ever asked for was some man to make her cry for joy, and no bastard had ever done it. Including himself.

With a dawning horror that compelled him and repelled him all at once, he knew what he had to do. Dear God, he was going to fail her now, as he had on the drystone wall but not in any way she imagined. When this night finished, she would be angry, but he knew an effective way to guide a woman into his dock.

He took the few steps needed to stand beside the bed, then knelt on the floor, tipping her shoulders to the pillows. He removed his pistol, placing it by his knees. "Are you sure you want this? Because you're in a delicate state of mind and I'm not. In a delicate state. I'm feeling like one hell of a rogue for how I'm about to pleasure you."

Her lips plump and red, spread into a luxurious smile, a dimple creasing one cheek. The sort of smile which might be called wicked on anyone else. On her, it invited tasting. It drove him insane.

"I'm ready to be bad." Her breath came shallow, fanning his neck.

He shook his head and prayed he could keep himself on the bloody floor without climbing on top of her. Why did she demand more control than he ever had the presence of mind or body to possess?

He moved a piece of her chemise, revealing the nipple that refused to be covered, and pinched the taut peak. She moaned and shifted. Her eyes glazed, half shut.

He stopped. She crested on a fine line between normality and breaking into oblivion.

"Kiss my breast again," she entreated. "Just like…"

He put his finger against her luscious lips. "Quiet. Let us have quiet. I am the expert."

"I never make a sound," she whispered.

He clenched his jaw. *Fuck*! "You may be as loud as you like. I want you to disturb Hermit's Peace like it has never been disturbed before. Cries of joy, remember? Like the maid. Waves crash loud when they break upon the shore, and so must you."

The dimple in her cheek gave a shy peep.

He leaned forward and licked her nipple. She moaned.

"Better," he whispered. "Just so."

Her hands were still extended, but now he grasped her by the wrists, holding her arms above her head. He stared at her, drawing her nipple into his mouth again, teasing it harder this time.

She groaned again and closed her eyes, moving as if to thread her hands through his hair, but she was bound.

"This is for you." He spoke into the swell of her

breast. "It is my turn to make you cry for joy."

"Oh but John, you were right all those years ago. I never—" He silenced her with his mouth, plundering her sweet taste. Once she had given up, the words dissolved in silence, then he moved his free hand down, down across her breasts, meandering over her stomach, to the frills of her skirt.

He ruched the white lacy froth which would bring him deep into the heart of her.

When he parted her thighs, she groaned into his mouth, his fingers opening her moist hot center as he plunged his tongue into her mouth. His finger and thumb slid into her moist cleft, finding her swollen pearl of velvet desire pulsating and eager. Giving it a gentle tug, he soothed it, and with a gentle twirl, waited for her shattering response. When she groaned and lifted her hips for more, he repeated the movements flicking and sliding over her delicate slicked flesh, taking her closer and closer to the edge.

Her small body shook beneath him with a series of mighty reverberations. Her eyes flew open, her pupils wide with such hot desire he wanted to come. Ah, but she did not know what was in store. He released her mouth, putting his lips to her breast, her soft moans and spasms building to a crescendo.

"Let me go," she implored, but he slowed, then increased, for this was how a wave broke against the reef, in patterns and rhythms.

"Don't stop. Please do not ever stop." She was hot and swollen, and her thighs were stretching. Then, her manner changed. She rode the peak and he joined her, her body shivering with swollen expectation, where the tide and flow could build no more, so it teetered at the edge of disintegration, a force of nature powerful, beautiful, terrifying to behold…

She screamed for joy, her voice echoing through Hermit's Peace disturbing the night birds and creatures, and even the horses stomped and whinnied, and he was shocked by her release, so loud and unbridled it crashed around him in a flow, sweeping him with her, knocking the breath from his lungs, disorienting his thoughts, stretching every muscle, pounding him on a hard ocean floor to a grain of sand.

Exhausted, panting, she curled on the bed, rocking and washing gentle in the ebbing tide. His knee ached beyond pain to numbness on the bare boards, but he didn't move.

Hell, but the woman was crying. Crying! He kissed away the tears and drew her to his breast, curling her hot body against him.

"I never knew," she whispered.

After all these years, she was his.

Chapter Seventeen

Friday, May 8

Anne woke, the scent of the room reminding her where she lay, daylight breaking so a soft gray light filtered through the trees and sky. A bird called in the distance, the first to wake as her heart burst. Her eyelids flew open finding him asleep in the chair by the fire. Why did he not stay with her in the bed?

Should she be peeved by his distance? Yet of all the men she knew, John stayed the closest. She drank in his presence. His boots and cotton stockings gone, his bare feet large and proportioned, high arched from the pitching and rolling of decks. His cravat draped over the back of a chair, so his long neck and chin with its dark stubble lay exposed, the barest pulse throbbing the skin at the base of his throat. Soft skin where the scent of him was strongest.

The rise and fall of his chest set a warm regular rhythm filling the room, and in the graying light his eyelashes fanned, still and dark and long against his cheek. She might run the tip of her finger along his forelock, the texture of hair waving smooth at the base of his neck where one curl snuggled.

She belonged to him, heart and soul, no matter feuding families or her marriage, his other women, or their tumultuous history. This man would keep her present firing hot.

She could whisper in his ear, into his dreams and tell him he was no rogue and she had never been fooled. She loved him for his ocean wide and deep honorable romantic heart. She always had.

His lips parted on some half spoken words, which drifted through the cool early morning air as shadowy as the light. Foreign lands and adventures, what dreams possessed him now?

The instant he woke, she determined to possess John's body, the way he had taken hers, that she would show him she could be adventurous. Except the memory of the letter from the archbishop regarding the special license intruded into her peace, swamping her in bureaucratic futility, sweeping away her desire.

What if she was legally married to Howard? The answer came clear and immediate; she would engage a lawyer, seek Howard out, and insist he order a divorce, the procedure would be quick and definite. The steps needed to achieve the outcome formed in law, in documents, in words printed clear in black ink. Charlotte would hate her, but at least there was precedent and a road to redemption.

What if she was not married? She closed her eyes. If she weren't married, the problem would not be the separation from Howard; it would be the years spent in a lie. Extramarital affairs were accepted, even Aunt Bess knew it was so. A pretend marriage?

Never.

Charlotte would be devastated enough by a divorce. However, she would be mortified by no marriage at all. Charlotte's hard-sought social standing would be in tatters, the mother-and-daughter bond broken beyond repair, for Charlotte loved and idolized her father more than Anne. Always had.

And what of her liaison with John? He didn't even count Anne worth a relationship. He seduced her for revenge on Howard, or perhaps a rake's parting gift before he left for Botany Bay. Maybe he took pity on the murderer's wife or had fulfilled an adolescent romance. She did not want to believe it and yet, he had not said he loved her nor had he slept in the bed with her. He gave nothing of himself—never had.

A true rake.

At least, last night, he had given her something in return.

Careful to be quiet, she rolled onto her back. On the high beamed ceiling, light filtered through the leaves casting shadows as the birds began to pip and tweeter. A new day to fight old demons.

Murder spoke blackness and desperation. There had to be a reason why Howard needed a wife and why her?

She scrambled through the memories of their time together, flashing through them like cards in a deck. Howard didn't prefer the company of men, and neither did he prefer the company of women. His monk-like habits had never been disconcerting. It was his inability to show affection, his occasional rapid and aggressive flares of temper and lack of humor, his arrogance—these were the essentials of the man. In fact, the one thing she could reliably say was Howard liked listening to gossip and planning functions.

Anne paused and frowned. When she put her mind to it, Howard had always been secretive, but those little things didn't seem to matter because they had no significance she could ascertain—which made her appear shrewish if she objected or queried the episode.

Like the Turner boy capturing sketches of her—not that she had ventured mentioning the occurrence to Howard, not after she had seen his reaction to her question about the message he had received late at night. There were inconsistences. Like many years ago when Howard first told her he would be visiting her father, so she'd sent a letter to Graystone enquiring if Father had had a nice time—a simple letter. The general had written back with a diatribe reminding her Howard was in the army and would be staying in barracks, not gallivanting around the countryside visiting relatives like a woman. She ventured to enquire about the confusion with Howard when he arrived home from God-knew-where, but he had been angry and obtuse, so she never asked his whereabouts again, but thereafter when he told her he'd been visiting Graystone and the general, she didn't believe it. Strangely, it sometimes seemed as if Howard told these lies tempting her to question him and provoke his anger, or so he might gauge her honesty. Anne called them open lies. There had been many.

What did it mean? The secret of the wedding, the murder, the note about his death, the visits to her father, and other little things like Howard never mentioning his family, never meeting his parents or siblings, never meeting friends. She expected he would be friendless; they had even discussed it. He said he was a commander, a leader of men, and others were prone to jealousy, yet she had this certainty Howard needed a woman beside him at social functions, because? She struggled. He hated women. Always put them down, treated her like chattel. He was capable at functions, far more social than her! It was as if he wanted to appear normal because underneath, life was abnormal.

Was this the key?

He needed a woman who wouldn't ask questions or lie to him, a perfect mate, a woman who would be grateful, and do his bidding. No doubt Anne's illegitimate pregnancy and her father's social rectitude had given him an opportunity at the cover. Why? To what purpose?

Anne's stomach shifted and turned. She and Father had praised Howard for his loyal offer of marriage. They hailed him as a savior, a man who had acted with unselfish virtue. Her father believed this still.

A fine tremoring filtered through her body.

Often Howard burrowed down in a discussion at some dinner to get one little grit of information. She'd heard the rumors. Dankworth's Duck. It was true his apparent successes often backfired later. Like India…

She shook her head. She couldn't fathom his international military successes or failures. These were beyond her ken. It was at home, where the small things could be observed.

It was the gleaning of information, which pleased him. Even at the theater, he would use his lorgnette to read the conversation of others rather than watch the play. They had argued about it. Him telling her through clenched teeth and angry whispering while the cymbals clashed and drums rolled that he would do what he damned well liked, and she was fortunate he didn't hit her in public, as some husbands had a need to do, though she deserved it. She saw in his eyes he would, hard and fast, when they arrived home.

A few weeks later, Howard was commissioned to India, and she collapsed. He didn't come back to England for two and a half years. Not long enough for her bruises to heal.

A sensation skittered across her mind, so awful, she dismissed it, and yet it refused to go. It lingered, turning itself over and over in a cloud of noxious vapor. Could Howard own subversive sympathies? The notion, in itself, was absurd because Howard was the English national hero. Yet the suspicion lingered.

Her chest swelled, might explode but for John's steadying breath in the chair. Shadows on the ceiling resolved to a time at Covent Garden when "God Save Our Lord The King" played and Howard sat feigning sickness, disturbing the performance for guests around him and irritating her with his lie. Perhaps his objection ran deeper.

Her disquiet skittered like thunder, lightning, and torrid pelting rain through her veins. In the stillness of morning, she faced the demon. Who would believe her? Did she believe it herself? Perhaps not except for one important memory, some years old, when their French chef had first arrived and she had come across Howard and the chef in the kitchen sipping coffee, Howard talking French like a native, but the men had stopped their dialogue as soon as she entered the room. Howard said later his father spoke French. Strange how he never mentioned it before… Strange how she had not thought of it for years…

John grunted and opened one eye. Scrubbing his stubbled cheek, he gave her a warm sleepy smile. "How did you sleep?"

The simple question made her smile, dispelling the

hurricane. "I believe the exercise prior to slumber may have had something to do with my refreshing rest."

His eyebrow rose, a slight smile pulled at his sleepy plump lips.

"So…" she ventured, "do you think we might do it again? Right now. Although perhaps you could join me on the bed, and I could take the opportunity to touch you?"

He sat up. "No. No. We had better prepare breakfast. You must be hungry, without dinner last night. What would you like?"

"You."

He stood awkward, stuffing his firearm into his belt, while staring at her with a hot smoldering gaze, igniting her belly with a fierce hunger that had nothing to do with breakfast. As if he knew what she was thinking… He shook his head at the floor and swung his stiff knee until it moved smoothly, arching his back and rubbing his chest. All in a morning ritual. She noticed his eyes remained dark, sultry, and heavy, locking down on her every now and again as if to check she was watching him. No ritual there. She loved watching, yearned for his undivided attention on the pulsing wet region between her legs. She inched her shoulder forward and backward a fraction, so a hard puckered nipple revealed itself.

"Come on, John. Let us be bad."

"No. No. I can't. I've been awake all night thinking about it." He scrubbed his head again, tossing his hair into black peaks.

"Me too."

"Not that. Not that. Not you. I mean about the damned marriage. I was thinking about it."

"Forget the marriage. Think of us."

Hands on hips, he stared down at her, a frustration simmering beneath the surface. "Annie, I am thinking of us. We can't give Dankworth the opportunity to traduce you. The scandal sheets will be full of it, and the courts will be against us. Trust me. The man's intentions would be unreliable, blacker than you can imagine, and I have no doubt he'd make it painful for you, for both of us. He is a murderer. Nothing stops him. If he tarnishes your good character, we have no case. While ever you remain the good wife, we are protected."

"But I'm not a good wife! You know that."

"Well, yes," he groaned, "but you mean too much to me to have your reputation sullied. If I bed you now, really bed you, I would be the basest man. I am not using you. I don't want to use you like that when you deserve more. Anyway I can't. I can't let it happen again."

"Oh John, of course you're using me, but I don't mind. I am using you too. I'm thoroughly enjoying being used. I want to be used by a master."

"Listen, Annie, last night…"

"You were doing what I wanted."

"I…no…maybe…I'm not sure about…"

"John, please don't be coy. When Howard returns to Graystone, Father will inform him I have gone off with you, but it doesn't matter. Howard cares nothing for me. You saw it yourself when we were on the terrace, and I'm sure he made it clear when you spoke to him, though you still haven't confided the details of the conversation."

"Forget my conversation. Dankworth made it clear

he doesn't give a toss about anyone. What I am trying to explain is that your good wife virtue is his Achilles heel."

"Now, wait one minute. I will not have my virtue spoken of again—especially not by you, for I have none. John, I am not trying to discredit you, but at the moment, I'm concerned about my access to your body, and we can't second-guess the outcome of the archbishop's search, so while we are in this cottage, why don't you come to bed and touch me? I want your hands and fingers on me, probing places which make me tremble." She leaned forward so the breasts spilled free, her hair tumbling over a bare white shoulder. "I want to stroke you."

"Yes. Yes. Annie, please, don't tempt me. You must not. My name connected to yours will be your ruination. Why do you think we are secluded away in this cottage so society will not see us? I have a duty to protect your character. Me, the rogue and rake, trying to redeem myself by protecting a woman's reputation." He shook his head. "It is ridiculous enough."

"No! John, it's slightly ridiculous to do what you did to me last night, which was intimate and excruciatingly wonderful, and then stand in some court and say to some magistrate, 'Oh but Your Honor, I haven't slid my rod into her so therefore…' "

"Right." He took a step backwards. "I want you to think before you speak. You know your choice of language torments me, doubly horrible since I caused your exposure."

"I hope I am tormenting you." She sat up further, making sure her chemise fell down, baring both breasts, letting her hand wander into the valley, and he looked so ruffled with sleepy confusion touched by the morning rays of the sun, she itched to unfurl his clothes off him, run her hands over the rough hair on his wide chest and sun highlighted skin, grab the bulge in his groin, and titillate him as he had her. "The sight of you is tormenting me, John. I've been thinking about what you did to me all morning. It was glorious. Can you not hear my heart? It is beating hard with wanting and desire. If this is what rakes do, someone should have told me. I would have tried one sooner."

"Right. Well, you won't be trying any other rakes because I have the best reputation, so I've spoiled you for anyone else—and what the hell am I saying!" He threw his hands in the air. "There's no point discussing it. We will burn ourselves up if we discuss this any longer. I can't have all this talk, talk, talk. I'm a man of action, damn it. Blood and wounds, a man can only take so much!"

"Stop it, John. You protest too much. Don't you think we've already waited long enough? Remember the night in the carriage when you sucked on my nipple, and when we were at your house and we kissed and your tongue darted into my mouth and sent me to the stars? I want more! I know my reputation is non-existent compared to yours, but I feel with your tutelage, I could come to perform better. I crave your touch, your fingers deep—"

"I have to tend the horses." He banged through the door, striding into the early morning light.

She flew off the bed, barreling through the doorway to see him limping with empty pails toward the stream. His leg must be aching, but he moved quick, so by the time she had run to him, her breath came fast, half closed chemise forgotten, breasts exposed and her skirts falling, but she did not stop to adjust accessories. Better she stripped bare and let John see her naked, begging him to take her, than be clothed in restricting garments. He wanted her. He must have every last fiber of her.

"John, I swear I will do my best to give you pleasure, if this is what worries you. I may not be as experienced as those two women I first saw you with, but last night felt so good I can never…"

He stood there, already shaking his head. "Why are you always comparing—"

They were interrupted by thunder. Anne turned, expecting the sky to be black behind her, God raining judgment on her sins, before realizing it was the pounding of hooves at a gallop. A visitor would be upon them in seconds. Howard? Dear heaven! Her heart exploded behind her ribs… He would kill her. Where to hide? Where? She gathered her skirts to run. The house was too far to reach…

Suddenly, John's firm warm arm grabbed her around the waist and dumped her behind him, just as a stranger on horseback erupted onto the meadow.

John stood still, the empty wooden pail he'd dropped in his rush to hide Anne rotating on the ground at his feet while one hand snaked around to find the pistol in his belt. Anne held onto his shirt, her hands in fists, cowering, her knees weak.

The rider dismounted in one vigorous leap and came toward them. His footsteps were full of authority. A young man, he hesitated when he noticed Anne peeping out from behind John's back. His gaze dropped to the pail, then rose, taking in John's state of undress.

"My apologies, my lord." The boy's voice went a little higher, his eyes a little rounder. "I rode all night with a special message from the Archbishop of Canterbury. Your staff gave me the route to your abode." He hesitated over the last word. He held out a document. "I have instructions to wait for your reply."

John nodded and took the necessary step toward the boy, snatching the paper from his proffered hand with snapping authority. "You are lucky you came when you did. We were about to bathe in the stream. Bare feet in running water."

The boy's eyebrows lifted.

John pursed his lips. "It's supposed to diminish warts. It's a tradition in these parts. Come. Don't tell me you've never heard of it?"

"I'm not from around here, my lord."

"No. No. Of course not. Well, you wouldn't know, but now you do you can tell everyone. Running water at dawn for warts. Polly does it every morning, and she has no warts, do you, Polly?"

"None." She agreed while tying material, getting all the layers in the correct place and concentrating on the proceedings, which John seemed to be determined to complicate.

"Do you have warts?" John enquired.

"No, my lord."

John stared at the boy as if wart treatments might be more important than the document. After a few moments' consideration, he tore open the seal and scanned the papers. He took a minute to himself, then told the boy there would be no reply, but he was to return to Elfleet Hall where he should ask for Donovan, who would make sure he received a hearty breakfast and was paid handsomely for his speed.

The boy, looking relieved, swung his leg back over his horse and cantered off. As the beat of the hooves retreated, Anne came out from behind him. "Well?"

"Your marriage is invalid." He held out the paper. "No special license was granted, no reading of the banns took place, and no permission was sought nor given to your father. Also, you said your marriage was performed at night, and this also invalidates it. You, my darling, are free."

Anne's eyes read the words, but she'd barely finished before John grabbed her by the arms and set her standing before him, like a rag doll. "You are free! Imagine it! He cannot damage you now—so long as I keep you safe, this is your liberty."

"No. No. This is dreadful news."

He stared at her, one hand on her shoulder, whilst his fingers drew slow lazy circles across the nape of her neck.

Anne placed her hand over his. "No."

John frowned, leaning in to kiss her, when he stilled. "Did you not hear me, Annie? You aren't married. This is your honor restored. You will still be in danger from Dankworth, but now you have the protection of the legal system, of men who will value your honor and how you have been mistreated. We hold in our hands solid proof, and we can celebrate in all the ways you begged not ten minutes before." He trailed his finger across her shoulder.

"No." She took a step back. Like a prisoner released from his shackles, there was some stirring of relief, but it was all too soon overshadowed by the consequences... How was she supposed to exist on her own? People would blame her for Dankworth's deception, not pity her or want to protect her. John's work was done; he would sail away. Meanwhile, all England would blame her—the witch who conned a hero.

Unseeing, she walked to the edge of the brook. Years of her life used by another man, and now, here with someone else, who had not told her he loved her, wouldn't share a bed with her—until now, when all was lost, when she had nothing. Like a doxy whore… His favored type of woman…

She was unmarried.

But all she ever knew was how to be a wife. No. She'd never even been a wife.

John came up behind her, running his hands down her arms, turning her to face him. She couldn't feel the warmth of his hand, her body dense, like wood.

"Come inside. We need breakfast. We can discuss what to do next."

Eat? She wanted to plunge into the cold flowing stream and be carried out to sea or stand forever in this place till she rotted like an old tree trunk, all parts dissolving back into the dark wormy soil. She let him take her hand and followed him back to the house.

The bread, cheese, and eggs made her laugh. Such an ordinary way to start extraordinary days. Except, instead of laughter, what escaped her throat gripped and lodged and came again. Sobs. Awful big sobs, and from her eyes, big plopping tears. She tried to wipe her face, but her hand was not connected to her at all.

He came and put his arm around her, sandalwood enveloping her, pushing a large white handkerchief into her hand. She did not know where he ever kept these damned handkerchiefs that appeared on demand, which made her cry even more. Wracked with shudders, the sadness seeped into her soul, echoing years of emptiness. Tears for the woman she had been. The loneliness. Years of nothing. Years of shame yet to come.

"Annie." He tilted her chin up, so she might see him. "Trust me. We can make this information work."

"Trust you?" she echoed.

"We must approach your father first. Tomorrow."

He eased her into a seat at the table, then sat himself opposite, the sun falling around him, so innocent. Oh, but his thoughts and comments were black. She could not believe he, of all people, had spoken them.

"I am not going to tell Father."

"You must, and Charlotte needs to be given the truth now we can show her proof. Prepare yourself for danger too, as we may need to face Dankworth. I would spare you, but I cannot anticipate how he will—"

"John, I have discovered my marriage never existed." Her voice rose as though it were not connected to her at all. "I am not going to discuss any of it with Father or my daughter! Father approved Howard in the first place. Father has had his control, has played his part. Now I am in charge. As for Charlotte, I don't know. God, she will be devastated, and now I must exist with her hatred." She buried her head in her arms. "I need time to think. Think what to do."

John reached out across the table covering her hand in his own, his grip solid. "I will ensure your father does not bully you. I will be there with Charlotte too, for I fear you are right. The girl will be hurt, and you will be the easiest person she can strike, but both of them will need to know the truth because once we bring this to light, society will be cruel in their judgments. To have them know is to forewarn them. Dearest Annie, do not expect any of this to be easy. It will be the hardest thing of your life, but I will never leave your side. You are not married, Anne Gastrell-Smythe. Under law, I can protect you and keep you safe from harm."

She pulled her hand from his. What was he talking about? There was no law about pretend marriages! She needed space to think—hadn't she told him? She pushed herself away from the table and faced the windows, wishing she was a cloud and far away, looking down on the world, not connected with it in any way, as he went on and on with his honorable, respectable, virtuous ideals.

"I will help explain it to your father. You said earlier you feared for his mental state. You can't do it alone."

"Oh, for God's bloody sake, John"—she spun to face him—"and yes, now I am swearing and I don't care, because Father will be the last to know. He's part of the lie, as guilty as Howard. He controlled me, played me before Howard even existed. Always the girl who had to make a good marriage, and I failed. Father has no right to know anything. I told you I need time to think."

"Annie, we don't have the luxury of time. Dankworth has used it all. The way I arranged my contacts in Margate, and now we have documented proof of Dankworth's duplicity, today is all we have." He stood, softening his tone. "Please listen. Dankworth duped your father too. The social and military outcome from all of this will be enormous. I have not explained it all to you, but I must meet with your father. Only he has the military expertise and contacts required to bring Dankworth to account."

"What military expertise? It is my marriage that has never been ratified! Indeed, you sit here preaching to me about families and what they must hear!" Her voice rose. "You know nothing of their dynamic! Your mother died in childbirth, and your father was as old as the hills, too absorbed with gambling away his wealth and his grief to give a fig about his son. You've always been left to your own devices, to do whatever in the world took your fancy, yet you are upset because some rag labels you arguing over a lady's reputation while you take multiple women to your bed! For God's sake, who do you think you are to lecture me about duty and what I must do, when you, the roving adventurer, shirked even seeing your father on his deathbed!"

"Where did that tidbit come from? Some rag again? Allow me to correct you. While you were up north with your pretend husband, I held my father's hand to his final breath—a fact never reported because a rogue and adventurer doesn't make for a good story unless he's up to no good. That is what people want to read, and you, who knows me better than any living soul, believed it. For Christ's sake! I thought you trusted me. I thought you above salacious gossip."

"Originality of thought is a luxury. Whilst you careered around the world, free from worries, I was shackled to a carved boat for my dreams—there is my creativity, my originality." She pointed to the carving on the window ledge. "You were born a man, John, and

257

in my family gender counts for everything. Don't even pretend to understand my family, or tell me about truth and women, when you know nothing of my sex other than how we can be controlled in your bed. Don't stand before me now, at this moment, expecting me to believe you are above any of it. You no sooner hear of my marriage being void and you want to bed me—yet not ten minutes before, when there was a chance of me being married and I wanted you, I was ignored. Is that because I suddenly became slovenly and available? Is it my reputation, or yours that you protect? Is that what you like, John? Are those the sort of women you crave? Me and my bloody virtue don't interest you at all, do they? It turns you off, doesn't it? You didn't dare to take me when I was the wife of a hero!"

"I'm the one helping you in this predicament," he exploded, "offering assistance, yet you would rail against me too?"

"You want revenge because Howard spoke down to you—called you out for the man you are. Don't pretend at altruistic, heroic motives. You're here for yourself. You are as base as my murdering husband."

His voice went low. "You mock even last night's pleasure?"

Her body stilled, cracked, shattered, like fragile glass. "Pleasure for whom?" she asked as the splinters tinkled and fell. "You gave me a demonstration of your prowess—no commitment, no sharing, no honor, and no virtue. Your display was as fake and hollow as Howard's wedding scheme. Neither of you join me in the bed. I have run from one master puppeteer into the hands of another. More fool me."

"Anger makes you spiteful. It's not the truth and

well you know it."

"Truth? Don't make me laugh. You tell more lies than any of them."

He stepped away. "In my bed, Anne, there are no lies. I see every flaw and every perfection. The truth is, you aren't yet ready for my bed."

"Or perhaps the honest truth is that you were never ready for mine—to face your own imperfections!"

His countenance was stony solid. His jaw ticced.

She crossed her arms and smiled.

"Damn your eyes and blood, Anne Gastrell-Smythe. You are as vicious and dangerous as any man. The shot of a pirate to both knees is preferable to the sharp poison of your tongue."

All her life, wanting to hear a compliment, and it was spoken in bitter hurtful rage. Her eyes flooded tears. Her vagina still pulsed hot and swollen from his touch, yet her blood which had earlier boiled and bubbled, subsided to a flowing lava. She could inflict pain. The knowledge was no comfort, but it was the one sliver of herself which mattered above all else. In the cruel fury of his arctic eyes, a watery insubstantial reflection of herself shimmered, somebody who could influence another—not in love, for that would be too impossible. Yet she could inflict agony as it had been perpetrated on her, and somehow, this was the truth that mattered. This was the moment she must build her new life from. This was the bitterness, the resentment, the rage, and humiliation from which her future could erupt. The world would come to taste her hurt.

"For once, Annie, be honest to yourself. I will not be distracted with abuse. You denied Charlotte the truth about her natural father because it was easier for you and Howard, but I can't let you deny the same truth from your father. The general needs to know the marriage is false and I will tell him myself if I must because there is more to Dankworth's duplicity—deceits we are yet to understand."

She stared at him. "I don't want to understand any more. But if it is so damned important to you, do you think this news of Howard's deceit will be painful for my father?" She tilted her chin.

He gave one curt nod.

"Good. Let us go. He never lifted one damned finger toward my parenting, not even to pat me on the head. At least Howard did. He even bought Charlotte a doll. Yes. Let it all come together now and talk it through, and I pray he feels the bitterness of Howard's betrayal. Betrayal by a man he thought his wonderful son-in-law. Then I will be vindicated."

John took one halting step toward her, reaching out, then let his hand drop. He limped one step back, his face a mask. Anne hoped John was in pain too, that everyone was feeling something. He needed to understand she had lived too long with a murderer not to feel the edge of human cruelty and use it to her advantage. She was bad to the core. John had been warned.

"I thought you were used to the idea of not being married."

"I thought I had too." She took up her plate with a clatter as if housework mattered. "The reality is a bit different from perhaps. My life will now be scrutinized. Society will enjoy crucifying the witch who wrecked the national hero. Me, who thought to be a good faithful wife, so father would be proud and love me. My daughter's society marriage, which she had worked so hard to orchestrate, will be threatened beyond anything I can conceive. I have been left with nothing, not a father, not a daughter, not a husband—whole family gone—not even a friend. I don't even have a claim to a brick in the house." She paused. "Funny, when I started this, and first saw you, I thought to keep my family safe. I wrecked even this with my meddling—ah. You warned me, didn't you? Right at the start you said leave it to men."

"Bitterness doesn't become you."

Anne dropped the plate onto the floor with a resounding crash. "Bitterness does not become me? I have to repeat it to make sure I have it right because as far as I remember, I was always bitter, John. After my mother died, after you left me, after Blake died, after father married me to Howard. What do you think I have been all my life except bitter! I am practiced at it, and who are you to lecture me on the judgment of others when you have cultivated the reputation of a rogue when no such rogue exists! Are you also a rake? Are you also an adventurer? I disbelieve all of it—you, the great lover who can't even take me to his bed because of the shadow of my hero husband! You never felt a thing for me."

"I am a rogue."

"No, John. A rogue would never have assisted me against a decorated national hero! A true rogue would have bargained with my husband for common use of my body, did you ever think about that? No, because once again you think of my bloody virtue. Virtue, which I never had, will never ever possess!"

His eyes glittered. "A true rogue would walk away.

261

I did such a thing years ago."

"Agreed." She pointed at him. "But a bloody rogue would have forgotten it. You haven't. My God, look at you. You have the face and physique of a goddamned mythic hero! You talk of telling the truth to everyone but yourself. Bloody rogue be damned. I could teach you some things, John Wylde, for I have been lying to myself for years."

"Annie, I am a rogue." He took a step toward her. "Only a rogue would admit, at this moment, when you are most vulnerable and torn by emotion, that he loves you and always has, that no matter what happens in the future, he will stand beside you and be there shielding you from everyone who means you harm, even if it means killing in cold blood or keeping secrets from you for your own protection. I am a rogue, practiced in all this and more besides, and worse, I am a rake for I can think of nothing else but to ravish you at this moment, while your eyes are wet and glassy and your hair is mussed and your clothes are crooked and your temper is fiercer than an erupting volcano. I want to kiss your soft red lips and drown in them. It is all I have ever wanted. Not one woman counted for anything. It was all a diversion while I lusted after you, made them into visions of you—even stipulating they use violets in their perfume. I am an adventurer, for I want to take you with me into the future unknown—other lands and places, far from here where the sun is warm and the sands is white and the sea is turquoise blue, for I cannot answer as to what will be in your future in this gray England, and I want you to be with me till I draw my last breath, away from all the people and hurt and horror and loneliness you have had to endure. I am all the things rumor ever said I was, but I am double those things for you. I love you. Am helpless for you. So helpless I do not even know where to begin to seduce you. You are the one woman I cannot seduce."

She stared at him.

"Annie." He said her name in a rush. This was no small cresting wave, and it didn't leave an ache, but rolled and crashed against her in a mighty tidal surge.

He took her hand, running his rough thumb over her wrist. "I have always loved you," he whispered and he wasn't scared of her, even when she gave him the worst, the bitch whose appetite for hatred and inflicting pain was insatiable, instead he fought by telling her he loved her. What else should she have expected from a brave hero who faced pirates?

Always the hero.

"Oh, John…" She drank him in, his noble bloody intentions pouring a balm on her seething heat. All she ever wanted was here, offering himself, driving away the bitterness that foamed one minute like Medusa, and the next turned her into a whimpering love-struck mess. How did he spin her so quickly? How did he dive into her soul and wash away all the foul wickedness with some sort of sweet draught? Oh, there was magic in the touch of John Wylde; she'd always known it was so. The notion of losing him for even a second, because of her churlishness, chilled her to the bone.

"What would you say, Annie? Tell me. There are no oceans to fill my heart such as your love."

She pressed her finger into his lips and closed her eyes. "I never ever dreamed you would say such words, let me taste them and savor them. Oh, John, I am scared, terrified. For you are too good for the likes of me. I am no easy woman to understand or love, and you speak of beauty when I have shown you my worst."

"Give me your worst every day of the year, Anne Gastrell-Smythe, for you make me a man." He drew her tight to him, then swooped her up, his arm beneath her knees, and kissed her hard, the pressure of his mouth claiming her, taking everything, demanding the world.

When they broke, he nuzzled into her neck to feather kisses behind her ear. "I would take you to the drystone wall at midnight. We need to take our second chance."

"I am too old for stone walls, but the feather bed…" she whispered shaking with lust against his throat where the curl was tight. She slipped that curl over her forefinger, where it rested like an anchor.

"You will have to seduce me for I fear I am the novice in your hands," he said.

"I can do anything now I know you love me."

"Annie, in our future are two certainties. Us and Dankworth. Dankworth is dangerous. More dangerous because unlike you, he won't use words to fight. He will strike with a weapon in his hand."

"Why must you speak of him at this moment?"

His eyes twinkled, his dimples flashed. "Annie, the truth is you make me lose my head. To face Dankworth, I must be clear headed, and I need you to be prepared, for you will be his target. You are the threat."

"I need to prepare?" She let her head fall back so he had better access to her breasts, her chemise falling open wide, and the pulsing river of her desires snaking down between her legs. "How do I prepare?" God, but she ached for him.

And then the ground came firm beneath her feet.

His breath was torn; his eyes were black as he whispered in her ear, "How long since you last used a pistol?"

Chapter Eighteen

He reached up and placed a pinecone between the trunk and branch. "Not the silver birches," she called.

John put his hands on his hips and stared at her.

"If I hit the branch, the tree weeps. When I was a child I knew them as the crying trees. It's the sap."

John continued to stare. It sounded lame even to her own ears. "I won't hit the branch then," she mumbled. John continued his work.

Anne weighed the pistol in hand. John's own. It was a wonder he didn't hate the device. It caused him such inconvenience with his wound, and yet he never went anywhere without one tucked into his belt. She'd have to ask him about it. Dear God. She turned the metal over. She hadn't used a firearm in years. It had been her father who encouraged her because he wanted to show her to advantage on some foxhunt with the ton—a potential marriage in the offering, which never eventuated, despite, or perhaps because of, his aggressive posturing. In any event, the one benefit to come from those hunting parties was her unerring aim. John remembered it—then again, he would. Her father never spoke of it once she was married. Howard, when she bragged to him of her expertise, was skeptical. He used firearms to intimidate and kill.

The black metal in her grasp showed no reflection but absorbed the darkest and bleakest of her humanity.

The balanced smooth grip made it easy to kill, an extension of her.

"Ready?" John moved well out of the firing line.

Just then a russet brown hare, oblivious to all except his lunch, hunkered on the grass, nibbling, black tipped ears twitching, and mid-morning sunlight tipping its fur.

John pointed to it, indicating a new target.

Pistol in her right hand, cupping the dark wooden butt with her left, she lifted the black muzzle, her sight travelling out to her target, the pine cone some five feet above the ground. A gentle warm breeze, with spring sweetness, brushed her forehead, clearing the last vestiges of their argument as she focused on the wooden scales.

"Bang," she whispered.

"You were supposed to kill the hare." John came up behind her, lifting the weapon from her hand. "I'm guessing you haven't even loaded." He tutted as he checked the chamber. He rammed down the powder, then raising the pistol, his aim on the hare, he squinted.

She placed her hand on his elbow, where the sinews contoured skin tanned by a tropical sun. "It's God's creature. Leave it be."

He ignored the pressure of her hand, keeping his gaze steady on the hare. "When you were younger, you would have taken this animal with one shot from a crooked barrel."

"You always did exaggerate my ability, and cold disposition." She let her hand drop.

He turned his head, his gaze now focused with unnerving intensity on her. "Yes, I must have, for it takes courage to pull a trigger. Dankworth won't pretend. If you are in his sights, you will die."

She gazed up to the windows of Hermit's Peace, dazzling hard gold in reflecting sun. "Your words of love prove I shared Howard's name, not his nature. I fancied I had been sullied, but you saved me. I cannot stoop so low."

John stared down the barrel. "Dankworth's nature is to kill."

She stepped in front of the barrel. "Dankworth, yes, but not me or you." Her voice shook, the cold metal tube pressing into her breast as she stared into his eyes.

"I have killed, Anne."

"You did not like it though, did you?"

He stared at her.

"We will never be like him."

He dropped his arm, the firearm dangling near his thigh. "Do not despair, my love. I have talked with Dankworth once, and I too felt tainted by the experience. I can only imagine what atrocities he has perpetrated on you. I will not let it happen ever again."

She stilled, this man who killed pirates and bedded whores. This man who respected her virtue. He owned her heart. Simple, undying, eternal love that asked no questions. At last, she understood how such devotion lifted her beyond all substance, made her a better person for being by his side. In contrast, her fake husband contained more malevolence, sank her deeper, than she'd allowed. So if the man standing before her was rattled and wanted proof, she would comply.

She took the pistol from his hand and shot the pinecone. Dead center.

"Ah, my precious Anne. You are the one person in this world on whom I can rely." His words and breath came across her ear in a half-groan. "You know, a woman with a pistol has always given me irregular excitement. I remember you on those hunts, violet perfume and perfect aim, riding straight-backed, rocking with the horse beneath you. It was always my undoing when you aimed, my avenging angel."

Placing his hands on her shoulders, he turned her to face him. His eyes glittered black. For the first time in her life, she was master of it all, capable of instigating events, of taking the wildest man and taming him.

The way a woman should.

"It is the challenge," she whispered.

"A matter of honor," he replied.

She tilted her chin, a frisson quivering down her spine to the juncture between her thighs, the soft skin erupting in an instant tingling, ordering her to express a satiation of urges from years of frustration in this moment released. She was plump. She was wet. She was an aching void for him to fill.

"I call out your skill as a man, John Wylde. Do you accept my challenge? Code duello rules?" she demanded, the air from her lips hot with need as she aimed the pistol at his groin.

He smiled, a provocative twisting of his lips in wicked delight. "Duello." He took a step back and unbuttoned his waistcoat with deliberation, shucking it off his shoulders and throwing it to the ground. "I've chosen my weapon."

Her eyes widened. Her heart pounded a loud and hard applause. The ache in her womb screamed for his touch. So this was how it was to be?

He drew out his shirt from buff leather breeches, peeling it over his head, his shoulders broad and chiseled from pulling ropes and sails, caught the sunlight. The sort of shoulders that made her want to run her hands over them and press her thumbs into the iron hard muscle, the sort of shoulders which would rip his shirt in one tearing strip if he so desired. Bronzed and wide with dark hair across his nipples. This was where she would thread her fingers and take hold.

He stopped, his fingers twined through his belt buckle. "We don't have seconds."

"Your weapon is already loaded."

Her eyes fell to his chest where the hair became a thin line, pointing down to his breeches, where his manhood in clear evidence, throbbed. Now there was a prize flooding her with anticipation. He ripped the belt off in a fluid motion, followed by his breeches, throwing them with his pile of clothes. "I choose Hermit's Peace as a ground."

He was naked.

She took three slow steps toward him. Leaning over, she ran the muzzle of the pistol from the base to the tip of his shaft. He groaned.

"And I choose distance," she whispered. "Firing at pleasure. Agreed?"

She touched the pistol to his lips, the briefest touch, making sure the barrel grazed his taut stomach when she'd finished. A fine perspiration beaded on his brow.

"I like it when you fight for control, John Wylde, for it is your nature to be wild. Yet, you should not seek to tame yourself with me."

He stood still. "I am yours to command. I have given no other such a gift. Use it wisely. My control with you is not legendary."

She bent down to inspect his manhood, then raised

her eyes up to his. "I intend to bring you to your knees." She threw away the firearm and cupped his balls in the palm of her hand.

"Remember, Rule 22," he rasped.

She released him and took a step back. "Any wound sufficient to agitate the nerves and necessarily make the hand shake, must end the business for that day," she quoted, then smiled. "I haven't even begun to agitate your nerves." She ran her eyes over the long athletic legs. The scar on his thigh and calf glistened white. She inspected the spot where the skin was new, then went behind, following the angle where the shot had passed through his flesh.

And his buttocks, firm rounded globes before her. What those prudish women in Fernsby Ladies Literati would give to be here now.

She kept him standing there some time, before strolling to the front, as though in thoughtful consideration. "I like this weapon. It has fine balance. It is powerful and the sights are straight. I think I can use it to my advantage."

She pulled at the drawstrings on her waist, neck, and arms, peeling off her dress, undoing her chemise, and throwing it on the ground, so she stood before him naked, the sunlight warming their skin.

She walked over to him, close enough so her hard nipples pressed into his chest. He grunted. She took his hand, and put it between her legs, in the valley where she ached.

He looked at her one long minute. "I am about to perform, but I fear I will do my name an injustice. You sweep away all my experience, make me like a boy."

"Good—and this time I want to hear your cries of

joy."

He dragged her with such strength, into his arms, the air pushed from her lungs and his kisses so hungry she might be swallowed by him, and his hands spread and raked across her body forcing her to him so the kiss could deepen. He took total control.

"Stop!" She held him back.

He paused, but his cock glistened and his breath strained, every sinew in his body arched beneath the skin and the fine shimmer of sweat.

"You have learned much over the years."

"All for you."

"Show me what you've learned."

In one step, she was in his arms, laid on the blanket, her nipples and breasts teased and molded. He used his tongue to explore down further, until she gasped, cried, screamed, and squirmed, embarrassed, delighted, pleasured by the intimacy he took, which made her body as though his. He brought her to the cusp, then sliding his hands under her buttocks, opening her thighs to the world and his scrutiny, he slid himself into her, and she cried aloud, the thrust of him inside her, filling the void, owning her, stamping her.

"I've waited long enough for you, Annie." His voice shook rough and bad, as he shot into her hot core. "You win."

Chapter Nineteen

Saturday, May 9

They left early the next morning for Graystone.

With masterful hands, John gigged the reins, she sitting beside him, close, her hand upon his thigh, or sometimes higher when she sought to tease, her other hand clutching the brim of her hat, which kept catching the wind. As they made the journey, she looked out over the fields where a slight breeze bent the grasses. A perfect spring day.

"Howard will not be at Graystone. He'll be at Margate," she said over the pounding of the horse's hooves.

"I wouldn't count on anything with Dankworth. It is you and your father's safety that worries me. Perhaps even Charlotte will be at risk."

"At least I can take comfort that Charlotte has Joseph's protection and is no longer at Graystone. Father, however, is another matter. He will be upset at your presence today."

"Nothing changed then."

The horse's ears twitched, signaling to go faster, metal jangling with an upbeat tune.

"Do you have the pistol?"

"In my reticule."

He nodded.

"Annie, what was it about Dankworth during your marriage that you didn't seek out affairs? You would have been ripe for men like me," he asked, the question posed so quietly, his manner so concentrated on the horses, she knew her reply important to him.

"I am not the sort of woman men can love."

He kept his eyes on the road. "The old Annie I knew, the Annie who made love to me yesterday afternoon and again last night, would have demanded it."

She turned to him, needing to hold her hat tighter as the wind caught it. "I only ever demanded it from you."

He reached out and took her hand. "I will always regret I didn't make love to you on the drystone wall."

"Don't regret. We both made mistakes. I acted rashly having sex with Blake. I needed to grow up and learn to think with my head, not my heart. I paid the price by falling pregnant."

She should tell John that Howard had never consummated the sham marriage, that Howard could not function like any ordinary man, but the words caught in her throat, a bundle of knots impossible to unravel, tied to her lovemaking, notions of her body, man's pride, and passions discovered. It probably didn't even matter anymore, now she had made love to John. Nothing mattered but their love. He'd promised she would go abroad with him. Oh, but the world was a wonderful place and living in love was a joyous thing to behold.

John moved his bad leg, bracing it against the board. "Annie. I need to tell you something."

"Don't. Not now. I am already full with nerves and

you sound ominous. Allow me to relax before Father's onslaught."

"It's important."

"Important to me, father, or you?"

"Everyone, even Charlotte."

"I don't want to know."

"You must. I have kept something from you, a secret for your own protection, but now we have the special license, which is hard, incontrovertible proof of Howard's duplicity, I can tell you."

She looked over the fields toward some distant cottages. Howard's inability to make love did not need to be divulged. Nothing dark or sinister could hurt her now.

"How long have you kept this secret, John?"

"Since Margate. You never asked what I did that day. I should tell you."

"I trust you."

He stared at her with frank shock. "I thought you would hate me, abuse me, and rail at me about men keeping secrets."

"I thought I would too."

He drew the horses to a walk, turning to face her, his eyes searching her face, even while his hand reached out and caught a strand of her hair, pushing it behind her ear. "You worry me, Annie. Dankworth is dangerous, and you are fragile. He will stop at nothing to get what he wants."

She turned to him. "You will protect me. I give myself unconditionally to you."

His face broke into the open enjoyment she had seen in him as a young boy. "My God, I love you! You fill me with such pride and strength of purpose, such honor as I have never known. Ah, but you are right, of course. I'll protect you with my dying breath. Ah, Annie, you are as stimulating as a shifting trade wind, and you pull me up so it stings. God, but you have given your body to me, opened your soul, and I love every thought, every utterance, and every breath."

He took the reins and gigged the horses to a canter. "Come, my angel. Into battle we go."

How did she deserve such a hero?

They drove up to Graystone and, mounting the front steps, noticed the door ajar. Something was amiss. Anne hesitated, giving John a questioning glance. He pushed past her into the hall.

The house was quiet. No Haversham to meet them, or even Jenny, her maid. Yet a vase of rosebuds, all fresh and perfectly placed, wafted a gentle perfume into the still air. In silence, she walked ahead of John, putting her reticule on the table, lifting her arms to remove her hat, and placing it on the table, her footsteps reverberating in the empty hall.

"Father?"

There was no answer, but a muffled sound came from further down the hall.

John picked up her reticule from the table and passed it to her. "Keep it on you at all times."

She took it with a nod, then went carefully down the hall.

"Father?" She pushed open the library doors.

He was sitting at his desk, pouring measured powder into the barrel of his flintlock.

"Is the pistol for deterring the extended stay of houseguests?" She came into the room, hoping the small attempt at humor would alleviate some atmosphere in the house that enveloped them wrong.

"Anne. Your husband has been looking for you, but now he has gone. He was angry. He required you to accompany him to a dinner last night in Margate." The general's eyes lit upon John who stood behind Anne. "You are beginning to annoy me, neighbor. I was about to ask Cook to prepare luncheon, but I'll wait until you have departed."

John said nothing.

"Father, I must take this opportunity to speak with you. There's no way to make it easy but to say it outright. It is bad news."

"Never has been any good news in this family, has there? Certainly not my marriage, or your birth. A son, even a grandson, would have fixed it all, but maybe God knew better than to prolong the generations with our cursed lot. Would you like eel pie?"

She shot John a small frown.

"Father, I need you to listen. This is important."

John took a step toward her, standing by her side.

"General," John said, "your daughter has come here expressly to see you today because she owes you the respect of being the first to learn some distressing news, after which I request your ear and discretion with a military matter of the gravest importance."

"Respect?" He held the ball and cloth patch in place at the end of the barrel, his fingers extracting the ramrod from the pistol without taking his eyes off John. "Men like you don't understand the word respect. Men like you feed off our military success."

"Father, please, is this necessary? All I ask is that you listen to what John and I have to say." Anne stepped forward.

The general pushed the ramrod into the barrel and gave it two sharp jabs, his eyes dripped hatred. John's hand snaked around her wrist, drawing her away from the desk so as to be beside him, even a little behind.

"What are you doing there, General?" John enquired politely.

"I'm about to go hunting for my supper, merchant man. Want to come? No. I can see the answer in your yellow-livered eyes. Such sport isn't for the likes of fools who prefer to pay for their food with coin rather than earn it through an honest chase." Spittle flecked across the desk.

"Father." Anne stepped forward despite John's hand on her wrist. She pulled herself free and came to the edge of his desk. "We don't have time for hunting. I am here because I have discovered my marriage to Howard has never been legitimate. In fact, Howard prepared it all as a hoax."

The general stopped. "A hoax? A hoax!" He laughed, laughed until tears were streaming down his face. "Let me guess who thinks your marriage is a hoax. None other than the famous rake, the Earl of Rochester. Oh Anne, you are so disappointing and so predictable. Another man, another mistake. Stupid, stupid girl."

John stepped toward the desk, taking paper from his inside jacket pocket. "My lord, we have documented proof of the fraud." He grabbed Anne's wrist again, guiding her behind him. "This letter is from the archbishop stating no special license was obtained. As you know, Anne was wedded at night, when she was underage, under extreme and rushed conditions. The service itself was set up by Major General Dankworth, possibly with the help of his friends. However, it was merely theater. Anne has only discovered the truth herself and is most upset. She believes the purchase of the special license came from your pocket, but no monies were ever forwarded to the archbishop."

The general scrutinized his pistol. "I am not so easy to fool as my daughter."

Anne shook herself free of John's hold, and placing her reticule on the desk, stepped toward her father, leaning closer to him. "Father, I suspected this document would not be enough to convince you. Perhaps this information might. My marriage to Howard was never consummated. I have had no other children not by reason of infertility, but from a disinclined husband who was no man. Howard is the reason you lack grandsons."

Behind her, John readjusted his stance. She turned, expecting him to be shocked and discomforted. Instead, his eyes were calm and deep. He took a step toward her, catching her hand, which was sure and full of promise, not to hold her back from her father, but to give her strength. She tightened her hand in his. All the courage she needed.

"Well, well, well, aren't all our lives a sham, a bit of pretend, like a rose, all beautiful bloom hiding nasty little aphids and mildew?" The general banged the butt of the pistol on the wooden desk, indicating with his other hand the room and the manor and world about him.

"Father, Howard killed Blake. Murdered Blake, in Margate, all those years ago."

"Oh, but Blake was terminally irritating," Howard said from behind.

Anne and John spun around, Anne clutching at

John's arm.

Howard lounged in the doorway, a cruel smile playing on his lips, twisting a pistol around his finger. "Blake was only ever interested in using his lorgnette to pry down a woman's cleavage. Devils like that don't deserve to live, do they, Anne? I killed that son of a bitch with pride, and I'd do it again."

"What are you doing here?" Anne whispered.

"Keep away, Dankworth." John's hand placed firm on her back, guiding her away.

"This merchant dandy has made vile accusations against your manhood, Dankworth," the general said, as if Dankworth's appearance in his library were a common occurrence. "I believe you should call him out. The fool thinks he can tarnish your good reputation, and he's convinced my silly daughter of his lie. Rochester asserts your marriage is a sham, and you killed Blake."

Dankworth sucked on his teeth and pushing himself off the doorjamb, took two steps into the room.

"Father, did you not hear or understand what Howard just said? Howard murdered Blake. Howard admits he committed the murder."

Her father gave her a pitying look. "Anne, really, does it matter after all these years? Death is about us everywhere, and the boy was on his way to the Americas. You wouldn't have seen him again. As for this one…" He pulled back the hammer and, taking a powder measure, poured a pinch into the pan. "He is already shot. Lame. In this household, Rochester, you are surrounded by heroes." He pushed forward the frizzen. "And we have one purpose in life. To stop rogues like you." He pointed the barrel at John's chest.

"Good show, General." Dankworth bounced on the

balls of his feet.

"Please, General, put down the pistol," John ordered while at the same moment, Anne screamed, "Are you insane?" She ran to her father. "Put it away! Someone may get hurt!"

Her father turned the muzzle toward her, his eyes blank, empty.

She pulled up short, not with surprise at his violence, but rather the vacancy in his expression. She had seen it occasionally, but today, the countenance settled into some awful permanency. "Father, think what you do," she whispered.

"Don't stop now, General. Both of them must die anyway. I hear the battle cry," Dankworth goaded.

"Father, put the firearm down. Howard, stop this. Stop it now. He's upset. You can see Father isn't himself. It's obvious."

"No, Anne," the general said. "The merchant man is making me do this. He wants to tear down our family, so he can buy our estates and consolidate his wealth. He wants our food, our produce. I think he wants to eat our kidneys."

"My lord, with all due respect." John kept his hands open, where the general could see them empty. His voice too was calm. "Your daughter and I are worried for your welfare. Could I pour you a shot of whiskey or rum?"

Anne looked from her father to John, even as John dropped his hands and went to take the general by the arm, guiding him to a seat. Her father had gone in the head. John caring for the man, pouring a glass of rum, whilst Howard did nothing at all but goad and bounce with a stupid grin stretched across his mouth as if the scene were but a jest.

She took a step closer to her father.

"General," Dankworth called from the doorway. "I believe Rochester wants to cuckold me and make a fool of you." Dankworth gave John and Anne a wide smile, adding as an aside, "You see, the general and I have worked together for a long time now, and he trusts my judgment, don't you, old man?"

"Howard, stop this. You can see he is poorly."

"A nip of rum, General?" John held out the glass. "It might improve your health. Might I suggest you put down your pistol, so you can hold the drink."

The general blinked at John, then looked at his daughter. Shrugging off John's arm, he went back to his desk, but he didn't put down the firearm, nor did he take the glass from John's outstretched hand.

"I asked for Dankworth to give Blake a bit of a roughing over and put him on a ship to America. I wasn't letting a common stable boy run off without consequence, shirking all responsibility, even to my horses. I had high hopes for your marriage, young lady, which you all but ruined. Except for Dankworth who came to your rescue and married you, you would have been out on the streets with the girl-child, but this is ancient history."

Dankworth chuckled.

The general continued, "Dankworth has been unselfish in his regard for you, Anne." The general studied the barrel.

The irony was three months ago Anne would have agreed with her father, but today the truth was revealed. A different person formed before her. A short stocky man with ostentatious hair and a cruel smile on narrow little lips. A murderer. A liar. A gambler. A drunkard. A cheat. A stranger. The man her father called son-in-law.

"Father, put the pistol down," Anne ordered, keeping watch of Howard, whose sense of enjoyment grew if the bouncing on his toes was any indication. "Father, John and I are explaining that Howard has used us, unmercifully for his own end." She picked up her reticule from the desk, feeling for the drawstrings which kept it closed, while keeping her gaze on the muzzle of the pistol her father pointed at John's chest. Her father, or her lover. Had it come to this? "Howard is lying to you, Father. He has been for years."

Suddenly, the breath was knocked out of her as Dankworth grabbed her around the waist and lifted her off the floor, her light weight nothing against his thick arms. "I think I might put the lady outside now, sir," he said to the general, impervious to Anne's scream of shock, arms flailing and feet kicking the air as her reticule flew from her hand onto the floor, sliding under a settle bench.

"Let her go!" John dropped the glass and raced for Anne.

"Stay where you are, Wylde, or I shoot," the general ordered.

"I believe we have to attend to men's business—not the place for a hen." Howard gave Anne a powerful shove out the doors, so she tripped on her skirts and skidded across the hall floor, cracking her shoulder into the cold wall with a force that stung like an arrow.

"Thank you, Dankworth. Then we can see to lunch." The general nodded, his pistol aimed straight at John.

John started to say something, but his voice, outraged and passionate, was lost as the study doors shut in her face.

Anne screamed John's name, throwing her body against the white painted woodwork, pounding her fists on the thick panel. She could hear John's heated mumbling from inside and Dankworth's softer reply. She screamed again, kicked and pounded, not caring about bruising, impervious to all pain, cursing at having lost her pistol when she needed it most.

In some corner of her mind, she realized no servants were coming to her aid. No one arrived to investigate her distress. Haversham was sympathetic to her. All the staff disliked her father's authority, were scared of him. They would help her. She knew they would. But where were they?

She lifted her skirts and ran through the house, careening around corners, clutching at balustrades and walls, falling down steps, and wrenching her ankle in the kitchen calling for Haversham, Jenny, or anybody.

Every room was empty, echoing nothing but her voice. Perhaps this was a nightmare and someone would wake her soon, for her heart was fit to burst, and her legs weren't running fast enough. The kitchen was tidy, not one item out of place—why wasn't Cook preparing luncheon? She ran to the door through to the kitchen garden, escaping into the sunshine, screaming for help, sending a flock of chattering, bickering sparrows into flight. She ran back into the house when, from the corner she caught the smallest movement—it might have been a wasp—but she turned and came face to face with Haversham's blue eye through the slit of the scullery door.

"What are you doing?" she half screamed, half whispered, for she feared now her sanity slipped, that this must be how her poor mother felt before she died of nervous collapse, nightmare and reality melding in this large house of hell.

"Are you alone, Lady Anne?"

"Yes, yes. God, what's happening? Help me!" Her voice rose, but Haversham indicated for her to be quiet. Beneath Haversham's face appeared the maid's. Anne pushed her way in through the scullery door, stepping down into the center of the room, beyond caring if staff gossiped of her behavior. "What are you all doing here? Haversham, quick. I need your help upstairs. It's Father. He has a firearm on Rochester and is threatening to kill him. We must break down the study door. Come."

"Lady Anne." Haversham did not move. "Your father has been sickly all morning, screaming and shooting. We are too scared for our lives. I have brought all the female staff here for protection. We will not leave until I know it is safe." He frowned. "What is Rochester doing here? He will incite your father further!"

She pulled her hands through her hair. "What's happened? I don't understand! Shooting?"

"It's Cook, Lady Anne," Jenny replied, eyes wide. "Cook died last night, and since the general was informed of her death, he's been in a shocking state. He thinks one of us killed her, but we ain't never. He wants Cook to bake his dinner. He's been ranting he loved her, and she was taken from him because it was an indecent love for a domestic, but—"

"All right, Jenny," Haversham interrupted. "Lady

Anne doesn't need to hear the gossip."

"It's not gossip, sir, and Lady Anne needs to hear it. It's true, Lady Anne. I swear on my mother's grave, everything I've told you is true."

Anne clutched her hands at her breast. It was true. Cook's death would devastate her father such as her mother's death never had. His concern for Cook, buying medicines at the local fair—he had never been so caring toward her mother. Dear God, he denied love himself, and so everybody else was denied. Anne rubbed her face in her hands. She had to get back. John depended on her.

"I need to get into the library." She gathered her wits. "Will anyone help me?"

Haversham shook his head. "I have my duty here with the women, Lady Anne. Your father is too dangerous, and if you'll pardon my opinion, you should be staying here too."

"No. I won't hide here quivering when my duty is upstairs. Howard is with them…"

"Ah, thank God." Haversham clapped to the sky as the other women in the room offered prayers of thanks. "Now we will be saved! Major Dankworth is our hero. He will know what to do. He will have the matter quickly in hand."

Her stomach heaved. "No. Haversham, no. Please don't ask me to explain, for I cannot, but you are wrong to trust Dankworth. I cannot stay hidden in the scullery when Lord Rochester is alone, attempting to—"

Suddenly there was a shot.

A couple of the women screamed; everyone cowered, and Haversham snapped she must either go or stay, but within seconds they would be barricading the door to keep themselves safe. Anne, already bunching her skirts in her hand, sprinted for the library.

She screamed John's name, unsure if her voice was being held to drift in space or falling on ears. She hammered against the library doors, throwing her shoulder into the wood. After some moments, Howard opened it. He held the firearm and indicated with his head he wanted her inside. She took a step backwards, not inclined to follow anything Howard might order, when beyond him a body lay prostrate on the floor, white faced, eyes closed, blood pooling on the carpet. John. No!

She flew to his side, crying, lifting and cradling his head on her knees, whispering for him to open his eyes and that she loved him, strewing kisses across his pale cheeks and threading her fingers through his hair. She ran her hands across his face, where her tears were dropping, across his thick eyelashes and square jaw and down across his chest, checking for the wound and heartbeat, imploring him to wake.

Her father and Howard watched on, for seconds or hours she would never know. "What have you done? What have you done! Help him!" she screamed.

The general looked nonplussed. "I warned you death was everywhere today. It is eating away at us. Rochester won't get this land from me. Do you know he had the temerity to accuse Dankworth of being a French spy? The man was insane, Anne. Insane. I had to shoot him to keep him quiet."

Anne stilled. Her father had shot the man she loved? She looked to Howard for confirmation. "Insane," Howard mouthed with a smile.

Her fingers shook as she caressed John's lips and

hair, finding strength from holding his head in her lap where she would keep him safe and protect him with her own body. Howard was a spy, and John had discovered it. In her heart, she had already known the ugly truth. This is what John had wanted to tell her in the carriage, and she had stopped him speaking, when now, all she ever longed for was to hear him talk again.

She looked up at Howard, then to her father, and back again to Howard who held the pistol aimed at her. These men standing over her, ruined her life, taking anything good and turning it bad. They saw only one wounded person in the room, not even acknowledging her heart bled equal drop for drop with John's. Ah, but they were military men, only ever caring for the wounds they could see. Howard laughed and winked at her father in camaraderie, as if reading her thoughts.

"What in God's name have I ever done to you? I even stayed silent for your beatings!" she whispered to Howard, heat filling her face like a furnace, her heart billowing inside her chest forcing lungfuls of hot air on the conflagration of her soul.

Her father answered. "For God's sake, Anne, get off the floor, and let the man go. The fool wanted to marry you. Had the indecency to claim your hand right here in front of your husband! I told him this idiotic bit of theatrics was irrational. Better to bed you and shut up. No class. Typical merchant. Wasn't that right, Dankworth?"

"Oh yes." Dankworth smiled. "I even told Rochester he was welcome to you. Told him a week or so ago when we had our little chat in the vegetable patch. Did he tell you our conversation? No. My offer was too blatant for him, robbed him of the chase to drop your petticoat. Rochester is more the sort of man who enjoys a good skulk."

Her hands stilled. She wanted to scratch out Howard's eyes, shred his smug face with her fingernails, and watch him bleed, ruin his life, maim him, the way he maimed and ruined her. Her gaze flittered to her reticule some four feet away. If she could only reach it... To think a few weeks ago she had asked John for his help because she wanted to protect her family. What family!

Dankworth moved to stand in front of her. "Of course now Wylde has made this ridiculous accusation of me being a spy, well, I'll have to kill you too. I mean, I can't have my manhood and my political reputation tarnished, can I?"

"What's that you say, Dankworth? No, I don't think Anne needs to die. One doesn't attack the women."

"Why not, General?" He stared down at her, his cold eyes piercing her soul, while he lifted the flintlock and aimed it at her forehead. "Why not kill her? The rotten whore has done nothing for me. Hasn't even provided you with a bastard male heir."

Anne stared into the black hole. She had been in this position too many times to recount. Cowered in some corner at the end of Howard's pistol. Did he really believe she would subject herself to this abuse when there was nothing to live for? When her lover lay bleeding, dying at her feet? There was no fear. Howard might believe her shrunken and fearful. Pity him.

The general moved another step forward. "No. Come, Dankworth. We don't want language like that in front of the women. How about I get Cook to prepare something nice for dinner. Venison? She has the knack of roasting it to just the right bloodiness. We can eat in the dining room."

"I think, Father," she said, raising her head, enunciating every syllable with excruciating care while she stared at Dankworth, "I think I saw an aphid on the roses this morning."

The general stopped and looked at her, his head inclined with interest, yet his eyes were dead. "An aphid! Oh no. I can't have it. The aphid will have to die. Breakfasting on my roses is not allowed. I tell you death is all around us this morning, and such a lovely day too, don't you think?" He stopped. "Anne, I think the fellow is bleeding on my carpet. Whatever is the matter with him? Did he prick himself on a thorn?" The general shook his head. "Everywhere." He walked out.

Howard chuckled, even as he locked the library doors behind her father's back, Howard's motions too fluid and quick for her to even attempt grabbing her reticule. Dear heaven.

"Always protecting your family, even your poor demented father. I've been watching him slide for years, but now it's come. Foolish woman. I will enjoy killing you and your father. I enjoyed killing the poetry boy," Howard said, his voice captured by the books, absorbed into the quiet. "It's Shakespearean tragedy proportions, don't you think? John dead in your lap. You dead on top. Father pruning flowers, soon to be dead in the rose bed. Even rhymes. I will be so pleased to be rid of this infernal England." He laughed.

John's pistol…

She kept her eyes pinned on Howard. One hand rested still against John's lips as her other hand snaked behind his back. Where was it? She needed the heavy certainty of its presence pressed into her hand even while her body revolted and shivered at what she was about to do. Darling John. It was a matter of honor and avenging all the wrongs.

Something of her manner must have changed, must have conveyed itself to Howard, for he suddenly became serious. "Anne, you were so dumb for all those years. What did I ever do to arouse your suspicion?"

Now she spoke the truth, no matter the cost, needing to keep Howard's attention, delay him, while her fingertips stretched for the metal. "I read the letter, the note that came here ordering you to organize the funeral for Howard Dankworth. Why would a note ask you to prepare your own funeral? It made no sense. I knew then that you were a devious sod."

"See, this is the trouble with dumb hen-witted women. Can't keep their noses out of a man's affairs. I should have given you a good walloping more often. Tell me why this bloody Rochester fellow. I mean, this is a comedown even for you. His rod has seen more movement than a conductor's baton."

Revulsion at Dankworth's coarse language shimmied down her spine. "Lord Rochester is involved because you were sloppy. You talked in India about our fake marriage, and one of your captains seized the opportunity."

"Oh dear dumb Anne. You can't live now. I wish I had killed you years ago. I planned I would, even employed the chef to deliver the poison, but on a whim I let you live. You see, I am too kind hearted, and you were doing such a job of pretending to be my good wife. Yes. Although this end is more fitting, in your father's house, lover by your side, all the truth known—society discussing your infidelity, don't you agree?"

"You couldn't kill me before because of Charlotte." Her fingers found the hard pistol. At last, this conversation was on equal footing, but she concentrating on maintaining her demeanor. She inched it out of John's belt, the places where metal touched his skin, warm.

Howard stilled.

Her finger found the trigger.

"Yes. Charlotte." His eyebrows drew down. "You could have told her the truth about her father, but you always let her believe it was me. I'll give you that. For a bloody Anglican, you had an ounce of conscience."

She swallowed, forcing herself to say the words which were so true, but so hollow. "Charlotte loves you."

He pursed his lips, then nodded. "You should die, Anne Dankworth. You have put up with the ridiculous fictional name for too long. Stupid woman. Except I see with Charlotte, you did well, and the fact you have been so hen-brained and stupid for so long works in your favor. It gives me some hope you will underestimate everything that has happened today and go on your way, making a house, dallying with embroidery, filling your airy head with nothing except your poor sick father—and be happy with your lot. Except you dragged Rochester into the mix, I might have let you live. I bet you're sorry you let his dick inside you now."

John's lips moved beneath her fingertips. Dear God, thank you. He lived. Yesterday she might have wanted to collapse and cry with relief, but not now. She was changed. Gone was the simpering good wife who cowered before Howard and all adversity, replaced by a strong and daring woman who would demand from the world what she deserved.

Howard went on. "I was hoping to kill you in Margate yesterday, where I could dump your body at sea as I headed for France, but it won't be possible now. I can't risk the attention your hysteria would attract. Women always do become so hysterical when they are in danger, don't you think? One wonders why they don't embrace it and be a little more like you. Dumb."

She swallowed.

"Charlotte will miss me when I leave," Dankworth continued. "But they need me in France."

Anne gave a faint nod.

"I wonder." He felt around in his pockets, shifting the firearm from hand to hand, patting. "Could you give Charlotte something for me, in return for your life?"

Anne stilled.

He drew out a small pendant, on a chain, a piece of wood covered in glass from his waistcoat pocket. "I am Catholic, you see." He held the pendant, swinging it before her eyes. "I could never marry you. It was sacrilege enough me entering a heathen church, and I would never have forsaken my belief to lie with you. If Charlotte takes this, it will protect her somewhat from your Anglican heresy. It is an ancient relic. A piece of the Crown of Thorns. It's been blessed. By a proper priest, not one of your vicars."

Anne stopped. If she withdrew her hand he would see the muzzle; if she let go, she had no protection. If she didn't take the chain, he might kill her anyway, and overriding it all was the sense he was toying with her.

The chain was flicked back into his palm.

"On second thought, I should give this to Haversham to deliver. He will say it with the right amount of detached English reserve."

Anne clasped the firearm.

"I think…" He leaned down and whispered, "I am about to become the most lauded French spy in English history." He turned toward the door, more words on his lips, but Anne didn't wait. John had never underestimated Howard. John had warned her Howard would kill. She owed everything to John, and while John breathed and moved his lips but a fraction, she would act.

She lifted the pistol and shot Howard through the back of his knee, the explosion resounding through the room as Howard spun around to face her, dropping his pistol, his mouth hanging open in pure outrage at her audacity as he toppled backward into the wall in a groaning heap.

"My avenging angel, I knew you would act!" John struggled to push himself up. Anne threw herself onto him, kissing him, putting pressure on his wound until Howard, who'd collapsed against a wall, stirred. He was gaining consciousness, dragging himself into a sitting position, his hand reaching and searching for his pistol. She would never underestimate Dankworth again. Never be his fool.

"Stay still, Howard," she said with icy clarity, standing, letting go of John, and finding the pistol, aiming it true. "Or I'll shoot you straight through the forehead. I will enjoy the opportunity of being the most lauded English heroine in history!"

Dankworth glared at her, his eyes black and

vicious. "You mean lauded dumb whore," he spat, though his pain must have been tremendous. "You don't have the powder loaded, you stupid bitch."

John was standing albeit none too steady, behind her. In his hand, Anne's flintlock became an extension of his arm. "Do not fear, Dankworth, I'll not let Anne kill you, even though she'd love to," John bit out, his other hand clutching the wound his side. "You are too precious to England murder outright. It'll be better to make sure the whole country knows the one person this hero could never duck was a woman." John blew out the other knee.

Dankworth fell out of consciousness.

John stared at him. "Always do as the lady asks. She holds the firearm."

John fainted.

Chapter Twenty

Two days later

Blood rushed through his chest. His ears thrummed with a pounding tide. Without wings, he propelled himself through oceans of air to the mountaintops of islands erupting from a clear aqua coral sea, breathing the heady rush stinging his upturned face, for she soared above him in the bluest heavens, and he was flying to take her into an eternal—

"John?"

The vision faded. Another world came into focus. His oak bed. A multitude of glittering candles. The green duvet and… "Annie?"

"My darling. How are you feeling?" Her fingertips caressed a trail across his brow.

He blinked at the sheer lightness of being, the limitless potential of his world. "Majestic," he croaked.

She moved toward him, the cream frills of her chemise framing her neck, dark hair, and translucent skin. She held a glass of water in her fine hand, the wondrous beautiful hand that put a bullet through Dankworth's blood and flesh. His heart skipped faster; this dangerous siren was all his. She placed her gentle hand behind his head and helped him take a sweet moistening sip.

"You've been sleeping these past two days. You

will be thirsty."

Her voice sounded like angels in heaven. He shook his head, his back and leg muscles wound tight, raising himself from the pillows.

"Don't move." She put her hand on his chest, the open palm halting him, while the warmth from her touch sank into his curling ribs and healed.

"I feel wonderful." He sat up further, pushing, resisting her, testing his influence, his voice and throat less sandy, more himself. "What happened? Why am I home?"

"You were shot, remember?"

"Of course. My side." He winced, touching the thick bandage.

"A through and through. I've already had a medical man look at it—not your ridiculous leech, but a proper medical man who's with the military. He sees flesh wounds all the time and knows how to make them heal. He has used an unguent on it."

The shape of her lips when she said the word unguent set his pulse to quicken.

"I don't need any medical man to tell me I'm fine. Thank you for the unguent." He sat up further, wincing at a stab of pain near his rib, but otherwise the deep lungful of air tasted sweet as he arched his back and rubbed his bare chest, blood tingling his veins. Then he took her hand, stroking the fragile skin, raising her wrist to his lips, kissing her, her violet perfume easing the discomfort, talking against her skin as if he would send his spirit thrumming into her bones.

"Where is Dankworth? Come closer, sit on the bed here, and tell me what's been happening." He nuzzled his mouth into her palm.

Anne perched on the bed as ordered, withdrawing her hand, shushing the forlorn look he gave her. "I can't think with you kissing me and being so close. In any case, we've all been terribly concerned about you. I sat with you day and night. Donovan's been saying prayers and holding vigils for your soul. He lit all these candles to ward off evil spirits and it has worked!"

He took her hand again, pressing it to his lips. "What about you? How are you?"

"I'm faring better now you have come out of your sleep. Dankworth is a different story. After you shot his other knee, he passed out."

"Tell me all."

Again she snaked her hand from his grasp. "Well, as fortune would have it, officers arrived from London soon after the shooting asking for you and Dankworth. They took in the situation immediately, dressed yours and Dankworth's wounds, and asked me about what had happened. I explained everything and they were most sympathetic, promising all discretion in the matter."

John groaned. "For the love of God, Anne, please don't tell me you are aiding Dankworth's health back to recovery in the next room?"

"No." She gave him a playful pat on the covers. "You are my patient. They took Howard away with them. I have no idea where. I asked one of Father's cronies yesterday, but he was evasive."

He pulled her closer. "My plan worked."

"Plan?"

"When we were in Margate." He ran his hand up her arms, the skin so soft he longed to kiss her all over, and he would, within minutes. "When I left you at the inn, I drafted correspondence to London officials outlining what I knew, making the accusation of Dankworth's spying and threat to national security. I invited them to visit Margate to interview a few key persons who would be willing to talk. Then, in case London didn't believe my claims, which I have to admit, was a concern, I called into Margate Harbor and just happened to mention to a couple of well-known French sympathizers that Dankworth was a double agent."

"John! How farsighted of you!"

"Not really, my love." He fingered the frothy material on her chemise till it loosened off her shoulder. "Alerting authorities is what any man of honor would do. I wanted to tell you, but you told me my secret would keep. Remember?"

She wriggled closer to him on the bed. "I thought you were going to tell me Howard was a spy. So what do you think they will do with him?"

"Swing, rot in some gaol cell, or they may give him a pistol and lock him in a room. Rest assured, they won't want the world to know England has been infiltrated."

"The military can't make a national hero disappear."

John shrugged. "It seems to me the press will make people believe anything. Anyway, the French would have him on the end of a bayonet for being discovered. Sending him to Paris would be an option. How is your father?"

"Not himself." She rubbed her cheek against his hand like a kitten.

A sharp rap came on the door. Anne pulled away,

fixing her chemise. John swore at the interruption, then looked to see Donovan in the frame and broke into a smile. "Donovan! Your prayers were successful!"

"Good afternoon, my lord." Donovan gave a slight bow accompanied by a slighter grin, then, "Lady Anne, there is a visitor waiting in the reception room. Miss Bess Belet. The lady claims to be—"

"Anne's aunt." Bess pushed past Donovan's bulk, twittering into the room in a froth of gray feathers. "Anne darling!" She gave her niece a hug. "How are you bearing up, my poor dear? I expected to find you here, and Lord Rochester, good heavens. Still in bed and wasting candles when it is a beautiful day outside! Come, Anne, let us leave him to dress. You may be the merry widow; however, it's not seemly to be in a gentleman's bedchamber with his chest exposed. I'm sure your man Donovan will agree with me. One has to observe a semblance of protocol."

"Stop!" Anne and John said together. They looked at each other, then back at Bess who had paused beside Donovan in the doorway.

"Miss Belet, if you would care for an explanation," John said. "I've been indisposed for a few days, and Anne has been ministering to me."

Bess looked first at Anne, then at John with frank disbelief. "I hardly think, young man, you can escape your obligations on such a flimsy excuse! Your reputation as a rogue and rake precede you. The bedchamber tableau before me confirms my worst suspicions. However, Anne, unfortunately it comes a little late as now that your husband is deceased, you will both have to exercise restraint whilst in mourning. There should be a distance of at least two feet between you."

John scratched his stubbled chin. Not much of Bess's last comment proved accurate. This scene for his bedroom was tame. Dankworth lived, although in honesty, the reference to him being a young man lifted his spirits.

"Aunt Bess, John is in bed because he is recovering from a pistol wound, but what's this about me observing mourning? I am not a widow. We shot to maim Howard. He is not dead. In truth, I am surprised you know any details. I was assured the events would be a guarded secret."

"My dear girl, the rags don't keep secrets. They make their money from informing the world."

John swore. "See, Anne, I warned you! Those rags have no regard for a man's privacy, and they tell the most despicable lies."

"My lord." Bess rounded on him. "With all due respect, I hardly call Howard's demise a lie! Our nation has had an outpouring of grief for our hero, whilst you have been holed up here enjoying a close encounter with his wife! I hardly think crowing lies you killed him in another of your famous duels will curry favor when everyone knows the poor man died yesterday at the hand of savages!"

John paused. "Savages?"

"Ireland. Those Catholics, and I won't have you disparage our papers. Intelligent literary men toil on our stories. Anyway, you will have a chance to redeem yourself at Howard's funeral in a few days' time. I'm here to help Anne plan it. There is nothing I enjoy more than a ceremony for the passage of a poor soul."

"Yes," Anne said, her voice somewhat distant.

"But now"—Bess cast a sideways look at Donovan—"I'll ask your man here to show me to my room. I'm not staying at Graystone, and I'd like a bite to eat. I left the Hatter's house in such a flurry, I'm parched. Are you coming, Anne?"

"I'll join you in a minute, Aunty."

Bess raised her eyebrows and with a warning stare at John, fluttered from the room, Donovan trailing.

As soon as the door closed, Annie climbed back onto the bed and gave a long sigh. "I love you, John Wylde. Do you think it wrong to feel so happy?"

He pulled her toward him. "I'm wondering how long I have to wait before I can have you naked in bed with me."

She walked her fingers across his chest, every step sending shivers of desire down to regions that had no right to feel so alive beneath the covers of a sick bed.

"I've been thinking, my love…" He stilled her hand. "Charlotte is much like her great aunt, don't you feel? They both enjoy organizing events."

"You're right. Charlotte and Bess would be more than competent at organizing Howard's funeral." Annie sighed. "I gave Charlotte the pendant Howard had in his hand. The relic from the Crown of Thorns. She loved it. Of course when I gave it to her, I had no idea Howard had died."

"She will cherish the gift from her father even more."

Burning sensations, relief and love, brimmed and flooded her body.

"It's our secret, Annie."

She wilted and sighed, a glorious delight, a lustrous pearl in his arms as he kissed her, warm, soft, and lingering. Annie snuggled deeper.

"Good Catholic Dankworth will be turning in his grave to know he's having an Anglican funeral, lauded as an English hero." His voice was husky after the long kiss.

"We don't even know the man's real name."

"Alain Piggot." John had the decency to squirm at Anne's surprise. "I am sorry, my love, but I couldn't risk having it come out. Dankworth was ready to kill you. If he'd thought you knew his real name, it would be your funeral Bess would be organizing."

"Piggot? It's almost as bad as Dankworth!"

"Yes, well, I'm not certain of all the details. A lot of it I've had to piece together. After talking to some people in Margate, it appears Dankworth became adjutant to your father so as to stay close to the smugglers who could pass information back to France. He used the excuse to visit your father as required. Marrying into the family provided excellent cover and quality information. He was known about the smuggling coves as Alain Piggot. I am assuming it is his true name, but I can't be certain."

"Argh!" She shuddered.

"As you know, Dankworth was planning to return to France," he continued. "However, while being so well known in England had its advantages for gathering information, the same could not be said for when he wanted to leave. He was proud, and it was his undoing. Instead of making a hasty retreat back to France, he wanted the grand charade of the funeral, and I gather, from what the men said at Margate Harbor, that the French weren't so supportive. The letter you intercepted when you first asked for my assistance referred to their plan."

"Smugglers in Margate told you all this?" She pulled away from him. "They seem unusually free with their information."

He grimaced. "I paid. It may not have been successful, except they were tired of Dankworth's duplicity. He became ruder, more demanding as the time approached for him to leave. They were furious with him and ready to talk to anyone who asked—including the English military. His self-grandeur had become a liability. If we'd stayed longer in Margate, I might have discovered more. Fortunately what we had was enough to alert the king, and combined with the lie about the special license, I was able to cast doubt over Dankworth's honesty. Any interrogation would confirm my suspicions."

She curled herself into the crook of his arm. "I don't know that Howard would admit the truth under interrogation. I don't believe he would be intimidated by cruelty," she whispered against his chest.

"My love…" He stroked her hair. "You are safe with me." He kissed her gently. "Now, we must turn our thoughts to where will we live—Elfleet or Graystone?"

"What of the distant shores you promised?"

"The Italian Riviera is as distant as you're getting. My usual voyages are not appropriate for a woman."

"But John, I don't like you making allowances for my sex. Surely after the current turn of events, I've proved my mettle. You wouldn't want to give up going to sea for the Italian Riviera, would you?"

"How I love and admire your spirit and courage. I am not sure I can ever be as bold or spectacular as you.

You moderate me."

She smiled and tweaked his chin. "I think we will get along together very well."

His eyes glittered, his dimples flashed. "You are a minx for getting your own way, but your father is poorly. I can't drag you away from him. It's time I embraced my responsibilities. I want to be by your side."

"But Charlotte is married, and I can't for the life of me imagine you with any responsibilities other than a crew and brace of pistols. Anyway, Father hates you."

"There's truth in that. Before he shot me, I asked for your hand in marriage. I obviously irritated him."

"Father prefers to arrange my marriages himself."

"Unfortunately, he makes a hash of it."

"Yes." She sighed. "And now we have to wait two years for the mourning period to end."

"Two years."

"Two whole years."

"Ah, come…" He roused himself. "It isn't so bad, is it? We can be together in private."

"John?"

"Yes, my love?"

"I won't ever wear diamonds again."

"No. They don't suit your skin at all. Far too hard for your coloring."

"Staying in England feels like diamonds."

He stilled.

"The pain of all those years reminds me of diamonds. Can you understand?"

He cleared his throat. "Why upset your father further with news of our intentions? However, I feel marriage is important."

"In truth, John, the word makes me shudder. Anyway, I am not convinced of the institution's worth."

"Unlike you, I've always fancied myself a bit of a romantic when it comes to marriage." He sighed and frowned. "Settling with the right lady, having her take my name, giving her a home. I want to give it all to you, under law. If we don't marry, everyone will accuse you of being a kept woman and me of being a rake. I won't tolerate any tarnish to your reputation. Although I am still a rogue. I enjoy being a rogue—it allows me a certain freedom. You will have to get used to that, I'm afraid."

"Darling. Prepare to meet your match for now I am unleashed, I fear I have an inner desire for rebellion against all I've ever known. Be that as it may, the scandal sheets will be believed. It can't be helped." She shrugged. "I don't care what they say, marriage or no marriage, so long as I am with you."

"Oh, but I do, my love. I have no choice but to make an honest woman of you. Blood and wounds, you deserve nothing less!"

"John, it's not possible for us to marry. The scandal would outlive us."

He gripped her hand tight and frowned. "Perhaps then, we have outgrown England. We should take an ocean voyage."

"This is the conversation I have dreamed." She inclined her head to his bedside table where the whittled boat and firearm lay side by side.

He smiled, a half twist of his lips. "The sea can be the devil of a mistress."

"I believe I can compete for your attention. Anyway, Charlotte would prefer me to be at a safe distance on foreign seas. Nothing keeps me here."

"What of mourning periods and your father?"

"For a man I never married? Anyway, Father has the means to procure better care than I can ever give. He never wanted me. Remember, I'm the reminder of the woman he loathed."

"My darling"—he sighed, his eyes glittering with devilry—"snuggle in, for I have an idea. Those rags can have their story. We will also make it our truth." She stared at him, not sure of what he spoke. He smiled his assurance, cuddling her in his arm. "The last time I was on one of the islands, I was invited to a tribal wedding. It was a wondrous celebration like nothing you have ever known. The men linked hands and carried the bride across the beach, through shallow surf. The bride wore strands of colored blossoms, through her hair, on her dress, everywhere. The procession of the bride was welcomed with a herald of booming conch shells, and she was carried to her groom."

Anne closed her eyes, his words flowing over her as soft as a tropical breeze stirring the fronds of palm trees, whispering across fine white sand, hot from the sun. The whittled boat of her dreams. Finally, her body could relax to the tingling of his promises meeting her dreams.

"John," she said into his chest where the skin was tender and her voice rumbled into his heart, mingling with his beating blood, taking her spirit into lightness. "I have waited so long."

He tilted her face to his. "Annie. You are my home. My family. You make my heart sing with adventures undreamed, yet keep me anchored and in safe harbor. You are the treasure I have waited to cherish, and now I have you in my possession, nothing will tear you away."

"We are family for each other."

"My first and only." He smiled, then kissed her, dragging himself away when Donovan's sharp rap on the door sounded. "Come in, Donovan, though it is poorly timed. Lady Anne and I were about to embark on more pleasurable pursuits."

Donovan took one precise step into the room holding a parcel wrapped in shop paper. "My lord. A delivery has arrived. It is a picture. The gentleman asked me to convey the message that his nephew has completed this watercolor for you knowing your love of the sun is matched only by his own. The boy, Joseph, trusts it will meet with your approval, insisting his experience must broaden before he can complete such an oil, as per your original request. He will not forget your commission and would have you accept this small sketch as a token of his good faith."

John took the package and, pulling aside the string, extracted a watercolor of Margate, the picture dominated by a sky fluid with light and clouds blown across the glimmering promise of a dawn horizon.

"The boy is a genius," John whispered. "Quickly, Donovan, empty my purse. Where is the boy now?"

"It is the uncle who waits downstairs. He says his nephew is shortly to attend the Royal Academy School."

"Then give the uncle this message for Joseph to take to the school. I support Joseph Turner without hesitation. The work is delicate and beautiful. Any recommendation I can give, I will. Do it, Donovan, and show him all courtesy—anything he requires and a generous handful of gold coin."

Donovan bowed out.

Anne studied the picture. "The boy's talent is obvious, though why did you commission a picture of Margate? Our experience of the town has not been hearty."

He gave her cheek a kiss, still holding the painting at arm's length. "I didn't. I told him to strap himself to the mast of a ship to experience the drama of the sea before he paints it. Then I commissioned an oil."

"Of Margate?"

"Of you."

"Me?"

He nodded. "I requested an angel, you, standing in the sun with a mighty sword drawn in your hand entitled *Avenging Angel*. When I was lying on the floor thinking myself close to death, God handed you a sword."

"Oh. Darling, I do think you need to rest. You're all confused. I used a pistol, and in all honesty, I'm pleased this young Joseph Turner wasn't able to complete the painting because you have it all wrong. I see myself as a devil. I must say, my lord Rochester, you have a strong tendency to romance."

"Yes, well, you're the one person in the world to discover that vulnerability."

"Are you disappointed with this picture then?"

"I am proud. The boy has to experience the battles of nature before he can paint them. I asked too much of him when he is young."

Anne was silent, staring at the painting at the peeping sun stretching rays over the edge of the world. "We asked too much of ourselves, all those years ago," she whispered.

"We did."

"Some lessons take a lifetime."

"Ah, but the greatest lesson came so lightly I didn't realize it had already been learned—that I've always loved you. From the beginning. To the end."

And then he kissed her.

A word about the author…

When not studying medical research in dementia care, Mary Macken escapes into writing historical romance—it's a yin-yang thing. She and her ever-patient husband, along with their two beautiful daughters, live beneath Mt. Canobolas in regional Australia. Her love of social history and the tranquility of landscapes, together with the cherished friendships of like-minded romance readers and authors, all play a part in the world she creates in her stories.

www.ingramcontent.com/pod-product-compliance
Lightning Source LLC
Chambersburg PA
CBHW071535260626
47170CB00002B/639